BLACK KING

MARK WIL

First published 2007. This editio
www.lulu.cc

Copyright © Mark Willis 2007, 2023

Mark Willis asserts the moral right to
be identified as the author of this work.

This novel is entirely a work of fiction.
The names, characters and incidents portrayed in it
are the work of the author's imagination.
Any resemblance to real persons, living or dead,
events or localities is entirely coincidental.

9 781447 779452

ACKNOWLEDGEMENTS

Excerpt from 'Promised Land' by Dennis Brown 1983 (Chapter 17). All rights reserved copyright control by original publisher

Excerpt from 'Hello Mama Africa' by Garnett Silk 1994 (Chapter 17). All rights reserved copyright control retained by original publisher.

Excerpt from 'Duppy Conqueror', by The Wailers, lyrics by Bob Marley 1969 (Chapter 32). All rights reserved copyright control ©Tuff Gong Music.

Excerpt from 'Jah Live', by Bob Marley & The Wailers, lyrics by Bob Marley 1975 (Chapter 32). All rights reserved copyright control ©Tuff Gong Music.

Excerpt from 'Rastaman Chant', by The Wailers, 1973, lyrics Traditional.

Excerpt from 'Rainbow Country', by Bob Marley & The Wailers, lyrics by Bob Marley 1969 (Chapter 32). All rights reserved copyright control ©Tuff Gong Music.

Excerpt from 'Exodus', by Bob Marley & The Wailers, lyrics by Bob Marley 1977 (Chapter 32). All rights reserved copyright control ©Tuff Gong Music.

Excerpt from 'Zimbabwe', by Bob Marley & The Wailers, lyrics by Bob Marley 1980 (Chapter 32). All rights reserved copyright control ©Tuff Gong Music.

Excerpt from 'Redemption Song', by Bob Marley & The Wailers, lyrics by Bob Marley 1981(Chapter 32). All rights reserved copyright control ©Tuff Gong Music.

Excerpt from 'Get Up Stand Up', by The Wailers, lyrics by Bob Marley/Peter Tosh 1973 (Chapter 32). All rights reserved copyright control ©Tuff Gong Music.

All other song titles and lyrics used consciously are gratefully acknowledged.

SIDE ONE: LONDON

1: **Sweet Reggae Music**   (Nitty Gritty)

2: **War**   (Bob Marley & The Wailers)

3: **Picture On The Wall**   (The Natural Ites)

4: **Declaration of Rights**   (The Abyssinians)

5: **Young, Gifted and Black**   (Bob & Marcia)

6: **Exodus**   (Bob Marley & The Wailers)

7: **Worries In The Dance**   (Frankie Paul)

8: **Harder They Come**   (Jimmy Cliff)

9: **Chalice In The Palace**   (U-Roy)

10: **Jah Live**   (Bob Marley & The Wailers)

11: **True Born African**   (U-Roy & Sister Audrey)

12: **Redemption Song**   (Bob Marley & The Wailers)

13. **Untold Stories**   (Buju Banton)

14. **Who Could It Be**   (Luciano)

15. **Burial**   (Peter Tosh)

16. **Sitting In The Park**   (Slim Smith)

SIDE TWO: AFRICA

17. Hello Mama Africa	(Garnett Silk)
18. Promised Land	(Dennis Brown)
19. Amazing Grace	(Sanchez)
20. This Train	(Bunny Wailer)
21. In My Father's House	(Aswad)
22. Zion In A Vision	(Garnett Silk)
23. African Tears	(Peter Hunnigale)
24. Ambush In The Night	(Bob Marley & The Wailers)
25. How Can We Ease The Pain	(Maxi Priest/ Beres Hammond)
26. Rub a Dub Soldier	(The Bloodfire Posse)
27. Raggamuffin Girl	(Frankie Paul /Apache Indian)
28. Border	(Gregory Isaacs)
29. Police And Thieves	(Junior Murvin)
30. Push Come To Shove	(Freddie McGregor)
31. Going Home	(Bob Andy)
32. Back To Africa	(Aswad)
Epilogue: Forward To Zion	(The Abyssinians)

LONDON

1. SWEET REGGAE MUSIC

Robbie opened the record shop door and the bass line hit him in the stomach, nearly forcing him back out into the street. Pushing on, he sauntered over to the revival section, casually nodding his head to the machine-gunfire drumbeat and harsh rasping vocals spitting out of the metre-high speakers on either side of the counter. The floor, walls and windows were rumbling with the bass, as was everything in the shop, including his own internal organs, which was one of his favourite feelings. Flicking through the CDs, he wondered why he always felt slightly self-conscious in this shop, even though he had been coming here for over ten years, ever since he could hardly see over the counter. This was not strictly true, as he was thirteen at the time and quite tall for his age. But it is how he liked to remember it, being ushered up to the counter through the clouds of smoke and crowds of customers to part with his money in exchange for a small amount of credibility and the disco 45 that had topped the reggae charts for most of 1986. He was fairly confident that his mild awkwardness now was not consciously to do with the observation that he happened to be the only white person in the shop. This was quite unusual, as the record store, set in the trendy heart of Notting Hill, attracted a wide variety of patrons seeking out the best in reggae. He was annoyed with himself for even noticing this, as it always irritated him the way some people made a big deal about being the only white person on a bus or in a club.

Growing up in London, Robbie always felt it was a bit odd when it was the other way round, and he got nervous if he found himself surrounded by white faces, in case he had stumbled into a group of off duty policemen going to a line dance in aid of the Conservative Party. No, the usual feeling was probably something to with the fact all the best new tunes were behind the counter, and buying one involved the embarrassment of having to shout over the deafening volume for some obscure title. They would invariably turn it down for him halfway through, to leave him yelling something like 'Love Me Big Batty Gal by Colonel Lizard and Squiddly Banton' to the rest of the shop. In his younger days, he used to think it would be the best job in the world working here. Lately he had noticed that most of the guys behind the counter, who worked here all day and then played on sound systems all night, wore earplugs to cope with the occupational hazard of deafness and had developed a sophisticated level of lip-reading the names of artists and records requested by customers.

The tune came to an abrupt halt, and the other turntable flicked into action. The crackle of needle on vinyl gave a fleeting moment of peace before the opening drum-roll and spray of horns sent a familiar shiver down Robbie's spine. He stopped dead still, closed his eyes and was taken away by the sweet melody and heart-stopping rhythm. That was it. He loved this music so much it was embarrassing. Inside, he wanted to start skanking, wave his hands in the air and shout out his appreciation, but he knew if he did any of these things his faint self-consciousness would turn into a deep sense of shame and he would never set foot in the place again. Robbie remembered the day this reggae revelation happened inside him. It was on the way back from a school football match when he was twelve years old, and there was a group of about six or seven older boys at the back of the coach playing a dancehall tape on a ghetto blaster. The Pull Up Posse, as they were known, were the best football players on the first team and the coolest kids in school. The sharpest dressers, they even made the school uniform look good and always got away with wearing the latest non-regulation gleaming white Nike trainers. All the girls fancied them, and probably some of the boys as well, but this was generally left unspoken in an inner London comprehensive. They were funny and cheeky to teachers, but mostly avoided serious trouble. They were hard – they had to be to deter the few racists hanging around the school gates – but they were never bullies and nobody messed with them. They were not cool just because they were black, of course, there were a lot of other black kids in Robbie's school who wore NHS glasses, played the violin and hung out at chess club at lunchtimes. Although their coolness was inextricably linked to their blackness, they were role models in street credibility for the whole school.

Robbie knew the music the Pull Up Posse were listening to had to be wicked, even though it was mostly unintelligible to the untrained ear. But this tune just grabbed him and he started hearing it everywhere he went. Before then, Robbie had quite liked Bob Marley and appreciated his next-door neighbour cranking out some old bluebeat on a Sunday afternoon, but this was like a sudden discovery that this music was speaking directly to him, taking him over and controlling him. From that moment on, his ears pricked up every time a bassline boomed out of a market stall or a passing BMW, and he scanned the FM dial on his bedroom radio for pirate reggae stations. Like a lot of other kids at school, black, white and Asian alike, he tried cultivating a Jamaican accent for a while, but when he said tree instead of three and tink for think, it came out more Irish. He taught himself to play his dad's bass guitar, but his advert on the school notice board for a drummer, preferably called Sly, remained unanswered. Robbie's mates all became equally obsessed with hip-hop, indie or acid house in the late eighties. They liked the odd crossover reggae tune or listening to dub while sharing a spliff, but he knew they did not understand it, did not feel, live and breathe it, the way he did. It was a constant soundtrack to his teenage years, and every song reminded him of a girl he fancied, or a summer evening doing nothing hanging out with his mates, or a row with his parents. Now, nearing the age of twenty-four, he was stuck in the same adolescent vacuum where music expressed the feelings that his heart could not articulate. Years of listening to sentimental lovers rock lyrics had left him emotionally stunted, with impossible dreams and unattainable expectations. There were not many women he had met and liked who did not have one of his unique, homemade labour of love compilations buried somewhere in their tape collection. But reggae was still his first and unrequited love.

Robbie recovered himself and continued examining the CDs on display, although he was pretty certain he would not find what he was looking for. The newly released compilation he was after had been on display in one of the mega stores, but he had not bought it at the time. This was partly out of loyalty, and his desire to support small local traders rather than boost the profits of multi-national chains. He felt that an unfaithful purchase elsewhere could lead directly to specialist stores closing down, and the mega stores would then probably stop stocking reggae if it fell back out of fashion the next week. Importantly, CDs were also a pound cheaper here. The problem now was that he could picture the cover but for the life of him could not remember the title. He moved towards the counter, which was lined with serious customers piling up dozens of 7" singles fresh from Jamaica to entertain dances all over London. He was on nodding terms with the boss by now, although it was hard to tell as everyone was nodding the whole time anyway. The boss was universally known in the reggae world as Scotch, and his name on a poster always guaranteed a crowd at dances over the past twenty years. Robbie had wondered if he was so named because of a drinking problem or a liking for hot peppers, as he had never noticed a Caledonian lilt to his Jamaican accent, but the true reason was a lot more obvious. In fact, considering Scotch's school friends in St Ann's Bay had grown up stuck with nicknames like Uglybwoy and Smallhead, he counted himself quite lucky, especially as his long-forgotten real name was Hamish MacIntosh, after his Glaswegian grandfather, who went for a walk when his ship docked in Jamaica in 1921, and never left. They exchanged nods of recognition and Scotch raised his weary eyebrows slightly to let Robbie know he was ready to take his custom.

'HAVE YOU GOT THAT NEW COMPILATION...I CAN'T REMEMBER WHAT IT'S CALLED ... BUT ON THE COVER IT'S GOT - ' At this point Scotch took down the music.

'- A BIG PICTURE OF...Haile Selassie?'

Robbie trailed off sheepishly and the music filled the shop again straight away, sparing his blushes. As the other customers looked faintly amused, Scotch scanned his memory for a few seconds, mouthed 'hol' on' and disappeared beneath the counter. He was gone so long, Robbie began to wonder if there was a trap door and stairs to a basement behind there. The white furry hat eventually popped up again, followed by a gold-toothed smile and a vinyl copy of the album he wanted.

Everyone in the shop was drawn in hypnotically by the image of one of the icons of the twentieth century. They glanced over Robbie's shoulder to admire the album cover, which was even more impressive on 12 inch. His Imperial Majesty, the last Emperor of Ethiopia, stared up at him through soft, knowing eyes. It was a stylised image from an original photograph of the recently crowned young king, taken back in the thirties. The sleeve artist had brought the image a supernatural force, embellishing the face and beard with shining gold and rich ebony hues, surrounded by a glowing halo of flames, on a background of the red, gold and green Ethiopian flag. Across the bottom of the cover, the words of Marcus Garvey were emblazoned: 'Look to Africa, where a divine black king shall be crowned'.

Robbie flipped the record over, checked the track listing, reached for his wallet, then paused.

'CD finish,' explained Scotch, reading his mind.

'Oh, are there any extra tracks?'

'Nah, mi nah tink so.'

'Alright, yeah, I'll take the vinyl please... Thanks.'

Stepping out onto Ladbroke Grove and into the cold November air, with the vibrations from the shop fading behind him as he headed for the tube, Robbie remembered that he had promised to go and see his granny.

2. WAR

'**M**essage from the frontline, your majesty.'

The emperor delicately took his hands off the anti-aircraft gun as if it was a matchstick model and he was unsure it would stand on its own. Being one of only eight his entire army possessed he currently viewed it as more precious than the Holy Ark. He had spent all day aiming futile fire at the Italian planes high overhead like a small boy throwing stones at vultures. This was the first time he had let the heavy gun go all day and it slowly came to rest on its stand, pointing at the feet of the intruder to the shelter. Removing his tin helmet, the emperor wheeled round and faced the trembling young soldier.

'Speak.'

'The enemy has unleashed poison gas on the imperial defences and the villages north of Dese. Hundreds confirmed dead, countless casualties, supply lines bombed. Thousands of homes destroyed, refugees heading south. Enemy encampment at Maychew.'

The emperor held up his hand and closed his eyes, offering up a silent prayer for his lost subjects. He readjusted the collar of his uniform and smoothed down his tunic, which still gleamed immaculately despite the dirt and dust all around him.

'Very well. We shall advance through the night and meet the enemy at Maychew,' asserted the emperor coolly.

Fitwrari Tessem, the emperor's closest adviser, looked horrified.

'Your majesty, the enemy's airpower is devastating, we will be crushed. Our only hope is to flee and wait for the British or French to intervene.'

The mention of these supposed friendly countries made the emperor's nostrils flare and his lips twitched as if he had been given rotten food to eat. For years he had persuaded patronising diplomats that his country was a civilised, modern state of equal standing and independence, a fellow member of the League of Nations. Now despite their supportive words, Britain and France had sat idly by and watched the injustice of an aggressor invading a smaller nation, emulating their own colonial scramble of forty years before. If they thought they could save themselves by forsaking his country, they would come to regret their cowardice, thought the emperor.

'We can wait in vain no more. Our trust is in our Creator. We know the enemy has the advantages of modern technology at his disposal, but we offer up to the Holy God of Ethiopia our fervent prayers and everlasting faith. He has bestowed upon us the hearts of lions and the fearlessness of the martyred saints.'

Tessem urged the emperor to retreat, but knew his words fell unheard into the dust. The emperor's eyes filled with fire and stared past him into the distance, towards the row of red, gold and green imperial flags fluttering on the hilltops. Exhausted by battle, he had become detached from the realities of military strategy and felt honour bound to lead his wounded nation in one last push to repel the invaders, urged on by the voices of his ancestors, recalling the heroic victory of Adowa in 1896 when his great-uncle Emperor Menelik II had turned the Italians back once before. His majesty inspired the remnants of the army to the final sacrifice, persuading them it was better to die in defence of their freedom than live as slaves. Thirty thousand men marched through the night in darkness. They were tired, cold and hungry as they had been unable to light torches or campfires for weeks because of the risk of making a target for the enemy. In the dim glow of dawn, they made out the swollen discoloured corpses of their fellow men, women and children by the roadside and under every tree and bush, where they had sought shelter in vain from the rain of mustard gas. Marching on into the misty morning across the barren hills, the enemy encampment was visible a few miles ahead.

The attack was a disaster. All day long, wave after wave of enemy airplanes filled the sky, blotting out the sun with dark clouds of bombs. The enthusiastic but poorly trained Ethiopian conscripts were no match for the might of a modern industrial military machine and were mown down as soon as they got near the heavily fortified enemy lines. By the time darkness fell, the emperor and his inner circle had run out of ammunition and were cut off from supplies, waiting for the inevitable ambush in the night. One by one, the emperor had watched as the positions all around him were picked off, knowing that members of his family and trusted friends were among those blasted into the dust that hung in the air, and wondered if he had been spared by the grace of God. His faith was strong, but he realised that the enemy wanted to capture him alive.

'For the sake of Ethiopia, your majesty, we must retreat,' pleaded Tessem, who had come to the same conclusion.

'We will fight to the death,' asserted the emperor.

'That would be a noble end, your majesty, but I fear the enemy will rob us of even that one final dignity. To be captured and paraded before your subjects and the world as a puppet would be a fate worse than death.'

The emperor nodded. He could not fault the logic of Tessem's argument and there were few other options. Looking down at his hands resting on the useless artillery, for a moment he wished the ring on his finger contained a cyanide pill beneath the black jewel engraved in gold with the royal seal, the Lion of Judah. If only King Solomon had the wisdom of foresight to know what would become of the heir to his throne, the bearer of the imperial ring, three thousand years later. The emperor clenched his fist and smiled at this thought, knowing that the destiny of the Solomonic line and the root of King David, as revealed in the bible, was not to be hunted into submission like a rat cornered among rocks in the desert. The conquering lion of the tribe of Judah would rise up and let out its mighty roar to echo across this land again soon.

For now, he turned around and led his men south, protected by the jagged mountains in the moon-less night, through which even the bravest Italian pilot did not dare fly. Within a week, the emperor was back in Addis Ababa, where he collected the Empress Menen and their children. In a calm, controlled operation over several days, most of the royal family's gold, silver, jewellery, art, antiques and furniture were carefully packed into heavy wooden boxes. As the Italian army advanced south towards the capital, the emperor ordered that his remaining valuables be distributed among the people of Addis Ababa. He then instructed his essential retinue of one hundred staff to load the boxes, themselves and his two pet lions onto a train bound for the Red Sea port of Djibouti. After two days and nights' arduous journey east, the emperor graciously accepted the British offer of evacuation by a merchant navy steamer, and reluctantly accepted the captain's advice that about sixty staff, several tonnes of cargo and the two lions would have to remain behind. As the ship left the shores of Africa bound for Palestine, the emperor vowed that he would reclaim his throne within five years, as long as it would take the rest of the world to wake up to the evil that threatened all humanity.

3. PICTURE ON THE WALL

'Who's this?'

Minnie peered at the figure in the doorway from her armchair. She was propped up with several pillows, a tartan blanket wrapped around her knees and a large print copy of 'Jane Eyre' in her hands. She squinted at him briefly through her glasses and then divided her attention between her book and the quiz show on television.

'Oh, don't be daft, its Robbie. Your grandson. My son,' Robbie's mum shouted from the kitchen.

'Roddy? Is that Roddy? I thought he'd gone to America,' Minnie turned back at Robbie, looking him up and down disdainfully for a few more seconds, then smiled to herself. Rummaging through the pockets of several layers of cardigan and body warmer, she unearthed a packet of butterscotch, unwrapped one for herself and offered one to him.

'No thanks, Nan. It's me, Robbie,' He yelled at her over the blaring television, enunciating his words slowly and clearly, partly out of the pointless technique commonly adopted when talking to people who are profoundly deaf, or don't speak English as their first language. This was almost the case, as his grandmother's hearing was by all accounts severely impaired, and she had spoken only Welsh up to the age of eight, although to be fair she had got quite good at English after seventy-two years. It was also force of habit, as even when she was in full possession of all her faculties, his grandmother had never been able to understand a word Robbie said in his London accent at normal pace. Throughout his childhood, he realised that she always smiled politely and then asked his mother for an explanation, so he had made an effort to make it easier for her. This was not quite fair, as she had lived all of her life in Wales and made no effort to tone down her accent.

'You're not Roddy. Roddy could never resist butterscotch.' Minnie eyed him suspiciously then turned back to the television. Her daughter, Isobel, entered the room, pushing Robbie in front of her and making him sit down on one of the two chairs either side of a folded-up dining table by the window opposite Minnie. Robbie sat down and joined his grandmother in silent concentration on the quiz question. Isobel bustled around the small living room, busying herself with dusting ornaments and picking imaginary pieces of fluff off the carpet as she spoke.

'You're quite right, mum, cousin Rodney is in America. You do have a look of him, mind you, Robbie, but he's about fifty. At least he is now, not when you last saw him, mum. You know who this is, even though he doesn't come to see you very often. It's my little Robbie.'

'Oh him,' continued Minnie as if Robbie was not there, 'Has he got a job yet? Youngsters today wouldn't last ten minutes in the old days. When I was his age we were all down the pits morning 'til night, never saw daylight except on a Sunday.'

'Don't tell stories, mum, you were a nanny in Bath, then you worked in the Co-op in Cardiff.'

'Same thing,' shrugged Minnie.

'Thanks for coming, son, are you having a cup of tea? What about you, mum?' Isobel didn't wait for any answers and her chatter was replaced by the sound of the kettle being filled and the cups clinking from the kitchen.

Robbie smiled and waved at his grandmother. She nodded vaguely, as if humouring him. As she was immersed in her book, Robbie studied her face. She looked thinner and more wrinkled every time he saw her and she seemed to be shrinking. Her eyes still had a mischievous, childlike twinkle and she appeared to be quite happy, as she nodded to herself in a satisfied way after each correct answer was announced. He felt bad that he had left it a couple of months and had only seen her a few times in total since she moved down from Cardiff last year after his grandfather had died. Then again, she did not seem too bothered about Robbie's visits, or lack of them, and he was fairly certain that the fact she did not remember him was more to do with her condition than his shortcomings as a grandson. She had settled in well to the sheltered accommodation, a bus ride away from his mother, who was not the only family she had left, but about the only person she recognised.

Isobel set down the tray with the teapot, milk jug, sugar bowl and three cups, comprising most of Minnie's beloved royal wedding tea-set. Robbie loved his gran and she was the only real connection he had left with his Welsh heritage, as his parents had lived in London so long. He liked to cling proudly to his Welsh identity, partly in an attempt to identify with the oppressed colonial peoples of the world, but now he cringed at the reminder of his grandmother's devotion to the British monarchy.

'Well, have you been telling your granny what you've been getting up to?' asked Isobel.

'Not really, we've just been wondering what is the tallest mountain in Africa,' replied Robbie facetiously, as he knew his mother could hear they had not exchanged a word since she left the room.

'Kilimanjaro!' shouted Minnie, who had an uncanny knack of listening to the television and answering the questions apparently without interrupting her reading.

'Well, you can tell us now. How's work?' asked Isobel as she sat down opposite Robbie, obscuring his view of the television.

'Its alright.... Oh, well done, nan,' he said, smiling over at Minnie and giving her the thumbs-up as the quizmaster read out the answer.

'How's Angela?' asked Isobel, as she distributed the tea.

'She's great, thanks.'

'When are you going to bring her round to see us again?'

'I don't know, she's quite busy at the moment, what with work and everything,' said Robbie.

'Any news on moving in together?'

'Not really, we are doing alright as we are for now.'

'Well, I don't like to think of you paying all that rent in that little flat on your own and her in that shared house when you could be making a home together.'

'Yes, well, we don't want to rush into anything. Anyway, how's Dad?' said Robbie, changing the subject.

'He's not too bad, got a bit of a cold at the moment, you know,' replied Isobel.

They sat in silence for a while, just the sound of the television and the three of them gulping down their tea.

'The blue whale!' exclaimed Minnie, winking at Robbie, who smiled over again, nodding in agreement.

'So what are you doing tonight? I take it you're not spending Saturday night watching telly with us, eh?' asked Isobel.

'Just meeting up with James and Ravi later, y'know, going for a drink, watch the footy.'

'Very good. How are they doing?'

'Fine.'

'And where have you been today, Christmas shopping?' asked Isobel, thinking this was like pulling teeth, without the screaming and the blood.

'Nah, just records for myself,' said Robbie, pointing at the bag.

'Sean Connery!' shouted Minnie.

'And what have you bought? Are you going to show us?' teased Isobel.

'I don't think you and granny are going to be too interested, its not Tom Jones.'

'Cheeky sod, don't forget I saw Bob Marley in London before you were out of nappies.'

Robbie sighed, as he was aware that this technical fact made him feel a mixture of pride, that his ageing hippy parents may have been quite cool at one point, and shame, that unlike most young people he had got into music that his parents did not hate. Although they were not so keen on the hardcore digital ragga.

'Alright, here you go.' Robbie pulled the record out of the bag and held it up.

As the image of the emperor caught the light, the red, gold and green background flashed around the room. The piercing eyes of the emperor gazed back at Isobel, and simultaneously at Minnie, as she was distracted from her book.

'Very nice. The artwork is amazing,' said Isobel politely.

Minnie started giggling uncontrollably. She pointed at the record and became quite hysterical. Robbie was a little taken aback, and looked at the cover again. While he was not remotely persuaded of the divinity of the late Ethiopian ruler, he did not see anything particularly funny about the picture, and felt this attitude was a bit disrespectful, even allowing for his grandmother's condition. Minnie continued rocking backwards and forwards, laughing so hard that he also became quite concerned about the risk of bladder incontinence. Robbie stared at her for a few more seconds, thinking that her condition was obviously a lot worse than he had appreciated.

'What's wrong, mum?' asked Isobel, going over to sit on the arm of Minnie's chair, and stroking her on the back.

Minnie wiped away the tears that were streaming down her face and caught her breath.

'It's your grandfather!' she looked over at Robbie as the words exploded, and then started shaking again, but it no longer seemed to be with laughter. Isobel sighed and shook her head, hugging her mother.

'It's alright, mum, I know.'

Robbie put the record back in the bag, mystified. He felt distinctly uncomfortable as the two women sat sobbing together and got up, gathering the empty cups onto the tray to do the washing up.

A few minutes later, Isobel tiptoed into the kitchen and patted Robbie on the shoulder as he stood by the sink. He had managed to take an incredibly long time to wash three cups, absent-mindedly trying to rub the smile off Prince Charles' face, and was relieved that it was now safe to stop.

'Is she alright?' he asked.

'Oh, she's been like this on and off for a year, ever since your granddad died.' Isobel dabbed at her face with a tea towel, where her mother's tears had mingled with her own, before continuing in a whisper, 'One minute she seems perfectly happy, the next something reminds her of him and she's off. You know her memory's going and I think she keeps forgetting that he's died, and then remembering suddenly and it hits her all over again. Can you imagine what that's like?'

'Not really. Terrible, I suppose.'

'She's asleep now, poor love. I hate seeing her like this, she's like a totally different person.'

'Is there anything I can do? I mean, around the flat?'

'No, don't worry. I did the cleaning earlier on.'

'Doesn't she have a home help for that?' asked Robbie, looking at the spotless surroundings.

'Yes, but I don't want them finding the place in a mess.'

Robbie looked at her, raising an eyebrow and wondering if this dementia was hereditary.

'Anyway,' Isobel continued, ushering him out of the kitchen, 'you get off now and meet your pals. It's good of you to come. Don't forget your record.'

Robbie stepped carefully through the living room where his grandmother was asleep in her chair. She seemed peaceful enough now. He paused by the front door.

'What do you think set her off just now?' he whispered to his mother.

'Oh, I don't know, maybe the question about Sean Connery. I always thought dad had a look of him.'

'Yeah,' Robbie chuckled, 'He had his hair, or someone's, anyway. See you then.'

'Cheerio, son.' Isobel called after him, 'You can pop in anytime you know, even if I'm not here. She does appreciate it.'

'Yeah, I will. See you soon, gran,' he shouted, forgetting she was dozing.

Minnie, half-asleep in her chair, smiled to herself and murmured.

'I'll be seeing ya.'

4. DECLARATION OF RIGHTS

The emperor held his handkerchief to his nose and breathed in its heavy perfume to drown out the smoky fumes that seemed to hang permanently over London. As the train ground to a stop and the clouds of steam lifted from the window, to his astonishment a crowd materialised along the platform, and for a moment he wondered what was going on. The British government had insisted that his status was strictly incognito when he was transferred from the navy warship in Palestine to a passenger liner bound for Southampton, and he had been assured his arrival would be announced discreetly to avoid any threat from Italian spies or assassins. Meanwhile in London, the press had got wind of events, and while the government-supporting papers had tucked the story away in a small inner paragraph, others had seized on the opportunity to express their opposition to Italian Fascism. Huge headlines splashed 'WELCOME EMPEROR' all over the front pages, which were now being waved joyously with other messages of support on placards along the platform. Besides the modest official delegation of crumpled bureaucrats on behalf of the Foreign Secretary, a five thousand strong unofficial welcoming party had rushed to Waterloo Station. The emperor was amazed to see African, Chinese, Indian and Arab faces, cheering heartily amongst the flat caps and top hats of the English, waving the red white and blue of the Union Jack entwined with the red gold and green of the Ethiopian flag, as his private Pullman car drew in.

'Welcome to the land of the free! Hurrah for the one and only Emperor of Ethiopia! Down with Mussolini!' came the raucous shouts from the platform.

The Foreign Office representative, Mr Harvey, stepped sheepishly onto the train and formally greeted the emperor, his wife, children and retinue, which had gradually reduced in number since leaving Djibouti. He then presented the distinguished refugee to a line of eminent friends of Ethiopia as he stepped down from the train. One of these, a Liberal Lord and vocal opponent of appeasement, unrolled an elaborate scroll and as the crowd hushed, he read aloud its heartfelt, though unofficial, message:

'We lament that Ethiopia has suffered invasion. We, with thousands of people of Great Britain, express the hope that the day will soon dawn when Ethiopia will regain her ancient independence and her rightful Emperor will return and, trusting in God, will continue to lead his people toward light and peace.'

The Ethiopian emperor clasped the British aristocrat's hands warmly as he handed him the scroll. He lifted his head towards the crowd and smiled, pausing for a few seconds, as he had not prepared any words for this unexpected ceremony.

'God grant that it may be so ... I come to England confident that I will obtain justice here ... May the British Crown and the British people live forever!'

The crowd erupted, startling the emperor and snapping him out of the depressive introspection that had travelled with him ever since leaving his homeland. Suddenly he felt that there was some hope, and that his planned appeal to the League of Nations in Geneva could gather the support of the British, then maybe even the French and Americans, to oppose the Italian invasion. Forgetting the security concerns, he found comfort in the enthusiasm of crowd and waved cheerfully as he waited on the platform, carefully counting his forty-two crates off the train, including the gold bars and Imperial treasure chest. The emperor, his family and luggage were then whisked away by limousine with a police escort through the London streets towards Hyde Park. Paperboys ran along behind the entourage, shouting the news and waving copies of the latest editions, swelling the crowd with curious passers-by, lining the streets and cheering all the way to the luxurious townhouse at No.5 Princes Gate, which was to be his temporary refuge.

A week later, in the cool air of neutral Geneva, nestling nervously between Italy and Germany, the emperor's reception was very different. The streets were empty and quiet, white faces looked down to the ground as he passed. As he arrived at the League's headquarters, suspicious security officials demanded to see proof of his status as a member, and grudgingly allowed him in. He allowed himself a small smile at this irony, as if they could confuse him with anyone else; he wore his full imperial regalia and it was the only time in the history of the League that a black African head of state had appeared before the congress of colonial powers. He entered the hall at the appointed time and stepped up to the lectern in silence. Glancing up furtively at the cameras, he touched the microphone in front of him before lowering his head to read the speech he had prepared for months, ever since the first bombs fell on Ethiopian soil. His voice faltered and he cleared his throat, unused to the cold, damp climate of Europe.

'I, Haile Selassie the first, Emperor of Ethiopia, am here today to claim that justice which is due to my people, and the assistance promised to it eight months ago, when fifty nations asserted that aggression had been committed in violation of international treaties. There is no precedent for a Head of State himself speaking in this assembly. But there is also no precedent for a people being victim of such injustice and being at present threatened by abandonment to its aggressor. Also, there has never before been an example of any Government proceeding to the systematic extermination of a nation by barbarous means, in violation of the most solemn promises made by the nations of the earth that there should not be used against innocent human beings the terrible poison of harmful gases. It is to defend a people struggling for its age-old independence that the head of the Ethiopian Empire has come to Geneva to fulfil this supreme duty, after having himself fought at the head of his armies. I pray to Almighty God that He may spare nations the terrible sufferings that have just been inflicted on my people, and of which the chiefs who accompany me here have been the horrified witnesses. It is my duty to inform the Governments assembled in Geneva, responsible as they are for the lives of millions of men, women and children, of the deadly peril which threatens them, by describing to them the fate which has been suffered by Ethiopia. It is not only upon warriors that the Italian Government has made war. It has above all attacked populations far removed from hostilities, in order to terrorize and exterminate them.'

The emperor paused as he became aware of a murmur from somewhere in the hall and looked up to see the Italian delegation talking and laughing among themselves. His eyes blazed a fire of fury for a few seconds before he gritted his teeth and continued with his speech. As he went on, the jeers and abuse from the Italian diplomats grew more distracting, and he frequently had to stop and look around for the chairman to intervene, to no avail. The emperor stuck to his speech with steadfast determination, describing in detail the atrocities waged against his people, the infringements of international law committed by the invasion, and the moral and legal obligations of the gathered member states to safeguard a smaller nation, and thereby save themselves. While paper aeroplanes sailed down from the back of the auditorium, accompanied by the sounds of bombs and hissing of gas, the emperor spoke undaunted for thirty minutes.

'Representatives of the world I have come to Geneva to discharge in your midst the most painful of the duties of the head of a state. What reply shall I have to take back to my people?' he concluded with the question, which echoed around the hall for a few uneasy seconds. Even the Italian delegation went nervously quiet, in case the emperor's passionate oratory may have had the desired effect and the powerless puppets that attended the League would take back to their leaders some of his fire. The delegates all looked down or around, avoiding the emperor's burning gaze, which seemed to be directed at each individual personally. He stepped slowly down from the podium, but as he did so, he murmured clearly, within range of the microphones and reporters:

'It is us today. It will be you tomorrow.'

5. YOUNG, GIFTED & BLACK

As he reached the shared front door to his flat, Robbie could make out two unmistakable figures looming out of the darkness between streetlights at the far end of the tree-lined street. Ravi, towering over James by about a foot, bounced along the middle of the narrow pavement, while his short friend weaved in and out of his footsteps, bowing in a gentlemanly fashion as he stepped aside for a surprised old lady. Robbie just had time to nip up the stairs to his flat at the top, grab a beer from the fridge and put his new record on when the buzzer went.

'You ready?' Ravi shouted impatiently into the intercom.

'No, come up.' Robbie buzzed them in and heard heavy footsteps bounding up the stairs, followed by a slower, lighter tread.

He shook hands with each of them in time-honoured fashion. He was not really sure why they still did this every time they met and parted; it was a habit that had evolved out of the increasingly awkward touching of fists they had adhered to when they were younger. The three friends had all known each other since attending the same local school. However, at the age of thirteen, James' parents took out a second mortgage to send him to a private school after an incident involving the headmaster's car, demonstrating his emerging talent as a graffiti artist, a vocation of which his parents disapproved. This left him with a previously unpredicted university place and a habit of straying between a faintly upper class English accent and London street slang, although occasionally he also slipped into a vague approximation of New York for no apparent reason. Ravi had done a filmmaking course and was still looking for his big break while working as a van-driver. After varying paths of re-sits, college, university and travelling, the three of now found themselves back in the west London suburb where they started.

'Sit down, I've just got in. Do you want a beer?'

'Nah, just move your arse, man,' said Ravi as he flopped down on the sofa.

'No thanks. We really should be making a move - kick off is eight. Where we gonna catch it?' said James.

'Well, it's getting a bit late so we might as well just go somewhere local, alright?' said Robbie.

'Yeah, well, depends, who are you going to be supporting?' Ravi asked Robbie.

'Mate, I've told you, I'm a quarter Italian and the rest of me is Welsh, there's no way I can support England.'

'Oh, fuck off, I'm all Indian but I'm supporting England. Haven't you heard of Norman Tebbit?' replied Ravi.

'Leave the guy alone,' interrupted James, 'He is entitled to support who he likes. It makes him feel like he's an ethnic minority. But if you cheer when Italy score,' turning to Robbie, 'we don't know you.'

'Look, my mother's father was Italian. It's in my blood, the dark hair and eyes, olive skin - I can't help it, its where I get my good looks from,' replied Robbie.

'Yeah, that's a fair point. I always used to fancy your mum when we were kids. I mean she's getting on a bit now, but I'd still –'

'Please!' Robbie held up a hand to stop Ravi's train of thought, preferring not to know where it was heading. 'I'll just change my shirt and clean my teeth, and we can go. Make yourselves at home,' he said as he went through the adjoining door to the bedroom.

'What's this shit you're listening to?' called James after him over the first track of the compilation, which consisted mainly of chanting and drumming. Robbie ignored him. James picked the record sleeve off the armchair by the stereo and inspected it.

'What?' asked Robbie, putting his shirt on as he walked through the room and into the kitchen, still smarting slightly from the insult to his musical taste.

'It was a rhetorical question. We were just admiring this fine compilation,' said James, tossing the cover dismissively to Ravi.

'Don't dish the man's musical taste man. İ like a bit of rugga myself.'

Robbie was never sure whether Ravi was trying to invent some new talk of his own, so he let it pass.

'So, what you into this week then, James?' asked Robbie defensively.

'Garage, but it don't matter, cos what you picking up, I put down already. You don't realise that white people are the driving force behind black music. As soon as you guys get into something, we have to invent something new. Jazz, blues, rock'n'roll, ska, reggae, rap, house - same story.'

'Bullshit, white people have always been involved in black music. You just like what is trendy, you're not really into it.'

'Bredren, there is more to the world than black and white,' opined Ravi in a rare moment of clarity.

'Are you going like that?' asked James, looking Robbie up and down as he buttoned his crumpled shirt.

'What?' responded Robbie indignantly, looking down at his clothes.

'Have you heard of these metal things you can get now, that heat up?' added Ravi.

'Right. I can take a hint,' said Robbie as he went into the kitchen to find his neglected iron and board. 'Are you sure you don't want a beer? We'll be here a while now because this takes me ages.'

'Go on then,' said James.

'Cheers,' said Ravi.

The two of them sat sipping their beers watching Robbie fight with the ironing board, as there was nothing on television.

'We were just getting worried about you, there. Wondering if you might be turning into one of those white Rasta guys?' asked James, winding him up on his favourite subject. He liked Robbie a lot, and found his obsession with Jamaican music faintly amusing. Since university, James had noticed that nearly all his friends were black. This worried him faintly but he was fairly sure that it was not his fault, as a lot of the students he met appeared never to have encountered a black person before, and assumed it was necessary to initiate a conversation by asking if he liked UB40 or if he knew where to get some weed. James had made an effort to catch up with his old school mates, and was relieved, although slightly concerned, to find that Robbie and Ravi had not changed a bit.

'Yes, I mean we respect you and all for your dedication to reggae, but I am afraid I would have to stop hanging out with you if you started growing those nasty crusty rats' tails and neglecting personal hygiene,' contributed Ravi, helpfully.

'Thanks, lads. No need to worry,' Robbie reassured them, 'number two round the back and sides and a bit off the top. Anyway, you can talk Ravi, what about your flowing locks?'

'Yeah, but this is clean and smooth, and a big hit with the ladies,' said Ravi, in the semi-ironic attitude that he had been keeping up so long he could no longer tell how he meant it.

'Oh yeah,' snorted James with straightforward sarcasm.

'Believe, they can't help running their fingers through it all the time. It could do with a trim though, I'll give you that. Hey Rob, do you still go to that barber's on Beauford Road?'

'Yeah, usually, why?' said Robbie, not looking up from his ironing.

'Just wondering. Only I haven't been back there since he rested his bollocks on my elbow.'

'You what?' came the stereo response from Robbie and James.

'You know when you're sitting in the chair with your arms resting on the armrests, which is what they're for, I suppose. He leans over and rests his bollocks on your elbow. He apologised and everything, but I haven't been back there since. I was about sixteen years old at the time. I swear.'

Robbie and James just looked at him, not sure how to respond to this revelation.

'Well, anyway, I know the guy you mean. He's a racist fucker,' said James.

'How'd you mean?' asked Robbie, surprised.

'I went there a few years ago and he starting acting all weird about cutting my hair, like he couldn't do black people's hair. And then he started going on about how it used to be lovely round here, before all these foreigners moved in. I got the distinct impression he didn't want me in the shop.'

'Fair enough. Sexual assault and racial prejudice, I will have to find another barber. Funny, he was always quite matey with me.'

'Yeah, funny that,' remarked James casually.

'Hmmm....wonder why?' mused Ravi.

They sat in silence for a few minutes, listening to the next track as Robbie ironed.

'Look to the east, for the coming of a black king,
Don't be fooled, Jah is forever living,
He will return, cos he created everything,
Peace, love and healing he will bring.'

'So, why are these crazy West Indians still venerating a dead dictator?' James rudely interrupted Robbie's peaceful appreciation of the music. 'They might as well worship someone who stood for something, like Nkrumah. Now my dad always said he was a man you could really believe in. In the early days, anyway, I admit he went a bit astray later.'

The collected opinions of James' father were regular features in his conversation and they had to be respected. Mr Addo senior was one of the original 'verandah boys' in the forties; Ghanaians who had been well-educated abroad and fought for the British empire in the name of freedom. After the war they returned to their country to find that they now had to fight against British empire for their own freedom, and there was nothing for them to do but sit about on verandahs discussing how to bring this about. When they succeeded to become the first black African nation to win independence from the British empire in 1957, James' dad was one of the crowd holding Nkrumah aloft on their shoulders. He went on to become a high-ranking civil servant in the government but fled to London with his wife when he felt that Nkrumah had betrayed the ideals of the revolution. Ideals of justice, democracy and human rights, which he tried to instil into his only child, with some success, as James had recently decided to pursue a career in law.

'Well, you might as well ask why do Christians worship a guy with a beard who was nailed to a tree two thousand years ago? Come to think of it, why does my mum worship a guy with an elephant's head?' said Ravi.

The religious beliefs of Ravi's mother were vary rare features of his conversation, and were generally ignored. Mrs Gupta was a devout Hindu who had set much higher standards of religious observance and behaviour for her three London-raised children than she had left behind in Gujarat, but the temptations and evils here were so much greater, as she frequently pointed out. Ravi's older brother and sister had spent their teenage years fighting battles over being allowed out at all, being allowed out unaccompanied, being allowed out after six o'clock in the evening, and being allowed out wearing a short skirt. Ravi's sister took the lead on this last one. By the time Ravi was sixteen, his parents were old and grey and had lost the energy to keep fighting, so he found the rules could be bent and broken beyond recognition. Especially the ones concerning drugs, alcohol, and pre-marital sex, although he remained a strict vegetarian.

'That's no way to speak about your father, Ravs, but I take your point that all religions are based on superstition. I was directing my question to our resident expert on Jamaican culture.' James nodded at Robbie.

'Well, it started back in the thirties, during colonialism, he stood for independence and Africa and black pride and all that,' explained Robbie wearily, knowing he was being set up, 'but I don't know why there is a bit of a revival at the moment. Maybe to do with global capitalism taking power away from national governments.'

'Bullshit,' commented Ravi, 'they just want to get stoned.'

'You're quite right, it is bullshit,' answered James, 'but I feel it is because of a return to essentially reactionary, conservative values. I mean, back in the thirties Selassie was just as scared of revolution as the next western puppet. For example, lots of real African revolutionaries lived in Britain, but he had nothing to do with them when he was here. He was a totally conservative reactionary force, an absolutist monarch from the feudal era,' he concluded, leaning back with a self-satisfied swig of lager.

'Yeah alright, I never said he was a great guy myself, I just happen to like the music he inspired,' said Robbie as he held his shirt up and examined it.

'You missed a bit on the sleeve there – it's well creased,' Ravi pointed out.

'Hang on a minute, what was that you said just now?' Robbie stopped with a look on his face as if he had just remembered he had left the iron on, which of course he had, but he was still using it so this could not be what had suddenly entered his head.

'Just there, by the cuff,' said Ravi.

'No, not you, him – about Haile Selassie.'

'Er…western puppet…feudal monarch?' suggested James.

'No, no, did you say he was in Britain?' asked Robbie impatiently.

'Yeah, he lived in exile here for a while when Ethiopia was invaded by the Italians. Which is ironic, considering your allegiance tonight. Like I say, Nkrumah, Nyerere, Kenyatta, were here around the same time, at university. Selassie would not be seen dead with those guys, no offence. He was just interested in his own survival and ingratiating himself with the British ruling class.'

'Really? When? Where?' demanded Robbie, drinking from his can.

'Don't you believe me? I did study African history and politics for three years. He was in exile in the thirties. He came to London, and then lived in Bath, I think.'

Robbie spat out a mouthful of lager over his newly ironed shirt and started coughing.

'Fuck off. You're winding me up,' he said finally.

'What? He was, it's common knowledge. What is so unlikely about that?' replied James.

'Nothing, just something my granny said earlier on,' mumbled Robbie, recovering himself, he went into his bedroom and found a top that did not need ironing. 'Come on, let's go.'

'Wait up, I haven't finished this yet,' said Ravi, holding up his can, 'or shall I just spit it over your clothes?'

'Yeah, mate, that is one nasty habit. Please don't be doing that tonight,' said James as they left the room and headed downstairs.

6. EXODUS

Hot steam mingled with the cold morning mist to swaddle the train as it slowly pulled into the platform. The emperor was surprised to see his own breath vaporising in front of his face to add to the dull cloud that hung around him. It seemed as if winter had come early to London, and he tightened the belt on the greatcoat of his military dress uniform. Taking the hand of his valet to support him as he stepped down from the train, the emperor paused expectantly for photographers and to give the crowd an opportunity to see him. Looking up and down the length of the platform, he found that it was empty, save for a few passengers hurriedly making their way past him. His adviser, Tessem, looked over the imperial shoulder and muttered a few words of encouragement in his royal ear, speculating that the British government had kept secret his glorious return from Geneva so as to avoid a huge crowd. The emperor was not so sure, as the British had been very quiet after his speech in Geneva, and no one had spoken in his support. He glanced at the headlines on a nearby newspaper stand and saw that the main focus of interest had moved on to the civil war erupting in Spain, another arena where it appeared to him that fascism was spreading unchecked by the old powers of Europe. But his face did not betray his suspicions as he nodded his head and looked thoughtfully into the distance, maintaining his public air of omniscience. For the benefit of his family, Tessem and Solomon the valet, who were all he had left of his people, he knew he had to show them he believed they would all be returning home any day. He did not allow even himself to consider the alternative, and strode confidently down the platform, leaving Tessem and Solomon to sort out the baggage and hail a taxi.

Empress Menen gazed out across Hyde Park from the sixth-floor window of the luxury hotel, which to her was a prison. Desta and Sahle played on the floor with toy soldiers, re-enacting the battle for their country with a more favourable result. She longed to be back in her home, where the sun was always shining, where the trees and flowers gave off familiar scents and her family and friends were always around her. She knew her home had probably already been smashed under the jackboots of the Italian soldiers, and many of her relatives killed, but inside her head it would always remain the same. Nowhere would ever replace it as her home, certainly not this cold, unsmiling foreign place. While her husband had been to Geneva and back, it seemed to her that it had not stopped raining in London. The car drew up outside at the allotted time and the brief skip her heart felt on seeing her husband was replaced with a dull ache she knew immediately from her husband's countenance that the trip had not brought its desired outcome. Menen was quite a bit older then her husband and had spent all her life among the aristocracy and court politics of Abyssinia, and she knew that power could be a transient and fragile thing. All she could do was try to make life as secure and comfortable as possible. She really did not know what would happen to them now, only that her husband would never give up his own destiny, which he deeply believed was that he alone could protect and guide the Ethiopian people. Now his head was bowed and he did not look up to the window as he stooped hurriedly into the foyer. When he entered he embraced them all formally but there was no joyful reunion, as they knew they would remain separated from the place and people that made them who they were. The customary fire in his eyes had been extinguished and he seemed paler, as if the lack of sun had drained his natural colour, he was dishevelled and unable to smile or look directly at his family. Menen was reminded that without his throne, his empire and his people he was just a man; a small, slight, forty-two year old, brown-skinned man with a prominent nose. The emperor disappeared abruptly into the room that he had made his study for further talks with his advisers.

Menen kept staring out of the window at the darkening sky over London, watching the half-reflection in the glass of the room behind her as the hotel concierge showed in a thin Englishman wearing a grey suit. She continued looking away meekly as he bowed in her direction and shuffled hesitantly towards the study door. As the door clicked behind him, Menen decided to employ an ancient tactic her mother had shown her that had served her well over the years in the royal house of Abyssinia. She ran over and put her ear against the door.

'Your imperial majesty, welcome to Great Britain. It is my great honour to convey the warmest regards of his majesty the king,' said Mr Harvey, bowing obsequiously.

'We are eternally grateful for the kindness and friendship of the English people. Please express our deepest appreciation to his majesty the king,' replied the emperor.

There followed an awkward silence. The emperor knew that the king was probably not even aware of his presence in the country, as it was common knowledge in royal circles that he was preoccupied by an affair with an American divorcee. He also knew that the king would probably be embarrassed by his appearance, as he seemed reluctant to take any action that would impair his friendship with the Italian king and German aristocracy. The emperor was painfully aware that Mr Harvey was a representative of the Foreign Office, not the king, and his government had remained ominously silent throughout his speech to the League of Nations.

'Would you like a cup of tea?' interjected Tessem with impeccable diplomacy.

'Oh yes, please. Jolly good idea,' replied Mr Harvey with relief as he sat down and relaxed.

'So, have you news from Geneva?' asked the emperor.

Mr Harvey shook his head. 'As your imperial majesty is aware, the international situation is very delicate at the moment. We do not wish to take any hasty action that may precipitate another European war. Please realise how many of us lost fathers, brothers and uncles in the Great War. I am sorry that our diplomatic efforts have failed to prevent the emergency in your imperial majesty's homeland. I can only hope that your imperial majesty's stay in this country will be mercifully short.'

'Thank you. God alone has decided our destiny. Time will tell.'

'Indeed. Which brings me on to the question of your exact residence. Military intelligence tells us that Italian spies or even assassins may be at work in the capital, and a high public profile may be a cause of grave danger.'

The emperor raised his eyebrows in surprise, as such an eventuality had not crossed his mind. He replied immediately without a flicker of fear: 'We are not concerned with the actions of our enemy. We seek only to capitalise on our exile by making contact with influential persons, for which we feel we must remain in London.'

'I see. Of course, your majesty is free to come and go as you please…there is also the awkward question of the er…I mean I hardly want to bring it up, doesn't seem right…. but the cost of your current accommodation. Much as we would wish to extend boundless hospitality, sadly the political and economic realities of the day do not allow it. There has already been a leak to the papers and the opposition would have a field day if it went on indefinitely.'

'Of course, we understand,' hesitated the emperor, somewhat taken aback.

'My superiors have identified a suitable residence, which we believe will be easily affordable by the imperial treasure chest as checked in by our colleagues in customs and excise. It offers the safety of distance from London but has everything your majesty could require in terms of communications, transport and resources.'

'And where is this safe haven?' asked the emperor.

'Bath.'

'Bath? We are not aware of this place.'

'A major city in the southwest of England, with a long history of royal patronage. We have found an ideal property which will offer your majesty and family all the comforts and amenities you will require.'

The emperor understood that he had very little choice. His mind had already raced ahead, calculating how long the gold salvaged from the palace would last in real terms, and what sacrifices would be necessary. While Tessem made the arrangements, the emperor frantically prioritised the contacts he would need to make in London before they had to leave. He made a mental list of books and journals that he intended to use to lobby and galvanise support against the illegal Italian invasion. Empress Menen returned with the children and Solomon to Jerusalem, ostensibly to oversee the transport of the rest of the imperial belongings by boat. The emperor knew that this was her way of registering a protest, as she was deeply unhappy at the prospect of staying any longer in the wet, cold climate of England, and wanted them all to stay in the warmer climes of Palestine. He felt that he had already let her down and although he wanted to make her happy he sensed the best chance of influencing the international situation was to remain in England and avoid getting caught up in the instability sweeping the globe. While he waited over the following weeks, alone except for his right-hand man, Tessem, the emperor sank into a deep depression, barely aware of his changing surroundings. Maintaining an outward obsession with organising delegations and meetings, compulsively scouring newspapers and legal journals for some hope that would change the internationally sealed fate of his people.

The emperor arrived at Fairfield House in Bath and was re-joined by his wife and children later that autumn, but he could barely bring himself to speak to them. All his hopes of a campaign to free their home had been dashed. Members of the British public, liberals and former friends in the establishment had exhausted their sympathy and disagreed with him that Italy and Germany posed an immediate threat to world peace. Giving up hope, the emperor judged that without his throne, his useful life was at an end and the only purpose by which he could serve his people and history was to write his autobiography. He buried himself in his past and remained in a detached state until the following spring, when looking up from his study with a mighty stretch and yawn he caught sight of his son and grandson playing in the garden with a young woman he had never noticed before. Something in her face and the way she made the children laugh suddenly filled him with optimism as the morning sunshine streamed into the house. She seemed to embody all his ideals of faith, innocence and freedom. For the first time he noticed the pink blossom on the trees, smelt the fresh scent of flowers coming into bloom and heard the sweet singing of the birds. The emperor looked down at his finger, the gold ring gleaming in the sunlight and thoughtfully traced the raised head of the roaring lion, the emblem of his lineage engraved on the black stone. Suddenly he realised that almighty God had not abandoned him, and this vision was sent as a message. He remembered that his destiny had been written and whatever the immediate fate of himself and his family, in the end the conquering lion shall prevail.

7. WORRIES IN THE DANCE

It was just getting dark again as Robbie went out early on Sunday evening to call for Angela, still nursing a faint headache from the night before. They had headed into central London after the match and spent the remainder of the evening in a pub arguing about which club to go to. James had proposed an old school hip-hop and funk night, while Robbie had unsurprisingly opted for the institution that was the only reggae night in the West End. Ravi's preference was for anywhere that cost about a fiver, with no queuing in the freezing cold, a lenient door policy, as he pointed out his trainers were brand new and cost three times as much as the others' shoes, and half a chance of pulling. By the time they finished their drinks, they had missed the cheap entry B4 11 and there were long queues of shivering flesh everywhere like a scene from the Long Good Friday. Eventually the warm, neon-lit doors of a cheap tacky salsa club seemed like a good proposition, where they all disliked the music equally and had to down several tequilas before hitting the dancefloor. It was a tactic that at first appeared to hold some success for Ravi, as he got on very well with three Danish girls, who he persuaded he would cast in his first film. Robbie and James did their best to dance with and talk to the other two girls, but neither of them knew how to rumba or even cha-cha-cha, and were resolutely faithful to their girlfriends. So, although they were acting out of moral support for their friend, Ravi blamed their lack of commitment for his failure to secure so much as a fake phone number. Then, after wandering the streets of central London, strewn with the usual puking, fighting and fornicating bodies, James insisted on going for a Chinese meal before waiting in the freezing cold for a night bus, so it was about five when Robbie got in.

'Hello gorgeous,' said Robbie as Angela answered the door.

'All right, babes,' said Angela, standing on her tiptoes to give him a kiss.

'Are you sure you want to go to this thing?' Robbie hesitated before entering the house.

'Nah, forget it. Bye!' Angela closed the door on him.

Robbie waited on the doorstep for a few seconds before she opened the door again, her dark curly hair falling over her face as she laughed. He found this mannerism particularly appealing, not to say that she was ugly and looked better with hair covering her features, she was of course very beautiful and even more so when she smiled.

'I just mean I know its not your cup of tea, you don't have to go,' he explained as they went inside.

'Well, it's a bit late now isn't it? You've got the tickets. And I can't have you going on your own like a sad bastard.'

'Yeah, well. You might like it. Did you listen to that tape I made you?'

'Er...yeah,' lied Angela. 'It sounds great. You know me, I'm easy.'

They exchanged suggestive looks and raising of eyebrows.

'Are Cheryl and Sarah in?' asked Robbie.

'What's that got to do with anything?'

'Y'know,' said Robbie, winking and nodding upstairs as if he had some sort of facial tic.

'Is there something wrong with your face?' she laughed, 'Don't worry, they won't listen. I've described it to them in detail already. Well, as much detail as you can give to two minutes. Come on then, you can help me get ready.'

She led him upstairs by the hand and they were kissing and tugging at each other's clothes as she pushed him through her bedroom door. Robbie loved the smell of her room, the lingering, concentrated version of the smell of her skin, he felt like he could sit there happily breathing it in forever. Except this would make him a pervert, and her flatmates probably would not be too pleased, not to mention the landlord, and after a while his own decaying stench would take over. Still, he loved the smell, but it was actually something of a disappointment to find out it was a body lotion involving cocoa butter rather than a unique aroma that emanated from her pores. Robbie had discovered this only the other day when a girl went past him on a bus giving off the same sweet scent. The fragrance was always so unmistakeably intermingled with her presence that he had started getting an erection, although this often happened to him on the top deck of a bus for no apparent reason. But on this occasion his penis and brain, if such a distinction can be made, were thrown into confusion by the mixed messages from his nostrils making him think of Angela and his eyes telling him that she was not there. Her mouth always tasted quite nice as well, he thought, it had a distinctive flavour of its own, no matter what she had had for lunch, which today seemed to have involved garlic. Moving his hands slowly up and down her back, he started doing the things he knew she liked, although this did not include buying her flowers or expressing his feelings spontaneously. They had been going out with each other for about six months, and by Robbie's estimations, they were getting pretty damned good at the sex side. To be fair, they had been practising quite a lot.

'Can I take off your bra?' he whispered.

'Yes, and don't ever let me catch you wearing it again.' Angela collapsed in a fit of giggles at her own joke.

'Do you mind? Do you want to do this or what?'

'Sorry. Yes. I'll just set the mood.' She turned the lights down low and pulled the curtain. Suppressing her laughter with a sexy pout, she leaned over to the bedside table music system to put on a smooth jazz CD, and then lay down on the bed, pulling Robbie on top of her.

They were as enthusiastic as the first time, and still kept up the effort of trying to impress each other without cutting any corners. This accomplishment in the bedroom department was something of a relief for Robbie, as his sexual endeavours had got off to an inauspicious start. He had the unfortunate distinction of experiencing a pregnancy scare and contracting a sexually transmitted infection before he had technically lost his virginity. Jane, his first girlfriend, had been a few years older than him and was quite taken with AIDS awareness campaigns and feminist literature that emphasised the pleasure to be had through non-penetrative sex. Although in later years, Robbie and several future girlfriends would come to be grateful for what this taught him, at the time he was very very very frustrated. To a seventeen-year old boy desperate to lose his virginity, non-penetrative sex was not so much a contradiction in terms as a cruel and unusual punishment. They would spend hours naked together, stroking, massaging, licking and nibbling each other senseless. Eventually the inevitable happened and during a delicate movement involving brushing his penis against her inner thighs, Robbie ejaculated copiously over the general area of her vagina, thighs, stomach and bed. Being a sensible sort of woman with some experience in these matters, Jane decided it best to take the morning after pill, just to be on the safe side. Unfortunately the imbalance of oestrogen led to an attack of thrush. During a subsequent bout of almost lovemaking, it was Jane's turn to be careless with her bodily fluids and another delicate brush with her vaginal juices passed the mild yeast infection into Robbie's urethra. Mild and easily cleared up, but to a seventeen year old virgin, any burning sensation and discharge from the penis was not a welcome experience.

Now this was all a damp memory and Robbie was confidently getting into his stride. He had rolled the condom on without disturbing the flow or snagging his pubes, and it had slipped in smoothly. Angela was making the right sort of noises, which was encouraging, and they were gradually working up a sweat. But something was not quite right. While twiddling Angela's right nipple with one hand and kissing her neck, Robbie deftly reached over to the portable stereo with the other hand, flicked it on to radio and located his favourite pirate station, where Gregory Isaacs purred over a gently rocking beat. Robbie nodded to himself and lifted his head up, watching Angela's face as she moaned softly and half closed her eyes while he pushed rhythmically in time to the music.

'As we move, inside the Cool Ruler singing out for the massive. Big up the man like Errol from Hanwell – you're safe every time. And now – gotta pay the rent...Don't forget the mobile number for requests and dedications is 07790 -.'

Angela stopped moving and opened her eyes wide, looking up at Robbie.

'Do you mind?'

'Sorry darling, I'll turn that off, they usually have a lovers rock show on at this time, I don't know why they always talk over the music...'

'Robbie, we've started.... talk about me ruining the mood!'

'Hold on...I'll just...' Robbie reached over to the bedside table and started leafing through her CDs and cassettes.

'For fuck's sake, Robbie, can't we just listen to my taste in music for once?'

'Hang on in there, baby. You know I like to listen to some sweet reggae music at times like this.'

'Do we have to? All that jink… jink…it's too…jiggy.' Angela demonstrated by jerking up and down quickly as if to a ska tune, causing a not unpleasant sensation for Robbie.

'Well, we are supposed to be getting jiggy with it, as they say.'

'No, but it's too …bouncy.' Robbie could not help taking his eyes off the CDs for a moment and glancing down at Angela's breasts bouncing obligingly as she amply illustrated her point.

'Yes, but that rhythm is always there, it's just like your heartbeat. If you want slow and sexy, you can move in time to the bassline. Where's that tape I made for you?'

'Er…isn't it there? Just put anything on before the vibe is completely ruined, please.'

'OK, here we go. Marvin Gaye.'

'Perfect.'

With a little help from the late soul man they regained the moment and were getting it on. In the back of his mind, behind the frantic long division calculations he was attempting to prolong his staying power, Robbie started worrying that this difference of opinion was indicative of a deeper incompatibility. Could he really love a woman who did not love reggae? Making love, or even just dancing with the woman you love in time to a sweet reggae beat was the best feeling in the world as far as he was concerned. But he did not think he could ever really share this with Angela. She had inherited a liking for jazz from her black American father's record collection and after he died it was all she had that made her feel close to him. He thought back to the days in school, when the other kids used to tease her for her music taste and generally being a swot and a square. This was also something to do with the huge glasses, quiet demeanour and wild Afro, which Angela's white mother had not really known anyone to turn to for advice on coping with. It was years later when Angela had discovered contact lenses and relaxers that Robbie suddenly noticed her. In the past year they had really got to know each other and he liked everything about her, except for the fact that she enjoyed listening to the sound of a cat being tortured. Maybe there was a perfect woman out there somewhere for him, who loved reggae as much as he did. But then she would not have Angela's personality, sense of humour and everything else he loved about her. These thoughts did not trouble him for long, however, as his impending orgasm emptied his mind of everything. As they lay together afterwards, sharing the heat from each other's bodies and fighting the temptation to drift off to sleep, this uncertainty popped back into his head. It bothered him again when he was in the shower, until Angela joined him, although the erotic potential of this experience was significantly reduced by her contortions to avoid getting her hair wet.

They arrived at the venue a couple of hours later as a queue was beginning to form outside in the rain. Robbie thought he was playing it cool arriving fashionably late but was secretly a bit worried as it always took ages to get through the metal detectors, and the show might start a bit early as it was a Sunday. Another two hours later, approaching midnight, the venue was getting packed and the air was filling up with ganja smoke, but there was still no sign of life on stage. The sound system operator was doing a great job entertaining the crowd, but the atmosphere was finely balanced between excited anticipation and an impatient suspicion as the evening went on that none of the artists had turned up. At last, the compere appeared on stage and introduced the support act.

'Who's this guy then?' asked Angela, shuffling from side to side, her legs aching after hours of standing around.

'Bernie somebody or other,' said Robbie, focusing his attention on stage.

Angela reached into the back pocket of her jeans for her ticket and peered at it as the lights from the stage briefly illuminated the darkness. She started laughing and nudged Robbie. 'Bummy Wanks – look, what kind of a name is that?'

'You should learn to roll your arse.'

'Look, I don't mind coming to these gigs with you, but if you think I'm going to start dancing like that, you can fuck off,' Angela folded her arms and nodded towards a group of girls in fishnet tights and gold sequinned bras who were taking it in turns to have sex with an invisible man on the floor.

Robbie smiled. 'No, roll your 'r's. It's Ranks, not Wanks. And that's a misprint on the ticket. It should be B – u – r – n – y. As in fire burning, it's an enduring image, very powerful metaphor.'

'Oh right, do you like him then?'

'Dunno, I've only heard a couple of his tracks, he's quite new.'

'Any relation to Shabba?'

'Could be.'

They remained standing in their position towards the back of the hall and watched as Burny Ranks launched into his first tune.

'He's a rapper then, is he?' asked Angela.

'Yes, well no, they are called deejays.'

'Oh,' said Angela, looking puzzled. 'But I thought you said reggae invented rap.'

'Well, yes it did, but you don't call it rap.'

'So what do you call those people who play records?' wondered Angela.

'Selectors, or operators. They are also deejays, but it's different. Anyway, can we just listen to him?'

'OK, sorry.' Angela bit her lip and concentrated on the stage, nodding her head politely. After a few minutes she nudged Robbie and shouted into his ear again. 'Why does he keep stopping every song as soon as it starts? Does he get out of breath or forget the words?'

'The idea is if the crowd like the song, he starts it again from the beginning,' sighed Robbie, '…although it does get a bit boring after the sixth time.'

Angela nodded again and continued paying attention to the stage, hopping from foot to foot self-consciously as she found it impossible to dance to the stop-start ragga beat.

'Are you alright?' asked Robbie, looking at her feet.

'Yeah, fine. Just my shoes are a bit tight. One last question, why does he keep grabbing his crotch?'

'I honestly don't know,' replied Robbie.

Burny Ranks continued for about twenty minutes, as a handful of fans gathered enthusiastically round the stage, while the majority milled about indifferently, waiting for the headline act.

'All right, London!' Burny Ranks caught his breath as the music stopped. 'Remember mi name Burny Ranks. Mi come fi burn fire on all evil-doers and iniquity workers. All rudebwoy, trow down de gun, trow down de knife. We need peace in de ghetto. Strictly love and unity me a deal wid. Black, white, let us get together and unite. Every man a mi bredren. Peace and love to every man and woman.' Robbie joined in the lukewarm applause for this sentiment, as Burny Ranks continued: 'Dis next one a de final one for tonight. Dis one mi new single, it name All Battyman Haffi Get Shot and Bury.'

At the front, the loudest cheer of the night rang out from a small contingent of enthusiastic young men. Robbie touched his forehead in embarrassment and glanced at Angela, correctly guessing she had stopped paying attention to the stage some time ago. 'Come on, let's get a drink,' he said.

They sat in the quiet area by the bar at the back of the hall, just in view of the stage.

'Didn't you like him then?' asked Angela, relieved for a seat and relative peace and quiet.

'Nah, not really. This song is a bit homophobic.'

'Is it?' Angela looked towards the stage and shouted 'DICKHEAD!' waving her hand in a clumsy attempt at the wanker sign, which she had never quite got the hang of, to Robbie's occasional disappointment and discomfort, so it looked like she was raising her fist in salute to the lyrics.

'All right, love,' said Robbie, looking around nervously, to find no one paying them any attention, just another couple arguing and a few people drinking and chatting, ignoring the stage. 'I'm sorry, I didn't know he was like this.'

In fact, it had not escaped Robbie's notice that Burny Ranks had interspersed nearly every record about love and peace with a passing reference to what he wanted to do to gay men, but he felt this last song was too blatant to ignore.

'I can't believe you took me here. That is the last time I am coming to one of these concerts,' seethed Angela.

'They're not all like that. It's just the way they talk - you should hear what they say about soundboys and informers.'

'Don't make excuses for it. It's pure incitement to violence. What is his problem? He's probably just repressing his own homosexuality.'

Their argument was interrupted as the whole venue suddenly went quiet. Burny Ranks had torn off his shirt and collapsed in a sweaty heap on the stage, still holding the microphone in one hand and grabbing his crotch with the other, his baggy pants falling halfway down his arse.

'All battyman, all battyman' he panted hysterically into the microphone. 'Shoot dem, burn dem, strip dem, whip dem, get a big stick and lick dem! Battyman…battyman…huh…huh!!'

Burny got to his knees, paused and looked around him, as if he had forgotten where he was, to find his trousers were round his ankles and his boxer shorts had slipped down to reveal a partially erect penis pointing sheepishly at the faces in the front row of the audience. The band had stopped in their tracks at this obvious diversion from the rehearsed set, holding their instruments uncertainly while he did the same. Burny peered up into the spotlight, squinting nervously through the smoky gloom at the audience. Like a bunny rabbit caught in the headlights of an oncoming car while stealing carrots, Burny Ranks had a look of guilty embarrassment and a dawning realisation that his brief career was over. The crowd collectively shuffled awkwardly, coughing and murmuring for a few seconds, before someone threw a plastic bottle at the stage and the whole place erupted in laughter and a hail of missiles. Burny Ranks exited the stage as quickly as he could while pulling up his pants and the sound system turned up the next tune, drowning out the shouts of derision.

Half an hour later, the atmosphere was hotting up as the new messiah of reggae was expected on stage. Robbie had confidently assured Angela that this singer would not express any homophobic or sexist comments and she had reluctantly agreed to squeeze forward nearer the stage. The sound system went quiet and an air of anticipation swept the hall. The vibes in the venue gave the impression that the assembled few thousand knew they were about to witness something special. This was the first and only UK date for the latest Jamaican artist to bring inevitable comparisons with Bob Marley. Darkness filled the stage and a spotlight picked out an image of Haile Selassie on the backdrop, bringing spontaneous shouts of 'Jah! Rastafari!' from the audience. A few seconds later, a sweet vocal filled the hall to rapturous applause as the diminutive dreadlocked figure casually strolled onto the stage. The lights went up and the band clicked tight into the first tune. As the song began, the venue filled with the sound of the audience singing along to the words as if it was a prayer:

'Look to the east, for the coming of a black king,
Don't be fooled, Jah is forever living,
He will return, cos he created everything,
Peace, love and healing he will bring.'

Robbie closed his eyes and let the music carry him away. He felt his old self-consciousness fade, as he merged into the anonymous crowd, moved by the positive vibe and the uplifting melody. The air was so thick with ganja smoke, he even felt a little high from passive inhalation. Dominating the stage, the backdrop of images of Haile Selassie and Africa were hypnotic in the swirling stage lights. The sound was clear, and the lyrics lingered in his head, reminding him of things past and giving him a feeling of déjà vu, as if he had known them all his life, like long-forgotten nursery rhymes. The singer had a truly charismatic stage presence and had the whole venue mesmerised with his words, sound and power for nearly two hours.

After the concert, Robbie was distracted as they studied the traffic slowly streaming away from the venue. A man in an unmarked car beckoned to them enthusiastically and they got in. Fortunately it turned out he was not a serial killer but a mini-cab driver, or at least someone who was happy to drive them across London for fifteen quid.

'Why the hell do they have these things on a Sunday? Don't they know people have got to go to work?' asked Angela as she settled into the back seat.

'Yeah, dunno really. I think the venues are cheaper or something,' murmured Robbie, still buzzing from the experience.

'Did you enjoy it then?'

'Yeah, it was magic. Did you?' asked Robbie.

'It was all right, bit too much preaching and bible-bashing at the end there for my liking. And what's with waving the lighters in the air? I thought they only did that at Barry Manilow concerts these days.'

'Yeah, I know what you mean,' agreed Robbie, thinking he should have learnt by now not to drag girlfriends to concerts with him. He would probably enjoy it more if he didn't have to worry about the person he was with having a crap time. He tried to imagine how she felt about reggae; apparently it all sounded the same and there were too many cover versions. This was a common criticism, but whenever he heard a pop or soul tune that he liked, he could not wait for the inevitable reggae versions, which were far superior to his ears. He just could not understand how other people did not love it in the same way. It was an eternal mystery to him why the likes of Peter Hunnigale and Beres Hammond were not on Top Of The Pops every week. It was useless, like trying to see someone he loved and knew so well through the eyes of a total stranger. Angela had a point about the bible bashing, though, as he generally did not have much time for religion. If he was forced to listen to Christian rock for five minutes he would have to contemplate suicide, but he could listen to deeply religious reggae all day and appreciate it without believing a word. Now he was not so sure, and he was a bit worried that he was having some kind of a religious experience.

8. THE HARDER THEY COME

As tree branches whipped his face, the thought flashed through Walter Livingston McIntosh's mind that he should just stop running and give himself up to the police. The track he had followed from August Town, outside Kingston, had dwindled and split so many times that he was not even sure if he was heading in the right direction. As long as he kept the setting sun on his left, he thought, he must cross the hills and reach the north coast eventually, to the relative safety of his uncle's house in Port Antonio. But the forest was so thick that the canopy above him only allowed in the occasional streaks of dusky orange light from baffling angles. Add to this the fact that he kept coming up against sheer rock faces and winding waterfalls that forced him to change direction, he had the distinct impression that nature was playing tricks on him, and he was wandering around in circles. Except he could tell by the aching in his calves that he was still going up, gradually. It was too late by now to think about going back, his main priority was finding somewhere to sleep before nightfall. Cold ground as his bed was nothing new to him, but he was frightened of what might be lurking out in the bush in the dark, duppy or gunman. Suddenly he froze, thinking that he heard a rustling in the branches to his right. He peered through the dappled light to see a lizard on a limb of a tree. The lizard was looking straight back at him and nodding as if he knew the way but was not going to tell him. With a flick of his hand, Walter sent it scarpering into the undergrowth. Relieved, he stood in silence for a few seconds, listening to the beat of his heart. It took him a few more seconds to realise he was actually listening to the distant sound of drumming, echoing around the hills.

Since he was a little boy, Walter had heard stories about the wild people who live up in the hills. Some of them were Garveyites, followers of Marcus Garvey, who his mother had warned him about. By her account Garvey was a hothead from St Ann's Bay who had gone around stirring up a whole heap of trouble by telling black people some nonsense about they were not British, they were African, of all things. Not content with upsetting the British governor of Jamaica, Garvey had gone to America and started trouble for Negroes there. The American government had imprisoned and deported Garvey, and many of his followers in Jamaica had fled to the hills for fear of arrest. The joke was that many of them had set up camps in the Blue Mountains, where they waited for the day when lights in Kingston harbour would tell them a big ship had arrived as Garvey had promised, to take them back to Africa. Walter had laughed at this foolishness, and always did as his mother told him, so had mostly avoided these troublemakers. However, it came as a shock for him to learn that the nonsense about coming from Africa was apparently true. He had checked with several of his friends' grandparents and all the elders in the village confirmed this was the case, and some of them quietly confided in him that Garvey was a great and wise man.

Rumour had it that the other folk who had been living up in the hills for centuries were runaway slaves, marooned and protected by the thick forest interior where the slave masters dared not follow them. They had become known as 'maroons' and were notorious for the warrior ways that had won them their freedom, so much so that ordinary law-abiding country folk had nothing to do with them. The maroons remained outlaws in the mountains, perhaps not even knowing or caring that slavery had been abolished throughout the British Empire in 1833. Of course, Walter had always been dimly aware of slavery, but he thought of it as something that happened in ancient history, to other people. That was certainly the impression he had got from the English church school in the village. He was quite taken aback when he learned from talking to the village elders that his own grandfather on his mother's side had been born a slave. Estimates of his grandfather's age when he died had ranged from ninety to about one hundred and ten, no one in the village knew for sure, only that he had been the oldest man in the village for as long as anyone could remember. Walter was only seven when his grandfather died, but still vividly remembered him. His own father was not around, so it was to his grandfather that he would turn to when he needed help or guidance. He now found himself wishing he were still around for some advice to get him out of his current trouble.

Yesterday had started out as a really good day for Walter. He arrived in Kingston after two days travelling on the back of a breadfruit cart, with the little bit of money his mother had given him. He also had a scrap of paper with a name, Hamish McIntosh, and an address to find his father. His mother had always told him that his father was a wealthy merchant trader from Scotland. She said that his father had to keep sailing around the world but promised to return to Kingston when Walter reached the age of sixteen and would be able to take over the business. Walter imagined that his father would be waiting for him when he arrived, but with hindsight he realised this was unlikely. Luckily, he made some new friends who were hanging around the market and would help him search around the docks area the next day. In the meantime, his new friends, Clifton and Jimmy, had suggested they go to the newly opened picture theatre. Walter had not wanted to look like a country bungle so he had agreed, even though it transpired that he would have to pay for his new friends, but he was very excited because he had never been to the cinema before. He had heard about it from a friend's older brother who had been to Kingston but could not believe his eyes as he saw people and places all over the world right there in front of him on the newsreel, ten feet tall. It was just before the main feature, something called 'Gone With The Wind', that things had started to go awry. There was a lot of excitement, as the whole experience was new to Kingston people, and one man started shouting back at the screen as if he was having a conversation with the characters. Another man in the seat in front of Walter started shouting at him to shut up, as he was a damn idiot and the people on screen could not hear him, but he was spoiling the fun for everyone else. The other man started shouting that the picture house was the work of the devil, and he would burn it down. People started throwing things at him, other people agreed that the cinema was indeed sinful and they should all leave. A fight broke out, during which Walter had instinctively intervened to try and protect a fat old man who had got involved. He could not really see what was happening until the theatre lights came on, the police arrived and took down Walter's name and a statement before closing the cinema halfway through the picture, as the situation deteriorated into a near-riot.

Walter's new Kingston friends had invited him to stay with them where they all slept on the floor in a relative's shack. The next morning as he was sitting on the street corner with Clifton, planning the search for Walter's father, Jimmy came running back from the shop waving a copy of the Daily Gleaner excitedly. He sat down with them and started reading.

'Police are searching for Walter Livingston McIntosh in connection with a fracas at the Kingston Palace Picture House last night.'

Walter's face folded up with fear as he looked anxiously over his friend's shoulder at the newspaper. He could recognise his own name and make out a few words, such as 'police', 'wanted', 'knife' and 'five pounds' but not much else. Clifton looked at the confusion on Walter's face and quickly took over reading in a grave voice, relating the story that police were looking for Walter in connection with the theft of five pounds from the fat old man at knifepoint, and that he had also been blamed for starting the fight and causing a riot which led to the cinema being nearly burned down. Walter panicked and started protesting his innocence and shouting that they had got it all wrong. Clifton warned him to keep quiet and that he would never be able to explain that to the police. He reckoned that Walter was looking at fifty lashes at least, maybe ten years hard labour or even the gallows. To Walter's relief, his friends bravely agreed to help him escape, and took him to the edge of the city where he could run to the hills. Clifton had the good idea of taking the rest of Walter's money off him, because if the police found it on him, it would be evidence of theft. After some debate, Jimmy gave him the newspaper so that he could explain things to his uncle when he got there. Walter did not know how to thank his friends, and waved emotionally as he turned on his heels and ran into the countryside.

Now, as night came crashing down deep into the hills, his brief career in Kingston seemed like a different world, a fading fantasy. Walter thought how disappointed his mother would be that he had returned within twenty-four hours as a wanted criminal. His plans of joining his father's business and sailing the world were now hopelessly ruined, and he wondered if he could ever face his family, if he would ever see them again. Walter decided to curl up under a tree for the night and folded up the fateful newspaper to use as a pillow. He was lost in a reverie, going over and over the last two days in his head as he gave in to sleep, forgetting about the drumming, not worrying about who might be out there and not noticing the twig snapping in the undergrowth behind him.   Moments later, he found himself wide awake, sitting in front of a campfire, deafened by rattling, rolling drumbeats and surrounded by the weirdest looking people he had ever seen. There were about ten men in a circle, dressed in tatters, who were drumming and chanting in a language that sounded familiar to him, but he could not understand the words. Their glazed eyes seemed to reflect the fire's red glow as they stared past Walter through the hazy smoke. The most striking thing about them was their hair, which they had left uncombed so that it had gone knotty, a dreadful sight as if snakes were growing out of their heads. A few women in long flowing robes were dancing in a strange manner, bouncing and rocking in time to the rhythm of the drum. Walter wondered if these crazy marooned Africans were going to eat him.

'Don't be afraid, boy. Eat some food. You look like you haven't eaten all day.'

Walter was surprised to hear the gentle accent of the Jamaican middle class come from the mouth of a bare-chested drummer with long straggly knots in his beard and a huge paper cigarette between his lips, which popped and fizzed as he spoke.

'Thank you, sir,' said Walter as he accepted a roasted corncob.

'My name is Shaka.'

'Mi name Walter McIntosh, from Clarendon.'

'Who you running from? Police? What trouble are you in?'

Walter nodded, too tired to concoct a story to explain his presence in the middle of the hills at night. By way of explanation, he handed Shaka the newspaper as he carried on eating. To his dismay, the rough, wrinkly face creased into a smile and his beard shook as he guffawed with laughter.

'You can't read so good, can you, bwoy?'

'No sir. Me only learn the bible.'

'Good, but I know they teach you to recite the bits they want you to know, not to learn how to read it for yourself.'

'Me know this newspaper say I man wanted by the police but is a mistake – mi try fe stop a fight.'

'Hmmm…you are right. It says here the police are looking for one Walter McIntosh. But they want to give you a reward from the owner of Kingston Palace Picture House – apparently you saved him from a madman with a knife who tried to burn down the theatre and then started a riot. Five pounds, if you claim it before the end of today,' Shaka shook his head and laughed, then felt sorry for the boy. 'Who told you it said you were in trouble?'

'Mi friends – well, me met dem yesterday,' Walter trailed off, embarrassed, cursing the double-crossing tricksters who had no doubt by now helped themselves to his reward, as well as the little money his mother had given him.

'Nah, worry, son. It not the first time someone from country come a town and get fleeced. You can go back in the morning,' said Shaka as he turned back to the newspaper and continued reading.

'Thanks. Are you people Maroons?'

'We are all of us marooned on this island. Yes, most of these people have been living up here for over a hundred years. I myself am a more recent arrival. Have you heard of Marcus Garvey?'

'Er…yes, sir,' said Walter nervously.

'Don't look so worried. I see they have done a good job on you. I worked with him for a while, I tried to start a movement for independence and repatriation here in Jamaica, but the British did not like my ideas, so here I am, waiting for the right time.'

Walter finished the corncob in silence and lay down on the ground by the fire. Suddenly Shaka leapt up, holding the newspaper, and pointing at a grainy photograph of an African in regal attire.

'Garvey's words come to pass: Look to the east for the crowning of a black king! He is here – look!'

There was a commotion as all the men who had been drumming crowded around Shaka and looked at the picture in the newspaper as he read on:

'His Imperial Majesty, the Abyssinian emperor, addressed the League of Nations in Geneva, Switzerland last week. Emperor Haile Selassie, privately known as Ras Tafari, wore imperial crimson robes bearing the royal insignia of the Lion of Judah as he made his unprecedented appeal to the representatives of the great world powers. It was reported that he was barely able to contain the anger blazing in his eyes as he condemned the Italian war against his humble people, in which his primitive army was crushed by modern airpower and poison gas with the tacit approval of the rest of Europe and America. His cutting words exposed the appeasement of the bully Mussolini making the world a more dangerous place for everyone and destroying an independent, historic African kingdom, the oldest ruling monarchy in the world. The self-proclaimed King of Kings and Lord of Lords of Ethiopia traces his ancestry back to the root of King David in biblical times.'

At that moment, thunder rumbled through the hills and lightning flashed around their heads. As everyone else cowered, waiting for the downpour, an old man dressed in rags with thick grey ropes of hair nearly touching the ground stood up slowly at the back of the group. He raised his right hand, clutching a copy of the Bible to the heavens and started to recite in a deep gravelly voice:

'I and I saw in the right hand of him that sat on the throne a book written within and on the backside, sealed with seven seals.

'I and I saw a strong angel proclaiming with a loud voice, Who is worthy to open the book, and to loose the seals thereof?

'And no man in heaven, nor in earth, neither under the earth, was able to open the book, neither to look thereon.

'I and I wept much, because no man was found worthy to open and to read the book, neither to look thereon.

'And one of the elders saith unto me, Weep not: behold, the lion of the tribe of Judah, the Root of David, hath prevailed to open the book, and to loose the seven seals thereof.'

'Revelation!' shouted the others. As if possessed, the old man, went on reciting passages from memory, still holding the bible aloft as the first heavy raindrops fell:

'His eyes were as a flame of fire, and on his head were many crowns; and he had a name written, that no man knew, but he himself.

'And he was clothed with a vesture dipped in blood; and his name is called The Word of God.

'And the armies which were in heaven followed him upon white horses, clothed in white linen, fine and clean.

'I and I saw the beast, and the kings of the earth, and their armies, gathered together to make war against him that sat on the horse, and against his army.

'And out of his mouth goeth a sharp sword, that with it he should smite the nations: and he should rule them with a rod of iron: and he treadeth the winepress of the fierceness and wrath of Almighty God.

'And he hath on his vesture and on his thigh a name written, KING OF KINGS, AND LORD OF LORDS.'

The old man was silent and fell to his knees, followed by the rest of the group. The rain pounded their bowed heads and extinguished the campfire. Through the darkness, illuminated only by the cloudy red moon, Walter peeked out of one eye and looked down the mountains where the lights of Kingston harbour blinked dimly in the distance. His fear had turned to relief, swiftly followed by an awesome feeling that he had just witnessed something he did not fully understand yet but knew was truly amazing. He knew that he was part of this now and the little boy that had run away from Kingston would never return. Shaka followed his gaze and stood up.

'The time has come. We must gather the children together and bring the king's message to the city. The people must be ready for when he sends us home to Zion.'

9. CHALICE IN THE PALACE

Somewhere deep inside the house, muffled by the thick walls and plush carpets, the chimes of the doorbell played out a classical tune, annoyingly reminiscent of a television advertisement. The short walk from the tube station had taken them into the wide secluded streets of the most expensive part of Notting Hill, where Robbie had to surreptitiously peek at a pocket A to Z. It would have been easier if he had just stopped under a lamppost and consulted the map properly but he felt that he had to distinguish himself from the lost tourists and Christmas shoppers looking for Portobello Road market, which had closed hours ago. Although he liked to think that he knew the area like the back of his hand, it was a cold day and he was wearing gloves. He very rarely entered this maze of crescents and gardens, and when he did there were police barricades blocking off every junction redirecting bladder-stretched carnivalling crowds. So, after taking a couple of wrong turns, Angela asked a passer-by, who despite being a tourist weighed down with what he mistakenly believed were bargain antiques, actually knew the street they were looking for. The turning from the main road seemed very quiet and dimly lit but this was because the houses were so huge and far away from each other and the pavement that it was hard to detect any signs of life. It gave them the paranoid impression that their faces were already being scanned by CCTV, and any sudden movement would set off numerous burglar alarms and intruder lights. They crept past looking for the right door number and wondering, a) how much space could actually be used by one person, however rich; and b) how many homeless families could live comfortably in each property.

'Do we have to do this?' Angela whispered nervously to Robbie as they stood outside, rubbing and clapping their hands in a general display of coldness.

'Well, it's a bit late now, unless you want to play knock-a-dolly and run away.'

'Hmm, well, at least it'll be warm inside… and we're getting some food.'

'Yeah, but it'll probably be that nouvelle cuisine bollocks, so we might have to get some chips later. I hate dinner parties anyway, they're so pretentious, especially with this lot. Oops, here we go.' Robbie silenced himself at the sudden sound of the door opening.

'Daahlings!' This was Fiona, who they had to keep reminding themselves was James' girlfriend, and that he must see something in her they didn't, except for being loaded and beautiful. Not to mention intelligent and compassionate, hopefully anyway, as she was studying to be a neurologist, like her father, whose house it was, well one of them.

Fiona and Angela exchanged kisses, and then Robbie awkwardly bumped his nose on Fiona's proffered cheek as they entered the flat. This was unfortunate, as the temperature outside was near freezing, and Robbie's nose left the cold wet impression of a healthy dog.

'This is my best friend, Pippa' she gestured towards a tall, curvy figure galloping towards them along the corridor with blonde tresses flowing. Something about her made Robbie instinctively think of horses. It wasn't that she looked, sounded or smelt remotely like a horse, he reflected while they exchanged introductions, and he wiped his nose on her cheek. But as he followed Pippa down the hallway an image of tight jodhpurs, leather boots and a riding crop popped momentarily into his head, swiftly banished to the dark recesses from whence it came as Angela whispered in his ear.

'Really, can't we make an excuse? It's like posh and posher.'

'Come on, babe. It'll be all right. Just put on a brave face for Ravi's sake.' He replied in hushed tones. It was common knowledge that Fiona's dinner party had been engineered to set Pippa up with Ravi.

'Hmmm …well, it's him I feel sorry for – she'll have him for breakfast,' muttered Angela as she loitered in the corridor removing her coat.

James was relaxing in the dining room, with his feet literally under the table, pouring himself a large glass of wine.

'Hello, come in, make yourselves at home. Red or white?' he asked as they sat down.

'Hi, James. Red please. Here's a bottle for later,' replied Angela.

'Alright mate. Got any beer?' asked Robbie. He always felt that James slightly upped his accent when he was around Fiona and her friends, to which Robbie reacted by adopting a style he believed to be considered common. It was not that James was being pretentious, he just had a chameleon-like quality of changing his demeanour to blend in with his surroundings but remained basically the same argumentative git underneath. Robbie, meanwhile, was pretending to be something he was not, like working class, but it made him happy, as he made a great show of resting his can of lager on the neatly set dining table. There seemed to be an air of excited anticipation around the room as they swapped pleasantries, mostly emanating from Pippa.

'So what's Ravi like then, you're his best friend, aren't you?' she asked Robbie.

'Don't worry, I told you he's gorgeous, that's all you need to know,' interrupted Fiona, dimming the lights.

The opening bars of the doorbell saved Robbie.

'This must be him,' gushed Pippa, downing a full glass of red wine and disappearing down an adjoining hallway into a bathroom. It was true that Ravi sometimes had this effect on people. From a distance or in the shadows of a club, Ravi appeared impossibly good looking in the stereotypical Adonis fashion; tall, broad shoulders, big dark eyes, high cheekbones and shoulder-length hair, like Shah Rukh Khan. It was an image he had painstakingly cultivated for himself after shaking off the childhood tags of Pizzaface, Goofy and Jug-head. Close up, most people still noticed his bad skin, and when he opened his mouth, the reason for his permanent pout was revealed to be huge teeth, while the long hair helped to hide his protruding ears. But by then it ceased to matter because first impressions last and when he entered a room, women and men involuntarily turned their heads. People often thought he must be famous just by the way he looked and the air about him. Robbie and James were always a bit ambivalent about this effect when they went out together, as it gave them a good chance of talking to women, but they were invariably only interested in their friend.

A few minutes after Pippa went in there, a completely different woman emerged from the bathroom. If Robbie had looked up the word 'vamp' in a dictionary, he was fairly certain there would be a picture of how Pippa appeared right now. Her face had acquired a soft-focus sheen and her hair had tumbled loose as if she had just emerged from a haystack. She was slightly out of breath and rosy-cheeked, while her lips were dripping with wet red gloss. The top two buttons of her blouse had been undone and her breasts, previously unnoticed by Robbie, which is saying something, were pushed into a gravity-defying horizontal cleavage and were clearly intent on participating fully in the evening's proceedings. She tried to walk with a slow seductive swing of her hips but tottered on her high heels and leant seductively against the doorframe instead, smoothing down the hem of her miniskirt. Timing her re-entry perfectly as they stood at opposite ends of the dining room, she laid her eyes on Ravi.

'You must be Ravi,' she purred.

'That's me. You must be the famous Pippa - they never told me you were so…mmm,' he said as he reached for her hand and kissed it.

The other quality Ravi had that greatly endeared him to the opposite sex was absolutely no shame at all. He used the tackiest lines and corniest compliments with a tongue in cheek humour and a smile that somehow allowed him to get away with it.

'Please, you two, sit down and talk like normal people,' interrupted Fiona, installing them next to each other around the table. 'Now, help yourselves to bread while I get on with the starter. Robbie - put some music on, will you? I don't want any fighting between you boys so you each get one choice from my extensive CD collection, OK?'

Robbie jumped to the bait and went over to the sideboard where sat a tiny music system, the quality and expense of which was in inverse proportion to its size. This was usually where he found himself at some point at most parties and he began his inspection.

First of all, no vinyl. Always a bad sign, indicative of a not very serious music lover, although he was fairly certain Fiona had a comprehensive collection of dusty Duran Duran LPs somewhere. Three tall racks, comprising a good number and range of CDs, for a girl, he could not help himself thinking. Mostly quite recent, which concurred with his existing impression that Fiona shopped a lot and money was no object. However, as to be expected, a high proportion of these were compilations, also a bad sign, of someone who views music as something to put on in the background at dinner parties, rather than to actually listen to. Now, what about reggae? Of course, Legend. Robbie took a moment to admire the photo of his beloved Bob in thoughtful mood on the cover but did not consider putting it on as all the tracks had been played to death, murdered by buskers and then their graves danced on by karaoke singers. He was reassured that it was there, he just could not understand why, after hearing Legend, everyone else did not go out and buy every album Marley ever made. 'The Best Reggae Album In The World...Ever'; he doubted that he would share the view of the compilers. That seemed to be about it. Lots of compilations containing the words soul, love, woman and numbers. Quite a few indie bands who he had never heard of.

'Hurry up, and none of your reggae crap, please,' said James.

'Yeah, try and find something we all might like,' added Angela.

'Oh, I love reggae. As long as it's the proper seventies stuff,' chirped Pippa.

Privately, if there was one thing that irked Robbie more than the fact that none of his black friends liked reggae, it was that most of his white friends considered themselves experts on it, despite thinking it had stopped being made two decades ago. Undeterred, he continued his search to impose his musical taste on a roomful of people. He was about to settle for a northern soul compilation, even though he had never heard of any of the tracks or artists, but he felt sure this was a good sign and it would liven things up a bit when he noticed a familiar label at the bottom of one rack.

'Where'd you get this?' he asked, holding up a recent collection of singers that he had briefly seen on import but was now quite rare.

'Oh, that - some guy gave it to me when I was in Jamaica last year. He fancied me, I think, but I didn't really like it, or him. You'd like it, put it on,' replied Fiona casually as she placed a bowl of warm, sun-dried tomato bread on the table, next to the olive oil and balsamic vinegar.

If there was another thing that annoyed Robbie, he thought as he tried to work out the controls to the CD player without interfering with air traffic, it was people who had been to Jamaica. He hadn't and he was jealous. There had been a vague plan to save up for a while, but he had not got very much yet and he was put off by the apparent choice between the exclusive, all-inclusive resorts and the slightly scary image of touching down in Kingston on his own. Deep down, he knew the violent, gun-toting stereotype was a tabloid myth, but he was not quite brave enough to put it to the test.

'I never knew you been to Jamaica. Was it good?' asked Robbie grudgingly as he sat down, nodding his head to the opening drumbeat.

'Paradise. Pippa and I went together.'

'Oh yes, it was beautiful, sunshine, beach parties, dancing to reggae all night. Feeling hot, hot, hot,' said Pippa, jiggling around in her chair.

'That's soca, usually associated with Trinidad and Tobago,' muttered Robbie, but he was drowned out by Ravi, taking the opportunity to flirt with Pippa.

'Yeah, I love a bit of reggae to dance to as well, you certainly look as if you know how to move your waist.'

'Hmm…maybe you can find out some time,' Pippa replied, taking another huge gulp of red wine.

'Anyway, why don't you go to Jamaica, Robbie?' asked Fiona.

'Yeah, one day. I just need to plan it - I wouldn't fancy going to the touristy bits.'

'I know what you mean, Jamaica was divine, but next year I want to discover somewhere completely unspoilt,' commented Pippa.

'Don't you mean spoil somewhere completely undiscovered?' asked Robbie, as Angela kicked him under the table.

'Have you been to Jamaica, Angela?' asked Pippa, undaunted.

'No,'

'Oh, it's just you look as if you might have done. I mean… where are you from?'

'Chiswick.'

'No, I mean originally.'

'Oh, right. Hampshire,' Angela waited a few uneasy seconds and then decided to let Pippa off the hook. 'My dad was from America, though, if that's what you're getting at, Chicago. He was black, which is different from being Jamaican. Don't think he ever went there either, though.'

'Really, well, this is practically the United Nations we have here, isn't it? That's what I so love about London. American, African, Indian, and what about you, you're Jewish, aren't you?' Pippa beamed and clapped her hands as she looked around the room without the faintest hint of embarrassment and gestured towards Robbie.

'Er...no.'

'Ooops, sorry, it's the nose, I just assumed - you look like a guy I met in Israel a few years ago. It's lovely, I mean, very regal. People must say that to you all the time.'

Robbie touched his nose protectively, going cross-eyed trying to focus on it.

'What about my nose? No-one's ever said that before.'

'No one is as tactless as Pippa,' explained Fiona.

'Well, I mean, it is an absolute corker if you don't mind me saying. And you are quite dark and exotic looking, are you something Middle Eastern, then?'

'No, sorry to disappoint you, I'm basically Welsh.'

'Oh, well, that is still quite exotic, I suppose, it's all relative.'

'Do you think I've got a big nose?' Robbie turned anxiously to Angela.

'Well... it's distinguished,' she replied, leaning over, and kissing its prominent bridge.

'She's not complaining, you know what they say about big noses!' shrieked Pippa.

'My grandfather was Italian, mind you. So, it could be a genuine Roman nose.'

'Really, Italian...mmm... that's more like it. What part? I love Tuscany. Daddy's got a villa out there. We go every autumn.'

'Er...well, I don't know, he ran off before my mother was born.'

'Oh, so, you're not really very Italian then,' Pippa could not hide her disappointment.

'Yeah – he just started supporting them in 1982 when they won the world cup!' interrupted James.

'Well, after being forced to follow Wales from an early age, I had to support someone else when we always missed out on qualifying.'

'Italians were originally from India, you know,' Ravi would say anything if he thought it would help him get into someone's pants.

'Really? …Well that explains why they are so sexy, then. Excuse me, I'll just go and help Fi in the kitchen,' Pippa winked and wiggled out of the room.

Ravi sat back in his chair, looking like the tomcat that had not only just got the cream but also the promise of sexual intercourse with a very attractive lady cat.

'I think I'm in there,' he reflected.

'Oh please...you can't possibly like her,' hissed Angela across the table.

'She's not that bad really once you get to know her, she's just a bit nervous, and over-compensating,' said James.

'Come on, she's a stupid posh tart,' replied Angela, a little too loud.

'Yeah, I know. Great, innit?' said Ravi, grinning.

'You men are pathetic. I mean, what about her ridiculous borderline racist views?'

'Hmmm…nice tits, though,' commented Robbie, which earned him a slap.

'How did you know we had made a butternut squash tart?' said Fiona as she emerged from the kitchen with a big round plate.

'Yes, with rice grits and steamed vegetables. It's based on a Peruvian recipe I picked up last year. Don't worry, it's all vegetarian, we didn't forget you're a Hindu, Ravi. And no pork for you, beaky,' said Pippa, laughing at Robbie's nose again.

'You see, you can't really object to that too much, because as you're not Jewish she's not taking the piss out of an ethnic characteristic, just your massive schnoz,' James joined in the laughter as they sat down and started eating.

Everyone complimented Fiona on her cooking despite Robbie expressing doubts that Peruvian peasants actually had time to make and eat this sort of thing, what with the struggle to hold onto their land under pressures from multinational conglomerates.

'So, have you been to India, Ravi?' asked Pippa.

'Yeah, loads of times. Gujarat. We still have a lot of extended family there.'

'Oh, I love India. I had an amazing time there a few years ago,' enthused Pippa.

'Is there anywhere in the world you haven't been?' asked Robbie, a little too aggressively. He had moved onto the wine by now but was still taking big gulps as if it was beer.

James neatly defused the tension by attempting to launch a heated debate.

'What my good friend is getting at is, has the third world become an adventure playground for rich western tourists?'

'Yeah, sorry, that's what I meant. I just hate the idea of going on holiday to a place where the people are starving and don't have clean water,' clarified Robbie.

'Well, not going on holiday doesn't change the fact,' retorted Pippa.

'And like it or not, all of us here, in a global sense, are rich,' added James.

'Yes, you're probably right, but what can we do about it? At least when we go to places the local economy benefits,' offered Fiona, as she cleared the plates away, slightly worried that her dinner party was turning into a forum for a global class struggle played out by Robbie and Pippa.

'Anyone mind if I skin up?' asked Ravi, the suggestion alone instantly lifting the mood. The debate petered out and the table amicably split up into three intimate conversations.

'God, what a nightmare,' whispered Angela.

'Yeah, I wish we had all just gone for a drink instead,' murmured Robbie in her ear.

'Well done, babe, it's all gone sweetly,' said James.

'Oh, I don't know. What about those two, do you think they get on?' Fiona asked needlessly, nodding surreptitiously across the table at Ravi and Pippa, whose heads were so close together that Ravi's hair was getting entangled in her earrings.

'In India, cannabis has been used for thousands of years to help meditation, you know,' said Ravi has he did a long slow lick of the Rizla.

'Hmmm…also revered in Surrey for its aphrodisiac purposes,' purred Pippa.

Ravi had put on a chillout compilation that seemed to have gone on for hours. Almost as long as it seemed to take him to roll a joint before going through the eventual formality of lighting it and passing it to his neighbour. Pippa tried to look seductive as she inhaled deeply, suppressed a cough, and closed her eyes.

'Here you go, Robbie, you must smoke a lot, being into reggae,' she said as she reached the spliff across the table, blue smoke curling upwards in the candlelight.

Unfortunately, this commonly held belief was Robbie's pet hate number six for the evening, and he had not even met Fiona's cat. Carefully taking the spliff from her fingers, he passed it straight on to Angela. He quite fancied a puff to ease the tension a bit, but he had already had quite a lot of alcohol and was worried the combination would trigger off his bowels. Also, he preferred to register his objection to this last comment on principle.

'I don't know why people always assume you have to be stoned to listen to reggae.'

'Whatever,' said Pippa, giving up saying anything to him and going back to examining Ravi's eyelashes.

Angela took a couple of draws and then passed it on to James.

'No thanks. I haven't smoked for years now. This studying is a serious business; I can't afford any memory loss,' he said, passing it on to Fiona.

'Trust me, I'm a doctor, you have to be using it heavily long-term - it's when you start repeating yourself that you need to worry,' advised Fiona as she let the smoke slowly out of her lips.

'In India, cannabis has been used for thousands of years to help meditation, you know,' said Ravi.

The evening meandered to a close and they all ended up hugging and kissing each other goodnight like bosom buddies, and then Angela and Robbie slagged the rest off all the way home in the cab.

10. JAH LIVE

The colonel listened to the old man's slow, laboured breathing in the darkness. It was midnight and the palace was silent. Deserted, now that he had dismissed the rest of the imperial bodyguard. He took a few steps into the room, his shiny new boots clicking and creaking noisily on the marble floor and was relieved to find the old man's snoring continued unabated. The colonel's eyes became accustomed to the dim moonlight seeping in though the heavy curtains on the huge window overlooking the capital. On the other side of city, the student riots had died down after reluctant soldiers had been sent in with batons and live rounds, on his orders. In the distant countryside, those among the peasants who were not starving had ceased their protests to save their strength for another day now that he had instructed the regional governors to redistribute the meagre supplies of grain. The once proud, independent nation that had survived the colonial era intact now teetered on the brink of collapse, an insignificant pawn in the cold war, reliant on overseas aid and wracked by internal rebellion. Through all this the emperor slept. By day he remained preoccupied with interruptions to his supply of caviar, the health of his pet dogs and his next trip abroad. The colonel looked into the emperor's face, and tried not to think of the blazing eyes, black beard and stern jaw of the powerful, inspiring image that he had grown up to love and admire. The beard was now grey and the face faded from endless days inside the palace, isolated from the fresh air and sunshine. Etched in the lines of his face were the pain and puzzles of growing old without wisdom. Standing over him in the darkness, the colonel shook his head at the thought of how long he himself had followed his increasingly disastrous orders. He laughed at the thought of a crazy bunch of foreigners who worshipped this frail old man as a god, while most of his own people now despised him as a cruel tyrant. Not that he was fooling himself that he was doing this for the benefit of his people or the nation, of course. He knew that if he didn't do it, one of his comrades would, leaving him in a weaker position. The ultimate goal was within his grasp, his only chance of power, wealth and freedom in this godforsaken country. And he could hardly do a worse job, he considered, especially as his friends in the KGB had offered him all the help he needed.

The colonel held the pillow in his hands and placed it squarely over the emperor's face. He enjoyed the feel of the cool silk under his fingers and chuckled silently at the emblem of the imperial lion on the pillowcase, helpless to save its master. For a few seconds he wondered if the way they had planned was the right way – maybe he should wake the old man up and explain his actions, then put a knife through his heart or a bullet between his eyes, so he would enter the next life knowing who had sent him there and why. He looked around the room but there was nothing but gold jewellery and expensive perfume bottles twinkling in the gloom. No, anything else would be too noisy or messy, and he did not want to make it look too obvious just in case he had misjudged the mood of the people. He wanted to be above accusation and yet cultivate an implicit understanding of his role in the emperor's timely demise. Reassured, he tensed his muscles and pressed down with all his weight. This was more than sufficient, as his young, strong muscles almost crushed the ancient delicate frame. The emperor let out a stifled snort and his bony arms flapped briefly before falling lifeless to his side.

The colonel stayed in the same position for a few minutes, waiting motionless. He looked down at the emperor's hands for any sign of movement and his eye caught a glint of gold in the darkness. Relaxing his grip on the pillow, he lifted up the old man's hand and inspected the ring on his finger. It was the emperor's most prized possession, handed down through the royal line dating back to Solomon, symbolising his power and justifying his reign. Solid gold set with a black jewel and embossed in intricate detail with the Lion of Judah. Perfect, thought the colonel, this would be the answer to anyone who questioned his authority, and if things did not go according to plan it would be the ideal insurance policy to guarantee a sizeable sum in future. He tried to prise the ring off, which proved much more difficult than killing him, as the dead man's finger seemed to resist his efforts and pull against him with the strength of a heavyweight boxer. The colonel had no time for superstition and figured this must be rigor mortis setting in already and carried on twisting and turning the ring against the bony knuckle in vain. As the cold, rubbery skin stretched and tore under his frantic grip, he stopped and calmed down, reminding himself that there was no one else around, he was alone with a corpse.

He contemplated hacking off the finger with a knife, but on second thoughts acknowledged this would ruin the appearance of a natural death. Walking away from the bed, he nearly gave up, thinking that he could do without this trivial souvenir, as he would have all the gold in the country. This thought triggered the opposite effect, as he was reminded that his was one of the poorest and most indebted countries in the world, and his position would still be very insecure until he could consolidate his power. Standing in front of the mirror at the huge, ornate dressing table, the colonel swore that he would never give up on his personal quest. Just as he took his knife out of his pocket, he noticed a small pot on the table. The colonel opened the lid and gave the contents a sniff, before dipping in and rubbing the pungent oily cream between his fingers. He returned to the bed, massaged the emperor's dead finger and slipped the ring off easily. Holding his hands up against the window, he placed it on to his own finger and raised his arms in silent victory, vowing never to remove the ring for as long as he held power. The colonel dismissed the burning sensation he felt, assuming that it was a reaction against the lotion, which turned out to be a haemorrhoid preparation. Clenching his fists, he strode out of the room and returned to his own sleeping quarters where he lay wide awake all night, waiting for the first signs of the rousing of the royal household.

At eight in the morning, the colonel listened to the footsteps approaching his door, as expected. He was a little surprised at the lack of weeping and wailing so far, but he reasoned that even here among his own entourage the emperor was as unpopular as among the rest of the people.

'Sir, Colonel, Sir!'

'Enter. What is it?'

The door opened and Tessem, the emperor's loyal and long-serving footman entered, wringing his hands, and looking anxious.

'It is his majesty, sir,'

'Oh no. What has happened?'

'He is gone, sir.'

The colonel paused and did his best to look shocked and upset. 'Our emperor is dead. Our nation is left fatherless, but we must remain strong. Even though his body is gone, his spirit will always be with us…'

'No, colonel, sir. I don't know, I mean, he is gone. He was not in his bed when I brought him his breakfast tray this morning. Has there been some emergency? Have you seen him? Has he contacted you?'

The colonel pushed Tessem to the floor and ran up the stairs into the bedroom he had only left a few hours ago. Bursting through the door, he could not believe his eyes. The bed was indeed empty, and looked as if it had not been slept in. He rubbed his eyes and blinked, not sure if he had been dreaming last night or was still dreaming now. He picked up the bed with all his strength and turned it over. With a flailing of his arms, he swept the perfume bottles and jewellery boxes off the dressing table and smashed his fists into the mirror. He opened the wardrobe and tore through the emperor's fine silks and gowns, pulling it down almost on top of himself. He kicked over the table, sending the breakfast tray with pot of tea, cups, plates, and cutlery scattering across the room. Swearing and shouting, he stormed through the palace, kicking open every door and searching every room in a blind rage. He called for his soldiers and immediately arrested anyone loyal to the emperor. In the belief that someone knew what he had done, and the body had been hidden in a conspiracy, the colonel quickly ordered the shooting of the footman and a few close members of the imperial family. Troops were sent out onto the streets in large numbers to secure all buildings of national importance under his sole control, meeting with little resistance and some jubilation. The emperor's popularity had been long eroded by his own ostentatious wealth and lavish banquets while peasants starved, and workers went on strike. His once astute political sense, which had seen him climb to the top of a feudal aristocracy in the twenties, had been undermined by the military, using the modern media against him. As part of this understanding, the colonel ordered the takeover of all radio and television installations and maintained a news blackout until he was ready to address the nation.

By nine o'clock that evening the colonel had appointed his clique of high-ranking soldiers to form a new government. In the newly refurnished and renamed presidential palace the radio microphones and television cameras were set up around him to witness the announcement of a new era in the nation's history. The cameras started to roll and all over the country people gathered around their radios and a few televisions in hotels and bars, eagerly awaiting confirmation of the rumours that had spread from the capital that day. The solemn music that had been playing all day stopped abruptly was followed by the hum of dead air as the colonel appeared on the monitors, staring blankly from behind a desk and rubbing his hands together nervously. Suddenly his air of power and confidence was visibly shaken. Sweat could be seen breaking out on his forehead and his mouth opened and closed several times with no sound. His hands twitched and he seemed to be cracking his knuckles in anxiety.

'Yesterday, the former emperor died. Cause of death was circulatory failure.'

The colonel recovered and gave the rest of his speech with his customary discipline. Only he had noticed what had momentarily thrown him. The emperor's ring, which had been stuck fast on his finger that morning, was not there now.

11. TRUE BORN AFRICAN

A week after his last call, Robbie followed it up with another visit to his grandmother, thereby doubling his previous three months' commitment to the institution of the extended family in one week. Before leaving home, he had warned her by telephone, and she seemed quite happy with the idea, but as he knocked on her door he still had a sneaking suspicion that she would think he was a door-to-door mugger. It made him wonder if he could get an official grandson ID card to slip through the letterbox. Instead, he smiled and tried to stand with his face in the light as the door opened slowly and braced himself for an attack of elderly person's self-defence.

'Hello gran, it's me - Robbie!'

'Oh, little Robbie! Of course it is, what are you doing here?'

'I rang earlier, remember? Just popped round for a cup of tea.'

'Oh yes. Come in out of the cold son, come and sit by the fire.'

Minnie seemed in much better form than at the weekend, practically shoving Robbie into the front room as she disappeared sprightly into the kitchen. He sat down and the laborious clanking of the kettle, teapot and cups began.

'I'll make it, gran, you sit down,' he shouted pointlessly, knowing she would refuse his help.

'Don't be daft, son. I'm perfectly capable of making a little pot of tea.'

Robbie felt it was better to sit and let her get on with it, rather than patronise her and try to stop her from her commitment to the tea-making ritual, which provided one of few breaks from her armchair and the TV for the day. He also knew that she would insist on bringing a tray laden down with teapot, cups, saucers, the milk in a jug, a sugar bowl, even though neither of them took sugar, a plate of biscuits and buttered slices of fruit loaf. It was all a very complicated, strict tradition and it was not his place to disrupt it by going in and chucking a teabag in a mug. Ten minutes later, the clanking stopped, signalling that preparations were complete. Robbie tore himself away from the comfort of the gas fire, armchair and TV, just as he was thinking he could get used to this lifestyle, went into the kitchen, and managed to wrestle the heavily laden tray from his grandmother's shaky hands.

Minnie poured the tea and offered Robbie the plate of biscuits and cake.

'Thanks, gran. That's lovely. How have you been then?'

'Oh, not bad. I felt a bit of the flu coming on at the weekend, but I think it's gone now.'

'Oh, that's good, are you going to get a jab from the doctor?' asked Robbie as he took a bite of his biscuit.

'Well, we didn't have that in our day, I don't really trust those jabs, you never know what will happen. Don't worry about me anyway, son, what about you? Look at you, you're all skin and bone. Here, have some of this fruit loaf.'

Robbie quickly grabbed a slice of fruit loaf to stop her from the painful struggle of getting up again to reach the table. Minnie relaxed back into her chair and smiled as he took a bite.

'Oh, I'm fine, gran. I've always been skinny like my dad.'

'So, how's the studying?' asked Minnie.

'Er…I finished university about two years ago. That's me there' Robbie reminded her, pointing at his graduation photo between the photo of his sister's kids and the picture of Elvis Presley on the mantelpiece.

'Oh yes, that's right. Is that you? Well done.'

'Thanks.'

'And did I ever tell you about the time I met Elvis?' Minnie asked excitedly, reminded by the picture in pride of place on the mantelpiece, next to the Queen Mother.

'Yes, you have, gran,' sighed Robbie, as he knew this, the only story she told lately, off by heart. His mother had assured him that she had made it all up and was getting mixed up with one of his films she had seen. It involved his grandmother meeting Elvis when he was with the US army in Germany in the fifties and him singing a song to her, so considering she had never been abroad in her life, he accepted his mother's version of events may be the more reliable.

'What's the matter, do you not like those biscuits?'

Robbie took another biscuit, aware that she had no intention of having anything on the plate but planned on watching him eat the lot. 'They are delicious, thanks,' he mumbled with his mouthful, taking as long as he could to eat it before she made him take another.

'So, how was America?' asked Minnie, her eyes brightening.

'Er…' Robbie hesitated, unsure whether to explain who he was again or just let her think he was this second cousin Roddy in America who he had never seen. Just as he was thinking that she seemed perfectly alright, this served as a reminder that her condition was pretty bad. According to his mother, it was the recent, short-term memory that was worse affected, while she could remember things from fifty or sixty years ago as clearly as if it were yesterday. Slightly selfishly, Robbie thought this could serve the purpose of his visit quite well, as it was what he wanted to ask her about. He had always felt a bit annoyed that his grandparents had never lived up to the stereotype of old people, not going on about the past and the war like they are supposed to, even though he would have been quite interested. It was quite tricky to ask his grandmother now, as he thought maybe there was a good reason that she never mentioned it, and it might dredge up some painful memories. Perhaps he should respect her right not to talk about it, but on the other hand, she probably kept quiet because she thought he would not be interested.

'…No, gran, you're thinking of your nephew Roddy. I'm Robbie, Isobel's youngest.'

'Oh yes, that's right, I know. You're the spitting image of him.'

'He went to America after the war, didn't he?'

'Roddy? Gone. That's right. He was only eighteen.'

'Why did he go?' asked Robbie, sensing an opportunity.

'Ah, there's a question. In those days there was nothing left in Cardiff for the young folk. I knew lots of people who went away. America, Canada, Australia. Never heard from most of them again.'

'Did you ever think about going to live in America?'

'Me? America? No, no, no.' Minnie laughed at the thought of it. 'I had your mother before I knew what I wanted to do; I wasn't going anywhere. Least of all America.'

'Is that because of the father?' Robbie asked, tentatively.

'Oh, you know all about that as well? Aye, that made it worse, I still feel terrible about it.' She looked down, sadness entered her eyes, and the room went quiet for a while. Robbie decided it was better to leave it. He took another slice of fruit loaf and sat back in his chair, trying to think of how to change the subject before she started crying again.

'Oh well, I don't suppose it matters now,' Minnie continued. 'Makes no difference if I tell you anyway. It's all ancient history to you.'

'It's OK, gran. You don't have to talk about it… but I am interested.'

'Oh dear, all those gangfights. My father and brothers and their pals going around looking for any Italian in Cardiff, it was terrible. So, I said he had gone to America, but that made it worse. They just took it out on anyone. But they hadn't done anything. Just like Gino Ginelli. It was the only name I could think of…and then my father went around Italian ice cream shops asking for Gino Ginelli… and because of the war, y'know, Mussolini and the fascists were on Hitler's side, all the Italians were rounded up. Oh dear, it all got out of hand, I can't believe they fell for it. You see, I made it up, there was no Gino Ginelli!' Minnie started laughing. 'He wasn't even Italian!'

'Wow!' Robbie was transfixed.

'And then your granddad came back from the war and took me and the baby on. Bless him, he had a heart of gold.'

'Yeah, he was a great guy,' agreed Robbie, wary that she might get upset again, but not wanting to disturb her as she sat reminiscing quietly. Minnie smiled at him, and he grabbed the last biscuit before it distracted her attention. He waited a few seconds to see if she would say anything more, but she seemed to have stopped. Robbie swallowed his biscuit and forcing his reservations down with it, bravely asked:

'So…who was the real father, then?'

Minnie laughed again for a few seconds, 'Oh, you really want to know do you? How long have you got?'

12. REDEMPTION SONG

A cool breeze drifted in from the bay, filling the hillside cottage with the scent of jacaranda, fresh from the storms of the night before. It was a beautiful sunny morning in May and the entire world had stopped to pay its respects, even the sea appeared still and calm as the tide lapped gently onto the beach. Gloria sighed heavily and pretended the pain in her chest was her angina playing up. She tried to be happy, knowing that her nephew had chosen to go to a better place, but her faith was not quite strong enough to overcome the grief she felt. She could still close her eyes and see the skinny little boy running in from the shore with the fishermen as if it was yesterday. Even then she had known he was special, the way he was always singing and picking up a guitar, but she never imagined he would become a superstar, famous throughout the world. The extent of his popularity was hard for her to imagine and she was amazed at the steady stream of visitors to the village over the past few days, from England, Japan, Zimbabwe and places she had never heard of, all weeping and wailing as if they too had lost family. Nine days had passed since he had died and now she just wished for tomorrow's funeral to be over as soon as possible. A knock on the door disturbed her from her thoughts and she turned round to accept the condolences of the latest sympathiser. Her sister was sleeping in the other room now, for the first time in days. Gloria worried that she would break down completely and not make it through the funeral, so she had to protect her from unwanted intrusions.

'Sister, I and I come from the Free United Church of the Kingdom of Everliving Rastafari to chant some psalms and give thanks and praises for the life of Bredda Bob, who has chosen Zion and is truly in a holy place in the ever-loving arms of Jah. Rastafari.'

Gloria stared at the stranger, who wore a turban wound tightly around his dreadlocks and was dressed in elaborate white robes with red gold and green trimmings, carrying a staff in one hand and a bible in the other. She had never seen him before and had never heard of the sect that he claimed to represent, but she accepted his embrace and warmly welcomed him into her home. He stood in the middle of the room chanting from the bible for a few minutes in a faltering falsetto.

'Thank you, that was beautiful, - would you like a lickle someting fe drink? You know you never miss your water till your well runs dry,' asked Gloria with a chuckle when he had finished, concerned that his throat must be painfully dry the way his voice cracked as he sang.

'No thank you, sister. I and I come with a message from the elders. Bob was very close to our group in his last months, and converted to our way, the true Rastafari teachings of Haile Selassie, King of Kings, Lord or Lords, Conquering Lion of the Tribe of King Judah in this time, as revealed in Revelation.'

Gloria sighed; she had heard so many people repeating these incantations in the past few days that they brought on a headache. She was only a recent convert to Rastafari from a traditional Christian upbringing, and to her these were sacred words from the bible, a prayer with precious meaning. She was deeply suspicious of sanctimonious preachers who called on the Messiah's name at the end of every sentence. These various sects and self-appointed leaders confused her, as the thing that had attracted her and her sister to Rastafari was Bob's insistence that there was no organised church hierarchy, and everyone was equal in the eyes of Jah.

'Oh, really? He never mentioned your organisation to me. Is it part of the - what they call it - the Ethiopian Orthodox Church, or the Twelve Tribes of Israel? What is your name?'

'I and I name Bredda Benjamin. Ah true, sister. I and I represent the coming together of the Ethiopian Orthodox and the Twelve Tribes of Israel in one love and unity. Bob did see that when he came to his resting place in his final days.'

'Well, thank you for coming, Bredda Benjamin. We are all one family of Rastafari.'

Gloria stood up and prepared for him to leave. She too had not slept much for the past week and wanted some time to rest on her own before the funeral tomorrow. But Brother Benjamin remained stood still in the middle of the room, looking straight ahead, clutching his staff and bible as if he was about to preach a sermon.

'I and I come on a mission in the name of Jah Rastafari. Bredda Bob the prophet has – had - something that belongs to all Rastaman.'

'Hmm…and what might dat be?' asked Gloria warily. She had been fending off sharks and gold diggers ever since her nephew's first record sales but there had been a dramatic resurgence since his death, all after the same thing.

'Oh, a no big ting dis. Jus a lickle heirloom he wanted to entrust to the safe keeping of his bredren in the Church. Bredda Bob wore a ring –'

Gloria raised her eyebrows and kissed her teeth loudly and slowly. She knew what was coming and turned to look out of the window.

'Sister, the ring of Solomon is a sacred relic of Rastafari. It was given to Bob by the heir of Haile Selassie and rightly belongs in the keeping of his followers. It did not belong to Bob.'

'Well, it sure as hell nah belong to you! Come out a mi yard, man. Gwan!' she shouted, wheeling round, the stress of the past few days got too much, and her patience snapped.

Brother Benjamin dropped his staff as he backed out towards the door of the little cottage. As he stooped to pick it up, he protected himself with the bible in his other hand, fearing the old woman would cuff him round the head. She just glared at him as he turned on his heels and ran down the gully, his gleaming white robes dropping and trailing in the mud. Once he was safely out of her sight and her anger subsided, she sat by the window and allowed the tears to roll down her face. She almost felt like cursing this ring and the trouble it caused but knew how much it meant to Bob. She remembered how honoured and excited he was when Crown Prince Wossen, the only surviving direct descendant of His Majesty Emperor Haile Selassie, had agreed to meet him in London where he was staying for a while in 1977. Bob had phoned a few days later and told her that Prince Wossen had given him a gold ring that had belonged to His Imperial Majesty. It was set with a black stone on which was engraved the Lion of Judah, the same ring that Selassie had worn on his right hand all his life, given to him by his fathers, dating all the way back to King Solomon in biblical times. Bob never took it off again, even when he knew he was dying. Gloria knew it was not for her or anyone else to do any different as he lay in his coffin.

Early the next morning, Gloria felt like she was in a dream as they were taken to Kingston in an official car for the funeral service at the Ethiopian Orthodox Church on Maxfield Avenue where the body had been lying in state. The coffin was then taken to the National Arena for the state funeral and the award of the Order of Merit. She sat comforting her sister as politicians and pop stars paid tribute to her nephew, even those who had not had a good word for him when he was alive. One by one they went up to him as he lay, hands folded neatly across his chest with Selassie's ring shining in the candlelight. The thinning dreadlocks and emaciated face ravaged by cancer gave an image of how he would have looked as an old man, if he had lived another forty years. His real people, the poor people of Jamaica lined the streets in their thousands from Kingston to St Ann's Bay as the cortege drove across the island to the small village of his birth. They had built a small mausoleum on top of the hill in Nine Miles where Bob had grown up, opposite the renovated little shack where he was born, not far from his mother's new cottage in the village. At the end of what seemed like the longest day of her life, and the worst, she found herself inside the closed doors of the mausoleum. Her bleary eyes adjusted to the dim light, and she breathed in the cool, damp air. They shut out the crowds and the sunshine, and began the private ceremony. Just her, his mother, his widow, the children, and Bob's two closest bredren, Walter and Skill, stood around the modest wooden coffin. She touched Bob on the hand for the last time, and was surprised he did not feel cold as she expected, but the gold ring on his finger seemed to give off a warm sensation. The lid was placed over the coffin, and they all closed their eyes and bent their heads in silent prayer for a few minutes before the final ceremony when it would be sealed. A sudden knocking at the doors of the mausoleum disturbed their peace. Walter opened them and three Rastas in long white robes crowded into the tiny space around the coffin. Gloria recognised one of them as Brother Benjamin. He was standing behind an older man, who did the talking.

'We hereby demand by holy decree of the Free United Church of the

Kingdom of Everliving Rastafari that the ring of Haile Selassie, Jah Rastafari, be returned to I and I safe keeping before this coffin is sealed,' he said, stepping forward and lifting the lid of the coffin.

They were all too surprised at this invasion to stop it and before they had worked out what was happening, they were all looking into Bob's coffin again. Everyone stood in silence for a few seconds.

'Where is the ring?' demanded the Rasta elder, thinking they had played a trick on him.

The others were too shocked to speak. They had all seen the ring there a few seconds ago, and no one had had the opportunity to remove it. Bob's mother, who had barely spoken a word all day and appeared to others to be overcome with grief, smiled knowingly. She stepped forward and addressed the three intruders in a strong, calm voice:

'De ring gwan back where it came from, same as Bob.'

The self-appointed Rasta elders looked at each other and then back at the old woman.

'Where? What have you done with it?' squeaked Benjamin impatiently.

She realised they did not know and did not believe, despite the faith that they so professionally proclaimed. They stood in silence watching each other as the lid was calmly replaced and the coffin was sealed.

'De ring gwan back from whence it came. It back on His Majesty's mighty hand. And Bob is by Jah side.'

13. UNTOLD STORIES

'Hayley's a lassie! I'll be seeing ya; that's what we used to say, you know, so it sounded like Abyssinia. It was quite the in thing, and if someone said something you didn't believe, you would say: 'If that's true, then I'm Haile Selassie.' It was all the rage in 1936; he was in all the papers and on the newsreel at the cinema. I remember the pictures of the priests blessing Italian soldiers on their way. And then the fascists invading Abyssinia with tanks and poison gas, killing thousands of innocent men, women and children, and the emperor was forced out. All the British government did was offer him exile in England. I don't know why he ended up in Bath. Well, it's a nice a place as any, I suppose, very posh. Fit for a king. That's how we in Cardiff always thought of it, anyway, couldn't be more opposite. Cardiff in the thirties was suffering more than its fair share from the depression, thousands out of work, lining the streets. I was seventeen, had left school a couple of years earlier and was trying to bring some money home to help my parents out, as dad had lost his job and the rent was going up all the time. There was not much that I could do, but I was very good at English, always reading. I always thought it was because I was taught it late, after speaking nothing but Welsh until I was eight years old. When we first moved to Cardiff I did not want to be thought of as a country bumpkin, so I made a big effort, and learnt the King's English perfectly from my teachers. So anyway, I hoped to go into teaching, but in those days, people were just glad of whatever work came their way. So, I started looking after children, like a nanny, really. My mother used to do it, and she knew someone who could get that sort of work in posh people's houses, you know, the ones that send their kids off to boarding school and then don't even want to look after them in the holidays, they get someone else to do it.

'That's how I found myself being left at Fairfield House just before

Christmas in 1936. I answered an ad in the local paper – they wanted people from outside Bath for security reasons, you see, and then I had an interview with a man from the Home Office. I didn't really understand what was going on, but I was supposed to keep it a secret exactly who I was working for, on account of the threat of Italian spies assassinating him. I remember it like it was yesterday, the Rolls Royce in the driveway and the little red, green, and yellow lion flag fluttering above the doorway. It had been snowing, you know, real proper snow, not like the slushy stuff you get nowadays. The butler and the children came out to meet me. I had never seen an African in real life before. Don't get me wrong, there were always some living near the docks in Cardiff, but it was not the sort of place you would hang around, especially at my age. I remember thinking how dark brown tanned they looked in contrast with the deep white snow everywhere, beautiful. At first, I thought they all had grey hair! But it was the snowflakes settling in their black hair like diamonds against coal. They just looked so out of place, and freezing cold, poor lambs. It was a manor house on a hill just outside Bath, posh, but hardly a palace, and quite modest for an emperor and all his family. Apparently, they had to sell off most of the gold and silver salvaged from his palaces in Abyssinia to buy and furnish the place. It was sad really; he had been put up in London as a guest of the King earlier that year, but after his speech to the League of Nations I think we in Britain were ashamed of not helping him. Everyone forgot about him until the war started in earnest, and our boys pushed the Italians out of Africa in 1941, better late than never.

'Anyway, I was given strict instructions about looking after the two boys, told to stay in my room at other times and strictly forbidden from setting foot in the rooms occupied by the emperor and empress. The younger boy was Prince Sahle Selassie, son and heir of Haile Selassie, and Desta, the elder of the two, as it happened, was actually the emperor's grandson from a previous marriage. Both were very bright and keen to learn all about life in Britain. They had a reasonable standard of English, and my main job was to read to them and keep them entertained while the emperor received visitors and worked on his autobiography. The children thought it was a big adventure and were expecting to return home at any time. I never saw hide or hair of the man himself for several weeks. He was trying to gain support to fight the Italians and return to his country, but I remember the air of dejection and depression that filled the house when he was there that winter, it was clear that it would be a long, lonely exile in the cold. But he who fights and runs away lives to fight another day - that's what my dad used to tell my brothers. Anyway, the pay was good, and the butler seemed happy with my work, so I found myself back there again in the Easter and summer holidays.

'One day in the spring of 1937 I was in the drawing room teaching Sahle and Desta some nursery rhyme nonsense when they suddenly froze and went silent. I could tell someone had entered the room, you know, when you can feel their presence. I turned slowly and there he was, the emperor himself, a dapper little man, only about five foot, handsome and dignified. His skin was lighter than the children's, it almost looked faded, as if he had not seen the sun for a long time, which was true I suppose. Beneath his thick black beard and severe, unsmiling face he had an aura of goodness and wisdom. There he stood in the doorway, deep brown eyes shining like flames, looking at me down his Roman nose, like a great big beak. I thought he looked like an eagle about to swoop down, and I felt like a little field mouse. I had never been in the presence of royalty before, or since, and was not sure what to do, so I just sort of curtsied. He waited a few seconds and then asked politely:

'What is that you are teaching to the heirs of the Royal House of Ethiopia?'

'Er... s-sorry your highness, sir, it's Welsh.' I stammered. I was petrified; I didn't even know what to call him.

'Welsh?' He repeated, his English was excellent, but he had this funny accent, Abyssinian, I suppose, and he rolled the word around pronouncing each letter, as it was obviously unfamiliar to him.

'Yes, your highness, sir. The language of Wales, to the north-west of here.'

'We are aware of the country, but we were not aware that they possessed a separate language from England.' He was so funny the way he spoke, really like the royal family are supposed to, saying we instead of I.

'Yes sir, that was a song my parents used to sing to me. And Sahle has taught me some Abyssinian in return.'

'Amharic' he corrected, 'Excellent. It is only through education and understanding of our people that nation can truly speak unto nation.'

And with that he disappeared. I didn't set eyes on him again for weeks, but then he started sitting in with the boys when I was looking after them in afternoons in the springtime. He seemed very dejected about the fate of his people. Being around the children cheered him up. During the summer holidays, on fine days, I would be looking after the boys in the garden, and he would sit in as I taught them the names of our plants and animals. They were fascinated, as it was all very different from what they were used to in Abyssinia. I'll never forget the image of little Desta chasing a squirrel around the garden. Then, after the children had gone to bed, he and I would both just stay sitting there in the garden until it got dark, not saying anything, only smelling the flowers, listening to the birds and watching the sun go down. He was always the perfect gentleman, very polite, and at half past ten would say 'Good night, Miss Williams.'

'After a few weeks, as the summer faded, he started talking about his homeland, describing the golden sunshine, the flowers, the mountains, and the sky. It sounded beautiful; I always wanted to go there, bit late now I suppose. I was so surprised when he suddenly said something, I didn't know what to say, and I just kept quiet. During the days, he was dictating his autobiography to this little clerk with a typewriter, and in the evenings he would be talking aloud, working on what he wanted to say. He would talk for hours, a little bit about his childhood but mostly about his struggle to power and his mission to modernise his country. Obviously he was really homesick, and he was fed up of listening to the wireless, waiting for the rest of the world to stand up to Mussolini and Hitler. This was the time of appeasement you see, and he kept making these long speeches about how good must stand up against evil, with only the squirrels and the birds and me listening to him. In fact, I wasn't even sure he remembered I was there half the time, but he always turned to me at half past ten and said 'Good night, Miss Williams.'

'That was 1937, and it went on like that at half term and at Christmas, whenever I was there to mind the children. Nearly every evening that winter we would end up sitting in the living room, watching the dying embers of the fire. It was so quiet in that house, just his voice, soft-spoken but strong, talking about asserting rights that had been trampled on by fascist jackboots and choked by poison gas. He had these deep, black scars on both hands; mustard gas burns from holding onto his gun even while acid rained down from the skies, so I learnt. I remember the tears running down his face and into these dark pits on his hands when he talked about it. I think he had no-one else to talk to - I hardly ever saw or heard anything of his wife or the elder princess. God knows what they did; they must have been bored out of their minds. I went back home to Cardiff the rest of the time, when the children were at boarding school. Dad was getting ill by then and I helped my mother look after him while my brothers went out to look for work. They all thought I was working for a posh English family in Bath, I never told them that it was an African emperor. Dad would have had a heart attack, it would have finished him off. Mum would probably have wanted to go round for tea. My brothers would never have believed me, they would have laughed at me. So it went on like that through 1938 until September 1939, when the war broke out. You youngsters will never understand what it was like. Everything changed. Not straight away, there was the phoney war for what seemed like months, when we practised putting on gas masks and expected air raids any day, but nothing much happened. And then all the young men started to disappear. All three of my brothers joined up. They were looking forward to it, there was nothing left for them in Cardiff and the war was a chance for escape and excitement. Only one came back, of course. You remember your great-uncle David; he died a few years ago. We were too young to remember the Great War, of course, but our parents had talked about it all our lives. I don't know what we thought a war would be like, it was exciting, but we felt a mixture of fear and pride that this was what we had to do.

'This doesn't make it all right, of course. It was October 1940; we had known each other for nearly four years. I felt like I knew everything about him. I had heard most of his autobiography, his speeches on world affairs, his feelings about his occupied homeland and his adopted home. He had started asking me questions about myself that summer. He was very interested in my brothers and what they were fighting for, and how people in Wales felt about the British Empire. I probably sounded like an idiot, but I told him why we hated Hitler and what kind of a world we wanted to live in. Sometimes we would talk about nature and animals; he loved dogs. I was always hoping I would say or do something that he approved of, and make him smile. There was something irresistible about his smile, and I was always felt privileged when he smiled at me, it was like a rare gift. And then one night, after we had been sitting up talking for ages, it happened. My fault really, I was what they used to call a good-time girl in those days, and there were so few men around. Only the once, but that was enough as it turned out. I was going back to Cardiff the next day as the children were going back to school. When I came back for the Christmas holidays, Fairfield House was deserted; they had packed up and gone. About then I realised I was pregnant. The next time I saw him was on a newsreel at the cinema in January 1941, the Italians were forced out of Abyssinia, and he was restored to his rightful throne. And your mother was born on 15th June 1941.'

Robbie sat back as his grandmother stopped talking, and looked at the clock, it was quarter to twelve.

'So, nan, you're telling me that Haile Selassie is my real grandfather?' he said, incredulously, thinking she had completely lost it.

'That's right, son. You are the only person who knows the truth.'

'Haven't you ever told anyone else?'

'Not a soul…well, there was my best friend, Sally. When I came home the next week, I told her I had fallen in love with an African emperor. She just laughed, she didn't believe a word of it, more's the pity. I was so angry with her; I thought to myself that I would prove it to her. I went back to the house the next Sunday morning, knowing they would all be at church. I was just looking for a little souvenir, something to show that I was really working for an African emperor, not just some posh English family like I had said all along. I was upstairs for the first time and had a sneaky look on the dressing table. Just a little something…'

Minnie's expression changed at this point; nostalgic reminiscing was suddenly clouded by guilt. 'I was just looking in the jewellery box, and admiring it, looking at this beautiful little lion on it. I wasn't even thinking about borrowing it, as it looked so expensive, but then I heard a noise downstairs, and I rushed out of the room. The butler was pottering about in the kitchen so when I got the chance I bolted out of the front door, down the driveway. When I got to the end of the road, I looked down at my clenched fist, and there it was, still in my hand.'

'What was it?' asked Robbie.

'Here, you're tall, aren't you? Reach up to the top of that bookcase there. You see the little china puppy on the top? Pull that out; there should be an old biscuit tin behind it. That's it.'

Robbie carefully took the tin down, blew the dust off it and could just make out the typical forties style picture of a smiling golden haired child eating biscuits. He handed it to his grandmother, who prised it open and started poking through the contents. She handed him a newspaper cutting. The print had faded, the paper had gone brown with age and felt as if it was disintegrating in his hands. But there was no mistaking the subject of the cutting. January 30th 1941 – *Haile Selassie returns to Ethiopia... Emperor secreted from exile in Bath to join Allied forces forcing Italians back in North Africa*. Robbie looked up at his grandmother. She had found what she was looking for and a tear was making its way slowly down her cheek.

'I never meant to take it. I had it in my pocket that day when I went back at Christmas, but everything had gone. I loved him in my own way, and I know he liked me a lot. I hope he didn't think I was a thief...I was just looking for something to borrow to prove I had known him. But I was so mortified; I never even showed it to Sally, or anyone else. I laughed it off and pretended to Sally that I had been joking all along, made her promise to forget what I had said. She never mentioned it again, although she did raise an eyebrow when the baby came out so dark. That's when I made up the story about the Italian. There you go, son.'

Robbie peered at the object she had placed in his palm. It was a gold ring, set with a black jewel and embossed with some sort of insignia. Looking more closely, he could see the unmistakeable figure of the Lion of Judah, symbol of the royal house of Ethiopia, and cover star of countless reggae albums. He was speechless.

'Beautiful, isn't it? But it makes me feel guilty just thinking about it, it's stolen. I haven't even looked at it - it's been in that box for over fifty years. I've never stolen anything in my life...'

The tears started rolling down her cheeks now, and then she grabbed Robbie's hand and looked him in the eye.

'Will you give it back, son? Take it and give it back to its rightful owner. His son or grandson, whoever. Just take it, then I can rest easy in my grave.'

With trembling, wrinkled hands, she placed the ring on the middle finger of his right hand. It fitted perfectly, but burned his skin like fire, or so it felt for a few seconds.

Robbie looked into his grandmother's tear-filled eyes and promised her, 'I will, gran.'

Minnie was exhausted. Robbie helped her up out of her chair and she started getting ready to go to bed. He said good night and made his way home, breathing in deeply the stale traffic fumes and chilly midnight air. The roads around were quiet, just the hum of the Westway in the distance. His head was spinning. He examined the ring on his finger under the orange glow from a lamppost. It seemed heavy enough to be gold and the lion was correct in every detail. Where could she have got it? Robbie was mystified. Like all reggae fans, he knew the Rasta legend surrounding the holy relic of the ring worn by Selassie and given to Bob Marley, as seen on the cover of the Legend album, but he had taken it with a pinch of salt. Now what appeared to be a very similar ring was on his finger, and he was desperately trying to come to terms with what his grandmother had told him. Could it be true? Or was this just the senile ranting of a demented old woman with a royalty fixation? She certainly seemed to believe it, and obviously felt very strongly that he should take it back to its rightful owner. He did not know why he had promised her that he would return it, as this seemed to be an impossible task, it was just an instinctive reaction to make her feel better.

Robbie tried to distinguish facts from what could have been just pure fantasy. Apparently Haile Selassie lived in exile in Bath from 1936 to 1940, that much he would check out for sure from a library. His grandmother was from Cardiff. His mother was born in June 1941 – she had brown eyes, black curly hair and olive skin. His grandmother had given him a ring bearing the symbol of the royal house of Ethiopia. That was it. There could be an alternative explanation. She might have made up this fantasy to hide a more uncomfortable truth about the father. She might even have even started to believe it herself now that her illness was slowly detaching her from reality. The real father might have been an African living in Cardiff or just passing through on a ship, or a black soldier from an African or West Indian colony, based in Britain at the start of the war, or even an American GI. He might have spun her this whole yarn about Haile Selassie, and she might have believed him. It would not be the first time a man lied about who he was in order to have his way with a naïve young woman. He could even have given her the ring. It might just be a cheap imitation. Or maybe his grandmother had bought it herself – she worked in a charity shop in Cardiff a few years ago, maybe a local ex-Rasta had cut off his dreadlocks and given away his paraphernalia, and she had kept the ring for herself as a memento. Robbie laughed and muttered to himself, shaking his head as he walked, suddenly becoming aware that he probably looked like a madman, not that it mattered much in London at that time of night. He turned round and looked down the road to see his bus careering towards him in the distance. Robbie made a run for the bus stop ahead of him and got there just in time to hail the reluctant driver to a shuddering halt with a painful squealing of brakes.

'Careful darlin, min you don slip pon you foot and brok you backside,' offered an elderly West Indian woman walking past the bus stop.

This happened to Robbie a lot, elderly West Indian people saying hello to him. At least he thought it was just him. Getting on and sitting at the front on the deserted upstairs deck, he peered at his reflection through the dirt and tags on the window in front of him, illuminated by the lights inside the bus against the dark outside. He had quite a big nose, he supposed, but not a Roman one like Selassie. Brown eyes, but that was not unusual. And his hair was fairly dark brown, but pretty straight. He rolled the sleeves of his jacket up and looked at his arms. He was fairly white, there was no doubt about that, but Selassie looked fairly light skinned. Could he be a quarter African? More to the point, could he be the grandson of Haile Selassie? Robbie laughed to himself again at the absurdity of it, and shook his head, but somehow his life suddenly seemed to make sense.

14. WHO COULD IT BE

Monday evening, and Isobel was in the kitchen doing the ironing and listening to the radio while waiting for an oven-ready lasagne to be ready in the oven. Her husband, Tony, was asleep on the sofa in front of the football in the living room, sleeping off his take-away curry. Their eating and viewing habits had diverged dramatically over the past few years, but they were both quite happy with the situation. Placing a shirt on a hanger, she jumped as the harsh drill of the doorbell disturbed her peace and quiet. Slightly annoyed, she wondered whether she should just ignore it, as it was likely to be kids selling something or salesmen mucking about. Reluctantly, she made her way to the front door and was surprised to see her son for the second time in a week.

'What's wrong?' said Isobel, looking up and down the street behind him, half-expecting to see a police car or an angry mob to give some clue to his unexpected visit.

'Nothing, mum. Why should there be?' said Robbie innocently.

'Oh, come on, we don't usually see you for months. It's not Christmas for a few weeks yet, it's not my birthday, so what's going on?'

'Er...can I come in?'

'Hmmm...I suppose you'll be wanting something to eat as well?'

'Only what's going,'

Isobel ushered him past his snoring father into the kitchen and continued with the ironing while directing Robbie to put the kettle on.

'And you went to see your granny the other night, didn't you?' asked Isobel suspiciously.

'Yeah, that's sort of what its about.'

'What's the matter? Was she alright?'

'Yeah, she seemed fine, well, full of life, but I am not sure if she made much sense.'

'Oh well, she very rarely does these days, son. God, you had me worried there, I was going to pop round to see her later tonight anyway. So why the sudden desire to be close to the loving bosom of your family? Are you having some kind of quarter century crisis? Have you and Angela got a little announcement?'

Robbie gave her the same sarcastic sneer that had made her want to slap him on a regular basis during his teenage years. Isobel sighed and returned her attention to the ironing. She wasn't actually too bothered about weddings or more grandchildren; she just felt that if Robbie settled down, she wouldn't have to worry about him. Ever since the two older girls had got safely paired off and reproducing, she had felt the active service of motherhood was nearing an end. No one had told her children needed so much attention into their twenties and thirties, even. She was sure it had been different when she was younger. Eighteen and that was it. Sod off out of the nest and don't come back. Nowadays even if you could afford to pack them off to university, they all came back in a few years like boomerangs. Maybe student debt and London property prices were to blame. Anyway, she was going to retire next year, and now found herself having to look after her mother, so would feel a lot happier that Angela was looking after Robbie. Not that he needed a lot of looking after, she just felt that living on his own he was vulnerable to the usual dangers of depression, drug addiction and unspecified dissipation.

'Sorry. Angela's out with some girlfriends, I just thought I would pop in and say hello.'

'Ahh, were you lonely, son? What about your pals?'

'Dunno. Ravi is working on his film. James is studying, y'know, his law conversion.'

'Yes, now that is a good idea. Why don't you do something like that?'

'Yeah, maybe. Seems like too much hard work. I haven't got several thousand pounds going spare either.'

'Yes, I know, son. It just seems like you went off to university and came back and got a job you could have got anyway. What do you call it, data-inputting?'

'There is a bit more to it than that, mum. I answer the phone sometimes as well. Anyway, I might go travelling.'

'Of course, son.' Isobel sighed. He had been talking about that for the past couple of years, but he had enough difficulty organising a trip to the supermarket. She smiled at him, and he sat in silence for a while, hopefully trying to gain some tips on ironing.

'Mum, did gran ever talk much about your father?'

'Of course, she talks about him all the time. I told you she hasn't really accepted that he's dead,' replied Isobel absent-mindedly, as she pounded a delicate blouse with the steaming iron. She was actually a bit annoyed that the little time she had to herself had been interrupted by her son turning up asking stupid questions.

'Yeah, I know. No, I meant your real father, the Italian guy.'

'Oh, that sod. No, I'd forgotten about him, really. Your granddad was always there for me as my dad.'

They sat for a while longer in silence and Isobel set the table.

'Well, you are quite dark, aren't you? Even for an Italian I mean, it's quite unusual, for someone brought up in Wales.'

'I suppose so, which is why I used to get teased in school. Look, what is all this getting at, exactly?' Isobel was getting a little exasperated and put some peas on to boil.

'Oh, nothing. I was just wondering. He was an Italian ice-cream seller or something, wasn't he?'

'That's right and then he ran off to America when your granny got pregnant with me. It was just as well really, as your great-grandfather was ready to kill him, apparently there was a feud with the Italians in Cardiff for years after that. And then a lot of them were interned during the war, so he wouldn't have stood much of a chance. Dad had a heart of gold for taking the two of us on. In those days an unmarried mother was a real taboo.'

'Yeah, but I mean, how do you know that's true? Did she ever have any photos of him or anything?'

'Not that I know of.'

'How about a name?'

'Erm…I think she said it was Gino Ginelli or something.'

'Gino Ginelli? The ice cream seller? Come on, doesn't that sound a bit made-up?' asked Robbie.

'Well, maybe it is. She probably wanted to protect him. Anyway, what is your point, exactly?'

'Have you ever tried to trace him?'

'An Italian who went to America in the thirties? No. Needles and haystacks spring to mind.'

'And he's never tried to get in touch?'

'Not that I know of. He would owe me quite a few Christmas and birthday presents by now.'

'So you don't really know, then? You could be half-Spanish, Moroccan, anything?'

'In theory, yes. But Cardiff in the thirties was not the most cosmopolitan of cities and Italians were about the only foreigners around. It's not an issue, I am Welsh, my parents are Welsh, I may or may not have some Italian blood but this is about as close as I get to Italy,' Isobel took the lasagne out of the oven and placed it on the table between them.

'Yeah, alright.'

'So what is your point, exactly?'

'I dunno, it was just the way gran was looking at that album cover the other night. Y'know, the picture of Haile Selassie, and then she said something about my grandfather. I thought maybe he might have been Ethiopian?'

Isobel started laughing and nearly dropped the peas as she drained them over the sink.

'Oh dear. She's got Alzheimer's, son. You could have held up a picture of the pope and she might have thought it was your granddad. Mind you, where was the pope in 1940? You could be onto something here,' she laughed again as she served up the dinner, grudgingly dividing the lasagne for one into two.

Robbie felt a bit foolish, and they started eating in silence. Isobel continued examining the magazine on the table next to her plate, hoping Robbie would take the hint. It's not that she minded him coming round; she just wished he would watch the football and bond with his father in a silent male way. This was just a bit odd, and she thought he should be spending time with Angela or his mates. Isobel was tired after work and was looking forward to a quiet night to herself. The last thing she wanted was an uninvited interruption from her son, interrogating her about her biological ancestry. As a teenager she had dreamt about her real father being a rich, glamorous New Yorker, a gangster or a movie star, but she had not given it much thought for years. Frankly she thought Robbie was a bit old for such fantasies. Robbie was thinking the same thing.

'Sorry, I know it sounds stupid...it's just I was asking gran about the past, y'know.'

'Oh, right. That's nice, dear.' Isobel cleared away the plates and then went off upstairs with the ironing board and clothes in a clear display of disinterest.

Robbie handed her a cup of tea when she came back into the kitchen and carried on regardless. 'You see the thing is, she started talking about my real grandfather, your real father.'

'I knew it! It was the pope, wasn't it? Right, I'm going to sue him.' Isobel amused herself greatly with this idea and Robbie laughed politely but clung onto the subject.

'No, she told me this whole story about how she was working in some posh manor house called Fairfield House or something, teaching and looking after kids, and fell in love with their father... this rich mysterious bloke.'

'Oh right, that sounds familiar,' said Isobel casually.

'What, she's told you about it already?'

'No, I've read it, and seen the film.'

'Eh?'

'It's Jane Eyre. By Charlotte Bronte. You must have read it. Don't they teach you anything at university these days? She's a governess looking after children, Mr Rochester, madwoman in the attic and all that. It's your grandmother's favourite book, I think; she's always re-reading it lately. Mind you that's because her memory is so bad.'

'No, she told me it happened to her...'

'Yes, I've explained this to you before. It's Alzheimer's Disease. They have problems distinguishing reality from fiction. It's probably not that unusual that she gets mixed up between books and her memories, poor thing.'

'But...she told me the real father was Ha...an African, from Abyssinia, that's Ethiopia now, isn't it?'

'Well, who knows? Yes, it's the old name for that area, or Somalia as well maybe. Of course, it's crossed my mind before that he might not have been Italian. There were a few Somalis who lived near us in Cardiff when I was young. Not sure how they got there, but their language looks a lot like Welsh when it's written down, have you ever noticed that? Anyway, I sometimes thought it could have been one of them, but I gave up worrying about it a long time ago, I don't know why you're worrying about it now.'

'It's your roots, isn't it? And mine. You must think it makes a difference whether your father was Italian or African?'

'No, why? I've only ever known one man as my father, and he was a very good man from Caernarfon. You're the only one who ever made a big deal about being Italian, supporting them in the World Cup and all that, it's ridiculous. We have no connection with Italy or wherever else he may have come from. Now talk about something else before I get annoyed.'

'But...she said it was Haile Selassie!'

Robbie blurted the words out and regretted it instantly. His mother was clutching at the kitchen counter, doubled up with laughter and staggering out of the kitchen. She had to go and sit down, laughing so hard it was hurting her stomach, and she was snorting and getting out of breath. He had never seen her laugh so much. After about thirty seconds the laughter subsided, she wiped her tears away and caught her breath. Then she looked at Robbie and cracked up again. Robbie folded his arms and stood waiting patiently for his mother's fit of laughter to come to an end.

'All I'm saying is that's what she told me, I don't believe it, obviously, I just thought it was a bit of a funny thing to come out with.'

'Oh dear,' said Isobel, finally getting enough breath back to speak. 'Yes, it certainly is, funniest thing I've heard in ages. I've told you before, it's Alzheimer's disease. She makes up stories and gets mixed up between fiction and reality.'

'Yeah, but it's still a bit strange. I mean, if she'd said it was Elvis Presley or someone like that, I would have known she was making it up, but Haile Selassie is a bit obscure. Why do you think she came out with that?'

'Who knows? Maybe she saw a documentary about him or something. I'll ask her about if you like. She was probably winding you up; she used to have a wicked sense of humour. Oh dear, wait 'til I tell your dad, he'll love that. But please, do us all a favour; don't mention it to anyone else. They'll think you've been smoking that wacky-backy.'

Robbie was saved from further teasing when the phone rang. Isobel strolled off into the hallway to answer it, shaking her head and laughing again, leaving Robbie deep in his own thoughts. As he pondered his level of embarrassment, he became vaguely aware of his mother's voice in the background, becoming more agitated as she spoke on the phone. She came back into the room, her face drained and frozen, looking ten years older than a few seconds ago when she was so animated by laughter.

'What's wrong?' asked Robbie immediately.

'That was your granny's home help… she's dead.'

15. BURIAL

The wind was so strong that the icy rain was driving horizontally into the small crowd gathered together in a tiny village in north Wales for the funeral of Minnie Lewis (nee Williams). Huddled together outside the church, umbrellas flipped inside out and rendered useless against the midwinter elements. It had been Minnie's deeply held and often voiced wish to be buried in the village of her birth, even though now there was no one left living there that she knew from the old days. Her old family cottage was now second home to an English family who twitched their net curtains nervously as their extended Christmas retreat was interrupted by a steady stream of elderly women in black shawls saying prayers in Welsh outside the front door. This sort of thing could be expected on holiday in Tuscany or a Greek island, but not within a morning's drive from Hampshire. The procession of tiny evil-eyed women from neighbouring villages and as far as Cardiff had continued all weekend. Some said that she died of a broken heart and was never the same since her husband had passed away a year or so ago. Others shook their heads and mumbled that she should never have moved to London, it was the pollution and stress that did for her. A few muttered that things had begun to go downhill when she moved from the village to Cardiff. But that was over seventy years ago, so no one took much notice. Isobel thought these old crones had a damned cheek, as no one else was around to look after her when she got ill. Most of the other mourners had travelled long distances, missing Sunday shopping a week before Christmas to stand in the freezing wet and were hoping the family pallbearers would get a move on as they carried the coffin towards the plot.

Robbie was praying he would not slip or trip over. He was at the front, carefully winding his way along the path from the church to the cemetery, with his father to his left and his two uncles behind him. He could not understand how such a tiny woman could be so heavy, either that or why the coffin was lined with lead, as the edge dug painfully into his shoulder where he had linked arms with his father. They had not rehearsed this move, and he could not help but feel that they were all totally out of step, causing the coffin to wobble worryingly. This was made worse by the fact that they were walking slightly downhill and the uncles behind him were slightly taller than Robbie and his dad, so the coffin was pointing towards the ground at an alarming angle. He kept looking down at his feet, which lent him a suitably solemn appearance, but was actually out of necessity as he was concentrating on not falling over. It was not that he didn't feel sad; he had been shocked at the news and was sorry that he had only had one conversation with her that did not revolve around how tall he had grown or how grateful he was for the birthday money. He could not believe that she had been force-feeding him biscuits and chatting away to him a few nights ago, and now here she was, her stone-cold body a few inches away from his head. There had been no real sobbing so far; there was no one left who felt the loss as a real physical pain, the way she had felt when her husband had died, a gaping emptiness instead of the person she had shared most of her life with. Even Isobel had said they should be glad that she would be with granddad again, and that she died peacefully and painlessly before the illness robbed her of her faculties and dignity. Having said that, his grandmother had seemed very lucid the last time Robbie saw her, and he felt upset for the selfish reason that he could never ask her anything more about her story, or even find out if she would have told him something totally different the next time, like his grandfather was really Mussolini.

Looking up, Robbie saw that the coffin-laden foursome's faltering steps, with all the co-ordination of a newly hatched turtle, were veering dangerously towards a slope that led straight down to a boggy ditch. Suddenly alarmed at the prospect of all five of them falling headlong into the mud, he tried to see round the coffin to tell whether his father was looking where he was going or just looking solemn. The widest part of the coffin was resting heavily on their shoulders, so he could not crane his head round without dropping it. Their arms were linked, so he tried to push his father round by the shoulder to alert him to the approaching drop.

His father gave him a reciprocal squeeze on the shoulder, sharing a moment of mutually supportive grief, and continued heading straight towards the ditch. Faced with little choice, Robbie stopped sharply, causing the two uncles behind to almost bump into him and his father, and the coffin to carry on forward slightly with its own momentum. With the reactions of Olympic weightlifters, Robbie and his father managed to keep their hold for a few seconds, straining as they took nearly all of the weight at the front with a free hand each. Robbie coughed slightly as if to say, 'we are about to walk into a fucking ditch', causing the others to look up, adjust their footing and carry the coffin safely to the graveside.

The service went off without a hitch and an hour later the mourners were crammed into a distant relative's front room in the next village. They stood around uncomfortably, thick black garments giving off steam by the heat of the radiators as they nibbled cheese and pickle sandwiches and murmured in agreement about what a lovely service it was, as if a raised voice would disturb Minnie's peace. Robbie was relieved that after the stress of carrying the coffin had passed, he had got suitably in touch with his feelings and even managed a little tear. He had never actually listened to all that ashes-to-ashes stuff before, not being a big David Bowie fan, and found the vicar's words quite moving. He was even more surprised to find that he recognised huge passages of the bible from various reggae songs. Angela winked at him from across the room, where she was being harassed by several of his relatives on the subject of marriage. Weddings were the same, thought Robbie, if anyone ever actually listened to those vows or thought about them, it was hard not to feel touched. This reminded him that he had once heard somewhere that the power of a lot of religious stuff was in the beauty of the words, and he had meant to get round to reading the Bible or the Koran one day, but he could not face the idea of sitting on the tube with it. With this in mind, he sidled over to the man of the cloth, which judging by the wrinkled orange skin, appeared more like leather, who was at the buffet table helping himself to a slice of currant cake.

'More tea, vicar?' Robbie could not resist asking, by way of introduction.

'Ah, no thank you. And I am a priest, actually. Your grandmother was a late convert to Catholicism. Father Maximilian Miliano, but you can call me Maxi.'

'Hang on…that name sounds familiar, are you Italian?' asked Robbie suspiciously, mentally estimating his age and comparing the priest's nose with his own.

'Of course, my father came from Rome but he settled in Cardiff before the war. He knew your grandmother well.'

A tugging at the sleeve of Robbie's jacket interrupted his attempted interrogation. He turned round but could not see anyone. He felt the tugging again and looked down to a level of about four foot, to find a toothless grin and two beady eyes looking up at him from an incredibly wrinkled face, stretching at the neck like a hungry baby bird.

'Don't remember me, do you?' shrieked the old woman accusingly in a strong Cardiff accent.

'Ah…hang on…no, I'm sorry, remind me.' Robbie scanned his memory for great aunts but could not place the face.

'After all those times your granny and I would look after you in the summer holidays. I can still see you now, running about the garden in your Y-fronts.'

'Oh…that must have been a while ago…how old was I?'

'Well, I'm not talking about last year, that's for sure.' The old woman drained her glass of sherry and instantaneously exchanged it for a full one.

'Couldn't have been more than three or four. Same idiotic grin though. Probably the same Y-fronts as well!' She pinched Robbie's buttocks and cackled away loudly, causing the other mourners to turn round disapprovingly.

'No, I'm sorry, I'm hopeless, I can't remember anything from before I was about six. Were you and Minnie close?'

'Close? More than any of this shower of bastards here. I think I'll have another sherry. Why shouldn't I, eh? We were best friends since we were thirteen. Inseparable all our lives in Cardiff.'

'Oh, of course. You must be Sally. She used to talk about you a lot. I know she missed you when she moved to London.'

'Ah, I know she would never forget me, even though she was losing her marbles. Not me, though, I remember everything, like the way some of these HYPOCRITES – ' she spat as she shouted the last word and waved her arm around the room, spilling sherry on the carpet, '– the way they treated her when she fell pregnant, and when she was bringing up a child on her own – they never had a good word for her then, I can tell you.'

'Yeah, you must have been her only true friend back then,' Robbie encouraged her to talk a bit more.

'That's right. You kids don't understand what it was like in the early days of the war. Life was hard enough. Me and Minnie went out to work miles away from our families at your age. What are you, sixteen?'

'No, I'm twenty-three.'

'Well, you don't look it, never done a day's work in your life, I'd wager.'

'Well…' Robbie was about to justify the importance of his role in the world of statistical research, when he latched on to what she had said. 'What was that, where did you and Minnie work?'

'We were nannies, skivvies more like, looked after children, you name it, in posh houses all over, Bristol, Bath. We didn't know where our next meal was coming from, or if the house you left in the morning would be a pile of rubble in the evening. We had to pull together, but some people thought a girl bringing up a fatherless child didn't deserve any help.'

'Terrible,' said Robbie.

'Yes, it was only when Davy came back injured from the war and took her on that people started talking to her again. He was a good man. Fell in love with her straight away and loved your mother as his own. Minnie was never the same after he died.'

'No… but did she ever talk to you about the real father?' asked Robbie, gambling that Sally was not one to be coy talking about these things. However, her reaction took him by surprise, and he instantly regretted taking his lead from her tactlessness. She gasped and started choking on her sherry, coughing and spluttering, causing other people to look round in concern. After a minute or so, she beckoned for Robbie to bend down so that she could whisper something in his ear.

'I swore to her that I would never tell a soul. That will stay with me to my grave, not just hers.'

'Oh, I'm sorry…'

To his relief, Angela came over and interrupted them. 'Come on, we had better be going if we want to get to Bath this evening.'

'Yes, bye Sally, we've got to get going. It was really nice talking to you, I hope I'll see you again.'

As Robbie and Angela weaved through the room saying goodbye to his relatives, they turned to hear Sally shouting goodbye to them from across the room.

'I'll be seeing ya!'

Sally winked at him, took another gulp of sherry and cackled away to herself.

Angela sat in the car watching the drizzle on the windscreen and the headlamps on the buses struggling through the gloomy city centre and wondered why they hadn't gone for a cheap weekend break abroad instead. It was one of those miserable midwinter mornings when it hardly seemed to get light at all; as soon as the grey fog lifted it was getting dark again. Her friends had been telling her that Barcelona or Lisbon were very nice at this time of year, and flights were quite reasonable. Maybe even New York for a spot of Christmas shopping, people did that sort of thing all the time. And now that Robbie had been left a couple of thousand pounds by his grandmother, she thought he might have planned something special. But that would take far too much organisation of course, which borders on commitment. Helping Robbie bury his grandmother was just an unquestioned duty - she did not even remember being asked. He had just assumed she would take a day off work to go and stand in the freezing rain halfway up a Welsh hillside with him to pay her respects to an old dear she had only met once, when Minnie had confused her with a social worker and kept telling her to bugger off. Still, she did not mind coming along for support as Robbie had seemed surprisingly affected by her death and preoccupied the whole time. Then he had tacked on the idea of stopping off on the way back in Bath and staying in a posh hotel as a pathetic attempt to look spontaneous and romantic. True, the hotel was very luxurious, and they had made the most of it since arriving late on Sunday evening. She would have been quite happy staying in bed as long as possible, but Robbie had uncharacteristically got up early and insisted on going to the library to try to find some Roman tourist attractions open on a wet Monday in December. Angela could not ignore the nagging feeling of rejection that he had passed up a morning of hot love-making for a cold marble statue but reassured herself that this was maybe his way of coping with grief, he certainly had been acting very strange recently.

Robbie hurriedly twirled the microfiche reel backwards and forwards, flicking through headlines about the King's abdication, the Spanish civil war and tedious stories about local village fetes. He nervously looked over his shoulder in case Angela had decided to come in after him, but all he saw was the librarian eying him suspiciously. All Robbie had asked was why they did not have the local paper on a computer file that he could search and view, it was nearly the twenty-first century after all, and had been met with a snotty lesson in using microfiche files. He conceded that this was indeed a perfectly adequate way of storing old newspapers, as long as you have several hours to spare. Looking around, this seemed a plausible explanation for the presence of his co-researchers; a shabbily dressed old man who smelt of cat food and looked as if he had come in for the warmth, and a couple of sixth form students who were more interested in leaning over each other's shoulders in a flirtatious manner. Robbie felt a slight stirring in his trousers as he fondly remembered the erotic potential libraries held for bored and hormonally charged students who weren't allowed to see each other outside college. Just as he was drifting off into a memory of revising for his A-levels while trying not to be caught staring at the girl with the nicest legs and the strictest parents in west London, he remembered the job in hand. He was of course not contemplating an act of gross indecency in a public library, but an investigation into the passage and exile of the former emperor of Ethiopia in pre-war Britain. To make things worse, he only had a vague idea what he was looking for, and if it did happen, it could have been any time between June and December 1936. The pages spun before his eyes, pictures blurring and headlines merging into one, when suddenly he stopped and wheeled back. There it was, a small paragraph at the bottom of an inside page:

A HOME OF HIS OWN AGAIN

NEGUS TAKES UP RESIDENCE AT BATH

Deprived of their own home, in their own land, the Emperor and Empress of Abyssinia and their family have now found 'the next best thing' – a home at Bath. On Tuesday evening they took up residence at 'Fairfield', the beautiful Newbridge Hill house which was formerly occupied by Mrs Campbell White, a one-time Lady Mayoress of Belfast, and has been vacant since her death.

The Empress had remained at Jerusalem until the Emperor had finished his househunting activities, and only rejoined him last week. Soon afterwards, she paid a special visit to Bath, accompanied by her husband, to see her future home. A representative of this paper learned from a member of staff on Thursday that the family has quickly settled down. Except for a few details, the redecorations have been completed. They are unobtrusive, and typical of a tasteful English home.

NO ORIENTAL SPLENDOUR

It has been said in the city that the house has had its interior turned into a replica of an Eastern palace, but this is incorrect. The Negus is a great admirer of England and the English life, and he, and those with him, have adapted themselves very quickly to the new conditions. Unlike many Royal personages, they do not require a large staff. Of those in attendance upon them, several, including the chef, are English. The Emperor and Empress were busy this morning attending to certain household matters, and it is expected that in a day or two they will have settled down completely.

Robbie held his breath, half expecting to see his grandmother's face in a picture, or a reference to Minnie Williams from Cardiff. He stopped himself, realising this would be a little too much detail, but read the paragraph over and over again, his heart beating faster and faster. The basic facts his grandmother told him were true – Haile Selassie lived in Fairfield House, Bath from October 1936. She had not made that bit up -surely she would not have remembered it unless it meant something to her. There were three children, and he hired staff to look after them – why not his grandmother? Suddenly the crazy bedtime story that he thought was a side effect of too much Horlicks seemed plausible. He studied the grainy page, focusing in and out and trying to find some more clues between these few lines, before realising this was also pointless. Frantically rattling the microfiche files onwards, he scanned every page for the rest of the year for another mention, but there was nothing. It seemed the people of Bath had more important things to worry about, what with the rise of Hitler, the constitutional crisis and the rugby season, there was no more attention paid to the cold and lonely exile of a dethroned foreign king. Sitting back, as frustrated as the randy students opposite him, Robbie concluded that he would never find what he was searching for in a public library or anywhere here in Britain. Even if anyone else had known the truth about his grandmother's relationship with the emperor, it would probably never have been in the papers in those days anyway – this was years before the tabloids. He had found out all he could – it was possible, they were in the same place at the same time, but if he wanted to find out anything more, he would have to get closer to the real man who was Haile Selassie. He had to find someone who was there at the time – he had to talk to the emperor's descendants or even the butler's children – someone close to the royal family who might have kept such a scandalous secret all this time. Besides, Robbie had promised his grandmother that he would return the ring she had given him to the heir to the Ethiopian throne. This reminded him; he would have to try to take it off as it was making his finger feel red and inflamed. He twisted at his hand as he hurried out, ignoring the librarian's remonstrations to turn off the microfiche machine after he had finished with it. Grabbing a leaflet on tourist attractions as he passed through reception he looked down at his hand and was surprised to find that the ring was stuck fast on his finger and there were no red marks around it. Angela beeped at him impatiently as he hurried out of the doors and across the road.

'Sorry about that, babe. The librarian wouldn't shut up, you know how friendly these sad bastards are out here in the sticks. But I got it - a guide to Roman baths!'

'Great,' muttered Angela as she drove away.

16. SITTING IN THE PARK

Robbie was sitting in a pub in Hammersmith waiting for Angela, James and Ravi to turn up. It was a very quiet Thursday night in mid-January. It felt like the coldest day and the longest month in history. The pub was nearly empty, as everyone was waiting for the end of the month to pay off the excesses of the festive season. Like every other pub in London, it had been recently refurbished for what seemed like the fourth time in as many years, but this time they had managed not to make it look like a prison canteen. Big leather sofas and an open fire had replaced the long tables and hard wooden benches, making the place quite cosy on a night that felt too cold for snow. The jukebox had made way for a pair of turntables and a slightly embarrassed looking DJ, who kept Robbie, two old Irish men and a dog entertained with a Curtis Mayfield selection at an unobtrusive volume. Robbie plumped for the best seats by the fire, rested his pint on the table and picked up a free listings magazine for London's antipodean community, pretending to find something interesting in it as he nodded his head to the music and waited. James and Ravi arrived together as usual, and Robbie leapt up to greet them.

'Happy new year, fellas!' said Robbie, shaking hands.

'Happy new year, mate. Bloody hell, haven't we seen you since then?' said Ravi.

'Happy new year, Robbie. No, we haven't seen you since that night just after Christmas. How are you doing?' asked James.

'Alright, thanks. What did you guys get up to in the end?' asked Robbie.

'Y'know, the usual,' sighed Ravi. 'Paying fifty quid for an overcrowded club, trying desperately to get off your face before twelve' o'clock. Ended up snogging some Scottish bird.'

'Fiona and I went to that restaurant I was telling you about – you and Angela should have come along; it was very civilised. How are you anyway? You were a bit gutted about your grandmother last time we saw you, just after the funeral, wasn't it?' asked James sympathetically.

'Oh yeah, man. Forgot to ask you about that, you went to Wales, made a weekend of it, didn't you? Did you give her a good send off?' asked Ravi.

'Yeah, it was interesting. I was a bit sad about it, as it goes. I had only just started getting to know her properly, know what I mean? So, yeah, the festive season was a bit quiet for me. Stayed in with Angela for new year.'

'Ah, and here she is, speak of the devil,' Ravi got up and was the first to kiss Angela in greeting, 'Or should I say angel?'

Robbie tutted, although he was used to the way they flirted with each other and waited his turn to greet his girlfriend. Pleasantries over, he got the drinks in and they all relaxed around the table, Angela and Ravi sharing the leather sofa, Robbie and James taking an armchair each.

'Now, you may be wondering why I have gathered you all together. My two best mates and my beloved girlfriend.'

They looked at him blankly.

'Well,' he continued, 'I have an announcement.'

'Oh, congratulations, you guys. I knew you wouldn't hang around, mate. So, when did you pop the question? I bet it was New Year's Eve, eh?' said Ravi, tactless as ever, turning to hug and kiss Angela again.

'Er...no, leave her alone. That's not it.' Robbie hesitated, as a nagging doubt made itself felt that maybe this was not the best time to tell them, all at once, but he ignored it and continued undaunted. 'I'm going off travelling.'

'Oh, nice one, man. It's a bit late to be discovering yourself, but I'm sure you'll have a good time. Where are you thinking of going?' asked James cheerfully.

'Got to be India, init? I had a wicked time there, remember?' enthused Ravi.

They were both desperately trying to keep the mood upbeat; as it became blatantly obvious Angela was not sharing in Robbie's excitement. She sat opposite Robbie, staring at him.

'Er…no, Africa,' said Robbie. 'Just for a couple of months or so.'

'Oh wow, you will have to go to Ghana. I can give you my uncle's address.'

'Well…thanks, mate. I was going to start off in East Africa - Kenya, Ethiopia y'know.'

'Bloody hell, mate, why not try to get in all four horsemen of the apocalypse - war, famine, what else is there?' joked Ravi.

'No, things have quietened down there lately. Avoid Somalia, though. So, what about your job, and your flat?' asked James.

'Work are cool, they'll keep my job open for me, or so they said but I'm not to bothered to be honest, I could do with a change. And I was going to see if I can get housing benefit for a temporary absence, thought maybe you could move in for a while I'm away, give your mum a break?'

'Hmmm…I'll get back to you on that one,' considered Ravi, thinking the idea of a temporary shagging pad would be very handy without having to go through hassle with his mother of moving out permanently. 'So, where'd you get the money? I thought you were skint.'

'Ah, that's where my dear old grandmother comes in. She wasn't loaded but she left a couple of grand to each of her grandchildren. It's partly because of her that I'm going, actually…she told me my real grandfather wasn't Italian after all, he was from Ethiopia.'

Predictably, Ravi and James fell about laughing and even Angela managed a derisory snort.

'My long-lost brother…I always knew there was something about you!' said James.

'Of course, that explains everything…are you sure he wasn't Jamaican though?' teased Ravi.

'I know, I know it sounds crazy,' said Robbie, relieved he had not told them the full story, as he would never have lived it down, 'I think it might have been the Alzheimer's talking but it's not impossible. I mean they are quite light skinned, Ethiopians, aren't they? And if you look at my mum, she could be mixed race for all I know. What about that kid at school, Ben Michaels? Do you remember him? His dad was black, but you wouldn't have known by looking at Ben, would you? Except for the curly hair.'

'Yeah, I remember him…I was always thought he was adopted,' recollected James.

'No, Ben was Indian,' asserted Ravi.

'Get out of it, his dad was a black Brazilian,' Robbie informed them confidently.

'Now that is bullshit. Ben was never any good at football,' said James.

'Bastard. My mum was sure he was Indian. He used to come round at Diwali and eat loads of our sweets.'

'And Ryan Giggs – he's mixed race – and Welsh,' added Robbie.

'Also Indian. Real name Ryanjit Singh.'

'Don't take the piss, Robbie here is going back to his roots,' said James, getting on to one of his favourite subjects. 'I'm not saying you could not have any African blood in you, lots of white British people do without knowing. We have been here since before Elizabethan times, y'know, and after a few generations we get written out of history. But check out the literature – where do you think Shakespeare got the idea for Othello? And Wuthering Heights – Heathcliff is described as very dark, found on the streets of Liverpool, major slaving port at the time. Also Jane Eyre – the madwoman in the attic was mixed race, from the Caribbean.'

'Jane Eyre?' said Robbie, thinking he should get round to reading this book everyone kept mentioning.

'Yes, mate. And you think Cyrille Regis was the first black footballer? There was a brother playing for Sheffield United in the 1880s – he married an English woman and had children. Now his grandchildren or great grandchildren probably don't even know he was African. All I'm saying is in your case it is likely to be a delusion brought about by too much reggae and ganja.'

James and Ravi fell about laughing again. The three of them discussed the pros and cons of travelling to various parts of the world for a few more minutes, while Angela sat stony-faced and silent. Ravi and James finished their beers rather suddenly and stood up.

'Sorry, mate, I've got to go. I've got to get on with my coursework, big year this for me, y'know,' said James.

'Yeah, and I…er…promised my sister I would finish re-editing her wedding video tonight,' said Ravi uncertainly.

Robbie exchanged goodbyes and knowing looks with them and agreed to arrange a goodbye party. Thinking he could be in for a long hard time, he offered Angela another drink and she nodded. Coming back from the bar, he took a deep breath and sat down.

'I'm sorry, darling. You know I've been thinking about it for a while…I just thought it would be nice to tell you all at once. I'll probably only be gone for a month or so. It'll fly by.'

'Fine. It's nice that you mentioned it. I mean, where do I come after your boss, landlord, family, mates? Don't know why you didn't just wait until you got there and then send me a postcard to let me know.'

'I'm really sorry, honestly. I just got carried away with the whole idea and didn't think about your feelings.'

'Yeah right. And it obviously didn't cross your mind that I might like to come with you?'

'What? No, I mean… what about your career?' Robbie sounded alarmed.

'No, I don't want to, I was just testing.'

'Oh.'

'And what is all this about trying to find your long-lost grandfather?'

'I'm not. Just it would be interesting to find out if it's true, if possible,' shrugged Robbie.

'Yeah, but you're chasing a dream. You know my dad was American. I remember him telling me a story about his grandmother - she was a Native American Navaho Indian but what difference does it make to me when I have never met her? Do you see me spending my life traipsing around the mid-west American plains looking for my ancestors? My mum is the only parent I have ever really known - she's a middle-class white English girl from Hampshire and after he died when I was five, she brought me up on her own in Ealing and that's all there is to it.'

'Yeah, but at least you know that much, at least you know who you are and where you come from.'

'Robbie, if you don't know that by now you never will, trust me. It's not about the shade of your skin, it's about what's in here, and here,' said Angela, tapping her chest and her head.

Robbie kissed his teeth imperceptibly. He overcompensated by tutting and raising his eyebrows. 'Great, life according to Michael Jackson.'

'Sorry if I disappoint you, Robbie. Am I not black enough for you?'

Robbie sat back, hurt, and let the words hang in the air for a while, like a bad fart.

'I'm sorry, babe. I love you but you know I've always wanted to go to Africa anyway,' he offered.

'Good for you. Look, it's like this…' Angela leaned forward and picked up the ashtray. Robbie sat up and paid attention, looking down the front of her top. It amazed him that even though he had seen these very same breasts up close and naked many times, he still could not help taking another subtle peek when she was not looking.

'…concentrate, Robbie, and stop looking at my tits,' she continued, 'this ashtray is like your innermost soul, OK?' she placed the ashtray at one end of the table and moved the empty glasses in a line in front of it, forming a barrier. 'And these glasses are things like football, your mates, your obsession with reggae, and now this travel lark. And this over here,' she moved her mobile phone opposite the ashtray, with the line of glasses in between, '…is me. Do you understand?'

'Er…I think so.' Robbie picked up his drink, took a sip and hesitated. 'What's this?'

'That's a pint of Guinness, Robbie.'

'Phew… I thought I had just drank James and Ravi.'

Robbie tried a half-hearted laugh. The pub was filling up a little, and a group of middle-aged men occupied the table next to them. One of them came up and reached over Robbie and Angela's table.

'Excuse me, you don't mind if I take this, do you?' he said, picking up the ashtray.

'No, go ahead, mate,' said Robbie, and then whispered to Angela, 'Shit, that bloke's just walked off with my innermost soul, wasn't it?'

Robbie started giggling at this point, partly because he had drunk his first two pints rather quickly.

'God, you just can't take anything seriously, can you? Fine. Go to Africa, have a great time. I hope you find your granddad. Just don't expect me to be waiting here for you when you get back!' shouted Angela, getting up and heading for the door. She came back a few seconds later, picked her mobile phone up off the table, and stormed out of the pub.

Robbie considered running after her. By the time he had come to the conclusion that would be the right thing to do, he calculated she was probably nearly home, and finished his pint. He decided to walk home across the green to give himself some time and space to think things through. Sitting on a bench under a lamppost, he sobered up rapidly in the cold. Robbie pondered what he was doing. He stood to lose his girlfriend over this crazy plan. If only he had asked her to come along, they could have had a great time together. Feeling cold and alone in the London night, he suddenly realised how scared he would be stuck on his own in the middle of one of the poorest, most famine-ravaged, war-torn countries in Africa. What was he thinking of? He couldn't speak the language or stand the heat, was likely to catch some horrible tropical disease. All because of the ramblings of an elderly deranged woman. He did not seriously expect to find any corroboration of her story, even if it were true. As his parents had pointed out, two thousand pounds is a lot of money. It could go towards a Masters degree or something sensible to develop his future career plans, of which he presently had none. Deep in thought, Robbie did not notice the shadowy figure approach until he felt the bench move with the weight of someone sitting down next to him.

Snapping out of his deliberations, Robbie's heart rate quickened as he hastily ran through the likely options, without daring to turn round and look. It seemed doubtful that his uninvited companion was a mugger or axe-murderer, as he had given away the element of surprise, but this was still a concern. Robbie tried to peer along the bench out of the corner of his eye to make out the figure in the dim light of the lamppost. Male, short and old. This brought some relief, as he did not feel physically threatened, but was immediately followed by a different sense of panic as he concluded this park bench was probably a notorious gay cruising area, and the old man was trying to pick him up. Robbie prepared to walk off and make a run for it if necessary.

'Beautiful evening,' said the old man.

It was a surprisingly well-spoken voice, with an African accent, Robbie thought, from the way he placed equal emphasis on every syllable. Admittedly, he did not sound remotely camp, but you never can tell. As he turned to reply and get a proper look, Robbie saw that he had in fact been joined on the bench by a complete tramp. He suddenly felt guilty, as he realised he was probably sitting on the poor old guy's regular bed. The man looked about a hundred years old and was dressed in several ragged layers of what may once have been some kind of uniform, with plastic bags wrapped around strategic areas. He seemed to have based his entire look on a cross between Charlie Chaplin's classic tramp style and an extra from 'Night of the Living Dead'. Even in this half-light, it was possible to see that his face and hands were streaked with thick black dirt, and there was some sort of orange gunge matted in the grey knots of his beard. A pungent mixture of tobacco, special brew and urine wafted over Robbie, which would have given the game away earlier if the wind had not been blowing in the opposite direction.

'Yes, mate. Bloody freezing though,' Robbie sympathised, breathing sharply through his mouth and screwing up his nostrils.

'Ah, I don't really feel the cold. But look at the clear sky, the stars…'

Robbie waited a few seconds for the old derelict to launch into the traditional monologue about how he came to this way of life. He wondered if he should just give him a couple of quid now without being asked, or whether that would be likely to cause offence. Robbie had a strict policy of not giving to beggars unless they start to tell him interminably long, tedious stories about their predicament, usually involving a missed train, an estranged partner, and a cruel landlord, on the understanding that for some spare change they will shut up and go away. Not wishing to breach the etiquette in these situations, Robbie prepared to listen politely for a few minutes until the subject of money came up. He lifted his head and peered up through the orange glow of light pollution, the smoggy wisps of cloud and the little red and blue lights blinking from a queue of jumbo jets, and tried to make out some stars.

'Heh, heh, yes, they are not so bright here in the city,' said the tramp. 'But I grew up in the country, and closer to the equator - the sky is different there, so much bigger and brighter. You get to know each star like an old friend.'

'Yeah, must be amazing.'

'It is. But look, do you see that one?' The tramp raised his arm, unleashing an acrid vapour that brought tears to Robbie's eyes.

'Er…yeah,' lied Robbie, closing his eyes and holding his breath.

'Yes, in the east. The brightest one, you see it, yes?' said the tramp excitedly.

Robbie felt sorry for him, as he was probably very lonely, and he must have been someone's husband, father or grandfather once, so he tried to ignore the stench and humour the old man. He opened his eyes and looked up again at the night sky. Following the line of the tramp's outstretched hand, he made out a star shining slightly less dimly than the others, but he thought this meant it was a satellite. He nodded.

'What, is that the Great Bear or Orion or something, then?'

'No, no, I don't know about all that. You see, that star is not always there. It only appears every few years. I remember my father showed it to me when I was seven years old, and told me it appeared in the sky the night I was born.'

'I bet that was a while ago, eh?' said Robbie.

'Heh heh. Yes, a century has passed, and more. That star is a sign. It means something momentous is about to happen. Always keep that star in mind, son. When you see it, you know the time is right. You can take control of your own destiny. Seize it with both hands!'

'Right, mate. Thanks. Listen, can I give you the money for a cup of tea, warm you up a bit?' said Robbie, reaching into his pocket for some change and offering a few coins in his hand. The tramp unexpectedly enveloped Robbie's hand in his own rough, cold hands, turning the offering into a firm handshake. He laughed as he closed Robbie's own palm around the coins in the same movement.

'I told you, I don't feel the cold. And I have no use for money,' he said as he got up from the bench and shuffled off along the path.

'Oh well. Take care, anyway. Cheers. Goodnight!' Robbie called after him, but his words seemed to fall unnoticed on his back. The tramp took a few more steps and then turned round as he got to the lamppost. He raised his right hand and pointed up at the sky.

'Remember the star…. Rule your destiny…Goodnight!'

The tramp let his pointing finger turn into a wave, the lamplight revealing a big dirty mark on his open palm, and was gone. Robbie smiled to himself and then looked down at his own palms, wishing he had not let the filthy old tramp shake his hand. He peered and sniffed at them, but they seemed to be clean.

AFRICA

17. HELLO MAMA AFRICA

'Make a step down to Asmara, then we stop in Addis Ababa. Made our way to Shashemene land, riding on the King's highway,' murmured the dread in the window seat.

'Oh right, yeah, mate. Sounds familiar. I'm heading for Harar, myself, do you know it?' replied Robbie, leaning over, and staring excitedly out of the window of the Ethiopian Airlines plane, as if he expected to see the vast plains of Africa stretching before him, even though the plane was only just taxiing along the runway at Heathrow.

There was no reply and as the plane picked up speed, Robbie breathed deeply, yawning and chewing gum frantically in an effort to stop his ears from popping. He sat back and braced himself for the fleeting wave of panic and nausea he always felt as a huge metal container full of people separated from the surface of the earth. Science was one of the subjects he had dropped early at school, but even if he had not, he felt that he would never really understand how it was possible for planes to fly. Closing his eyes and praying to the patron saint of agnostics, he was relieved to feel the plane take off smoothly and start to climb into the sky over west London. Looking out over his neighbour's bowed head, he could just see the copper snake of the Thames glinting in the winter sun and strained to spot a familiar landmark as the plane veered to one side. In his head, Robbie said a final farewell to home, represented by Brentford's stadium with its message 'Next time…Fly KLM' and the distant green spectre of Hammersmith Bridge.

'Promised land. We're going to the promised land,' said his flying companion.

Robbie nodded, not sure how to respond to this slightly unusual take on the traditional in-flight conversation.

'Er…yeah. What are you going to Ethiopia for, then?' he asked.

His neighbour for the duration of the flight seemed intent on ignoring him and continued looking down, dreadlocks falling over his face as he nodded his head slowly. It was a bit of a stupid question, Robbie admitted to himself, but tried another one regardless.

'I mean, are you on holiday or is it a religious thing?'

There was still no response from the seat next to him. Robbie sat back, turning to the empty aisle seat on his other side, and resigned himself to a long and boring flight without any conversation, and hoped they would be showing a good film.

'Oh bloody hell. Thank God that's over,' came a northern accent from the window seat. 'I hate taking off, I always have to have these on, and imagine I'm lying on a beach somewhere. Used to get sick as a kid but I'm alright now, touch wood. Alright, mate? My name's Trevor.' Holding his dreadlocks back, he pulled the headphones out of his ears, and extended a hand for Robbie to shake.

'Oh, alright. I'm Robbie. Sorry, I didn't realise you were listening to music. Dennis Brown, obviously.'

'Yeah man. You know him?'

'Well, not personally, but I've got some of his stuff,' understated Robbie, aware that he ran the risk of looking like an idiot if he said how much he loved reggae as soon as he met a black person, he changed the subject. 'So, are you on holiday, then?'

'No way. This is a one-way flight for me. One stop. I am coming home.'

'Really? Do you know people in Ethiopia, then?'

'Well, not exactly, but I man a Rasta. I've got my people there. How about you? On holiday?'

'Yeah, y'know, just travelling around. Sounds like a really interesting place. I just fancied getting away from London for a while, somewhere totally different. So, … where are you from?'

Trevor looked him in the eye, giving Robbie a chance to study his face properly; late thirties, very bad razor bumps and a world-weary expression.

'Africa,' he said solemnly.

'Oh, right...I meant which part of –'

A wry chuckle interrupted him as Trevor's face creased into a smile. 'Sorry, I can't resist doing that. I'm from Africa, via St Kitts to Manchester, born and raised City fan.'

They both noticeably relaxed as the standard male conversation topic of football gave them something to talk about to fill in the hours between naps, while the hostesses blocked the aisles with never-ending rounds of tea, coffee, bar snacks and drinks, followed by an unidentified flying meal.

'So, what are you going to do when you get to Ethiopia, if you don't mind me asking?' ventured Robbie, after the tables had been cleared and he had accepted that Manchester City would be restored to their rightful place in the top flight within a few years.

'I hope to link up with some like-minded people and settle on a piece of land, become self-sufficient and help to rebuild the continent,' asserted Trevor confidently.

'Wow. Good luck to you.'

'Yeah, I realise that sounds a bit naïve,' Trevor laughed. 'But I'm serious. People are suffering. There must be something we can do. We can't go on living like we do in Britain, make out Africa has nothing to do with us, maybe give a little change to Oxfam and forget about it. I'm not just talking about black people, although obviously I have my own beliefs, but I'm talking about everyone. These are our neighbours, all of us.'

'Yeah. I have a standing order with Oxfam,' said Robbie.

'Top one, yeah, I'm not knocking that. I mean, look at me, I've been a Rasta for twenty years, most of that time I have been struggling to survive, working in a garage fixing cars for peanuts, building up a community radio station that keeps getting raided. I split up with my partner a while ago and I just realised there is no future left in the west. Friends my age have kids in their teens who are falling into gangs, drugs and crime. A lot of me Rasta bredren feel we should stay and try to spread the word but I know the right time come. Africa needs us now.' Trevor smiled again, getting off his soapbox. 'How about you? You wouldn't be coming to Ethiopia of all places if you didn't have some strong feelings about it.'

'Er...yeah, like you say. We've got to do something about unfair trade and debt...I remember watching Live Aid during the famine. Terrible.'

'Damn right, I hate Queen. But without His Majesty Haile Selassie to guide them, the people have been suffering.'

Robbie started to say something and then stopped himself for fear of causing offence, and then continued, reckoning that he could live with offended religious sensibilities for the remaining hour of the flight if necessary. There were a few things that had always bugged him about the Rastafari faith and although he knew a lot about it, he rarely got the chance to talk to a true follower when there wasn't a deafening bassline reducing communication to head-nodding.

'Correct me if I'm wrong here, but you guys believe Haile Selassie to actually be God, don't you?'

'That's right. He is a manifestation of Jah. Christ in His kingly character. Written right down in the bible, Revelation 5. *'Weep not: behold, the Lion of the tribe of Judah, the Root of David, hath prevailed to open the book, and to loose the seven seals thereof.'* Only one man on earth claims to be a descendent of King David, and all his life Selassie wore a ring on his right hand bearing the symbol of the Lion of Judah.'

'Yeah, I respect that, but he never produced any proof, like miracles or anything, did he?'

'One man's miracle is another man's coincidence. We don't need no proof, we know what is revealed in the bible is the truth.'

'But if he is God, and all-powerful and everything, how did he allow himself to be deposed in a coup? And the people of Ethiopia were suffering in famine and poverty while he was in power, how could he let that happen? And where is he now?'

Trevor shook his head and smiled to himself knowingly. 'Ah yes, these are common questions. But it is not for we to question. We do not believe the western propaganda about Him, and we know He is alive and doing His holy works amongst us. He revealed himself to the world, and it is up to us to give thanks and praise. We must be patient, a man cannot know why Jah has made the world so. All will be revealed.'

'Fair enough. I was just wondering. I'm a bit of an agnostic myself, could never get round the old why does God let bad things happen question.'

They fell silent. The conversation had exposed a rift between them, at the same time as the descent of the plane through the cloud cover had revealed the sprawling mountains and valleys of Ethiopia. United in their fascination, Robbie and Trevor were leaning towards the window and staring open-mouthed at the rugged highlands and sun splashed lakes.

'Wow!' gasped Robbie.

'Hello Mama Africa. I'm a coming home,' mumbled Trevor, causing Robbie to glance at his ears to check that he had put his headphones on again for landing.

18. PROMISED LAND

As the plane touched down back to earth with a bounce and a rumble, Robbie breathed in deeply. This was partly to fight off the urge to reach for the sick bag or shout, 'Oh my god we're going to crash', but also to tell himself that this was a truly momentous moment, as moments go. He thought to himself that his life would never be the same again, which on reflection, may potentially be true of any moment, but this felt different. Then began the usual scramble of people getting up before the plane came to a complete stop, falling into each other, opening the overhead lockers without due caution and finding that hand baggage had moved during the flight and fell on the heads of people who had formed a queue that did not move for several minutes until the doors were opened. Stepping onto the staircase at the back of the plane and into the bright midday light of Bole International Airport, Robbie felt the sunshine on his skin and the heat hit him as if he had just opened an oven door to check on some baked potatoes. The realisation simultaneously hit him that if this was how hot Africa was all the time, he would not last ten minutes, and he wondered when the next plane out was. Reaching the bottom of the staircase and resisting the temptation to kiss the tarmac, he turned round and saw that he had just stepped out of the plane downwind of one of the engines, which was still turning, making the air around it go wobbly with the heat. A cool, dusty breeze drifted across the open concrete plain of the runway and he sighed with relief that the Ethiopian Tourism Commission may not have lied to him, that most of the country, especially the highlands, had a pleasant, temperate climate most of the year, with sunshine guaranteed.

After collecting his rucksack, easily identifiable on the carousel as the only one in a luminous shade of orange, Robbie stood before the departure gates and prepared for the cutthroat chaos commonly associated with third world airports. He thought about what he was about to do. Setting foot in Africa; birthplace of humanity, dawn of civilisation, thousands of years of history of myriad ancient cultures and peoples. A continent torn into pieces by four hundred years of slavery that had wiped out millions of its children and scattered the survivors around the globe. Nations defined by a ruler on a map in a Berlin drawing room a hundred years ago, still divided and exploited today, long after the colonisers have gone. Beautiful faces, people of all races, thousands of different languages, traces of Arab, Indian, European, and Chinese influences. Addis Ababa: named 'new flower' a century ago by Queen Taitu, built by Emperor Menelik II as the seat of the Royal Court of Ethiopia, symbol of independence and black power shining through the dark long night of colonialism. Streets that had seen invasion by the jackboots of Mussolini's army, liberation by the Allies, celebration by huge crowds on the return to the throne of Haile Selassie. The city had survived a military coup, the cold war, and the famine that decimated the rest of the country, now headquarters of UN agencies and the Organisation of African Unity, the diplomatic capital of Africa. And there was Robbie with a bright orange rucksack – he felt like a right idiot.

Wishing Trevor goodbye and good luck for his internal flight connection north, Robbie passed through the arrivals lounge and cashed a traveller's cheque at a bureau de change. He approached a very helpful smiling buck-toothed lady at the tourist information desk, which was well stocked with information but deserted of tourists, who told him he could make a hotel reservation at a nearby desk. There, another very helpful smiling lady, who had a habit of gasping dramatically at each word he spoke as if he was confessing to a murder, and then sighing with relief as he asked where he could stay, booked a room for him and told him kindly where to get a taxi and how much he should expect to pay. Stepping out into the road outside the airport, Robbie was pleasantly surprised to find a queue of taxi-drivers relaxing, reading papers and drinking coffee as they waited patiently for their turn to pick up the next fare. On the other side of the road, a bus was slowly being obscured by loads of bags and a crate of chickens on the roof, people hanging out of the doors and a small elderly lady carrying a goat apparently sitting on the driver's lap. He felt as if he had just arrived at a small-town marketplace rather than a major international airport in one of the biggest cities in Africa. Suddenly he felt a tap on his shoulder. Robbie steeled himself, checked his wallet was secure and turned around to do the newly arrived western tourist hustle.

'Yo bro', did I hear you make a booking at the Blue Nile Ras Hotel?'

The voice made Robbie cringe instinctively. He felt that it told him all there was to know about its owner. The affected streetwise greeting could not hide the privileged Home Counties background, public school, university, no doubt with a job in the media or city lined up, taking a year out discovering himself, bankrolled by mummy and daddy.

'Er, yeah,' said Robbie as he turned round, and was not surprised to see a pair of rosy cheeks, blue eyes and a perfect set of teeth smiling at him from beneath a cluster of dirty blonde dreadlocks.

'Julian,' said his fellow traveller, extending his hand.

'Robbie,' he winced, on the end of an unnecessarily firm and enthusiastic handshake. In the past, Robbie had asked himself why he held an irrational prejudice against these people solely on the basis of their upbringing and accent. Was it their articulate confidence, their carefree attitude to money or their well-nourished appearance? Maybe that was it, their clear skin, bright eyes, and shiny coats. He had concluded that it was mostly his own inferiority complex at work, and he had accepted the theory that it did not matter where someone is from, it's where they are at. But he had then found that he still did not like most of the upper-class people he had met.

'Safe. I'm staying there as well. We might as well share a taxi, yeah?'

Julian turned to the nearest taxi driver and shouted something at him abruptly in Amharic with a posh English accent, pointing to himself and the rucksacks. Robbie hesitated briefly before shrugging and nodding his agreement. He then started to think about the idea and was annoyed with himself. Typical, he thought, you travel halfway across the world and end up spending all your time hanging out with a trustafarian from Surrey, talking about British universities and children's television programmes. He had been looking forward to an element of danger, a test of his character in a strange environment. Although Julian's kind offer was disrupting his own journey of self-discovery, part of him also felt quite relieved that he would not be totally alone on his arrival in Addis Ababa. Thinking about it, Robbie realised he was still just as alone as before, surrounded by strangers, but this one happened to share his skin colour and country of birth, and for all he knew he could be a serial killer. As Robbie was pondering the nature of humanity and whether it was really necessary to have something in common to forge a meaningful friendship, the taxi driver spat out a lump of vegetable matter that he had been chewing. He lifted himself off the bonnet where he had been leaning while chatting to another driver, opened the rear doors and nodded to usher Julian and Robbie inside, then chucked the rucksacks into the back of the Landcruiser.

As the vehicle lurched onto the main highway, Robbie stared out of the window excitedly, taking in everything he could. He breathed in the atmosphere hungrily, even though it was a mixture of traffic fumes, charcoal, open sewers and the heady scent of unfamiliar plants and flowers. They made their way through wide, open streets, lined with eucalyptus trees and punctuated by statues of the Lion of Judah and monuments of Soviet-style workers. Fading billboards and rusty signs flashed by, dedicated to the competing claims of churches, communism and Coca-Cola, and various other announcements in elegant Amharic script. The airport road cut through huddles of huts, with women sitting outside washing laundry in buckets by dirty-looking ditches and cooking over smoking fires, side by side with modern high-rise blocks, luxury hotels and gleaming offices. The taxi-driver expertly weaved his way at high speed around heavily laden trucks, brightly decorated buses, kamikaze motorbikes, oblivious bicycles, donkeys trotting intrepidly through red lights and goats grazing by the side of the road. A bus braked suddenly in front of them and they hurtled towards its back end, which was festooned with an array of lights and ribbons, a very skilful painting of Bob Marley and the slogan 'I know Jah will be waiting there', before they swerved at the last second to avoid finding out if this were true.

Robbie turned to Julian to share a few reflections on their surroundings, but found his companion was busily sorting through some cassettes and playing with his personal stereo.

'So, er…have you been to Africa before, then?' asked Robbie, aware that he was making a habit of asking stupid questions, but he was stuck for something to say. After all, everything about Julian's appearance seemed designed to render this question unnecessary, from the beads and bracelets to the Tusker T-shirt and loud patterned trousers, commonly described as ethnic, although the only group that wore them seemed to be white western European traveller types. Not to mention the fact that he had just hired a taxi in perfect Amharic.

'Yeah, few times now. It's more business than pleasure these days,' said Julian absent-mindedly. 'I went to Zimbabwe with my school when I was seventeen. Fell in love with African music straight away. Spent the last ten years travelling around in search of music – southern Africa and Zaire first, then spent some time in Mali and Senegal, last few years I have been coming to the Horn of Africa. Checking out up and coming local musicians and singers, listening, recording their sounds. I've set up a record label in London, trying to make some money out of them, or for them, I should say – that's why I'm here now, sorting out royalties and contracts for some of the artists.'

'Oh, nice one.' Robbie was gobsmacked. He had liked to think that he was fairly obsessed with reggae, but it had never seriously occurred to him to up sticks and go to Jamaica to be part of the music. Then again, half of the stuff he listened to was made in Harlesden or Crystal Palace, so he would not have had to go that far, but he had always been content just sitting at home listening to it. Julian had clearly dedicated his entire life to his musical obsession, and he felt a little envious and inadequate in comparison.

'Hang on…' said Julian suddenly as he looked out of the window for the first time, '…you don't mind if we stop here for a few minutes do you?'

Robbie shrugged as Julian had a quick word in the taxi-driver's ear, pointed to a house on the right, and the car skidded to a halt outside.

19. AMAZING GRACE

The house was set off from the road in a compound surrounded by a flimsy fence. Awoken from his afternoon nap, the elderly watchman at the gate peered in through the window of the car and, seeing Julian, opened the gate and waved them inside. A few children were running around barefoot in the dusty yard after a raggedy football made from tightly wound rubber bands and plastic bags. The ball rolled to a lopsided halt at Robbie's feet as he got out of the car, so he flicked it back to the kids. Evidently the children found this hilarious and immediately fell about laughing and shouting something at him. One of the boys suddenly pointed at Robbie's ear, and then held his own ear and shouted something to the other children, who by now were rolling around on the ground in laughter, forgetting about their football game for a few minutes. They then noticed Julian and started shouting his name enthusiastically and shouting rapid-fire questions at him in Amharic. He replied patiently and introduced Robbie, or 'Wobble' as the children instantly chorused.

'It's your earring, mate. It's not quite caught on for men in most of Ethiopia. You should have seen them the first time they saw me, a white guy with dreads – they were in shock for days. Say hello, or try saying 'teanastellen', they will appreciate that.'

Robbie gave it a go, and received a greeting in reply, but failed to stop the waves of laughter. He briefly thought that perhaps he had a natural gift that would make him a brilliant stand-up comedian in Ethiopia. Julian pushed him up the steps, through the open door and into the house.

The gentle drumming and singing that had been floating out from the house suddenly stopped as they entered the hallway and was replaced by pandemonium of women rushing around with cups, pots and pans, children running in excitement and a bewildering cacophony of shouts and greetings. In another instant, the room went quiet, and the crowd parted to allow a tall elderly man to stride confidently towards them. Dressed in a white dashiki with embroidered trimmings, loose fitting trousers and sandals, complete with a modest Afro and wraparound sixties style black shades, he looked like he had just stepped off the stage at Woodstock. Instinctively backing off slightly to avoid a collision, Robbie was surprised to find himself grabbed in a bearhug and being kissed on each cheek three times.

'As salaam alaykum. Julian, my brother! It has been too long. But thank heavens you have cut off those smelly dreadlocks at last! How are you?'

'Alaykum salaam. Sorry Omar, I'm back here, this is Robbie, a fellow traveller from England I met at the airport. Still got the dreads I am afraid,' piped up Julian, who was standing just behind Robbie in the doorway.

'Ah, so sorry. Robbie, pleased to meet you, this is the usual Ethiopian welcome for visitors,' he laughed and let the rest of Robbie go as he held onto his hand to shake.

'Robbie, this is Omar Hassan, Ethiopia's Stevie Wonder,' Julian introduced them, and it all clicked into place.

Omar then hugged and kissed Julian and they embarked on a series of greetings and asking after each other's family in English and Amharic that lasted about five minutes. Eventually, Julian gave Omar some papers and he disappeared into another room with a studious looking younger man in a suit. Meanwhile, Robbie was pushed into a seat. A cup of tea was poured from an ornate metal pot and a huge round flat bread pancake with dollops of brightly coloured stews was placed in front of him.

As Julian was made to sit down next to him, Robbie leaned over and whispered, 'It's safe, isn't it?'

'Yeah man, safe every time. Cool.'

'No, I mean is it safe to eat and drink?'

'Oh yeah, don't worry about that, I've never had any ill-effects. Anyway, if you don't eat, you will seriously offend them, and I don't want anything to upset this meeting. Omar has just gone to look over our contract,' said Julian.

'Oh right,' said Robbie, following Julian's lead and tearing off a piece of bread, dipping it in the stew and stuffing it into his mouth, he was pleasantly surprised by the delicately spiced, aromatic flavours. 'Is he a singer?'

'Yeah, he has an amazing voice. He plays the krar and guitar as well, fusion of jazz and traditional music. Brilliant. I swear, he could be bigger than Salif Keita, I just hope Island or someone else don't get to him first and try to make him change his style.'

'Wow. And is he totally blind?' asked Robbie, taking a gulp of hot, sweet ginger tea that made his eyes water.

'Er… I think he can see shadows and shapes, but he has been blind since childhood, not sure what was the cause. He has been pretty big in Ethiopia since the seventies.'

They continued eating while Julian introduced the rest of Omar's extended family and friends, and Robbie smiled and practiced Amharic greetings. Finishing his cup of tea and his share of meat stew and bread, Robbie found they were both instantly replenished, despite his protests. A worried look flashed over his face as he wondered how much he would have to eat to avoid offence, and whether there would be anything left for the rest of the family, he imagined the kids probably hated him for taking their dinner. Luckily Julian provided a distraction as he got up and went outside, returning from the car with a handful of pens from his rucksack as presents for the kids. In return the kids dragged them both outside to join in their game of football and Robbie found that they could have a perfectly eloquent conversation at the same time consisting only of shouting Ronaldo, Zidane, and George Weah. Strangely the children were not so familiar with the current Queens Park Rangers side. A few minutes later, someone called for Julian to come back inside as Omar was ready to sign the contract. Robbie was in goal between the gatepost and a tree, lining up three of the children in a wall to defend a free kick when there was a sudden commotion of shouts and wailing from inside. He nervously stepped back inside, worried that Julian had been caught trying to pull a fast one in the contract, and they were about to be run out of town. But it seemed to be nothing to do with Julian; he was standing on the edge of the room looking mystified. Everyone else was crowding round Omar, reaching up to him and touching him.

'Allah akbar!' shouted Omar, taking off his glasses to reveal tears streaming from his blinking eyes, repeating everything he said in Amharic, Arabic and English: 'My lovely wife! You are as beautiful as I had always imagined. Come here my wonderful children and grandchildren, let me see you for the first time. It is cloudy and the light hurts my eyes, but I can see! I can see!'

Robbie and Julian stood silently in the corner of the room, exchanging disbelieving looks. Omar walked out of the door and into the yard, calling out to the children, neighbours, and passers-by. As he admired the sky, the trees, his house, and everything around him, he asked his wife questions. She patiently explained to him, all the time staring into his eyes and holding his hand. Omar instructed the watchman to open the gate, where a crowd was quickly forming, as he wanted to walk around the city he had not seen for over thirty years. Julian suddenly jumped up as he realised the taxi driver was waving at them to get in before they were blocked by the crowd.

'Goodbye Omar! I am very happy for you! I will send you a copy of the CD when it is ready!' shouted Julian as he got into the car.

'Bye! Thanks for the food,' added Robbie.

Omar barely heard them amid all the other shouting, but they kept waving as the taxi moved through the crowd and into the road. Robbie caught a pair of misty brown eyes staring back at him as they moved off, and for a brief moment Omar seemed to pick him out and give him a knowing nod as if they had shared a secret. And then he was gone, traffic was stopping, people were shouting, and cars were beeping as the news spread. Julian sat back in his seat and wound up the window.

'Shit,' he said. 'This has totally fucked up my marketing. It's great for the guy that he can see, obviously, but how can you sell him as Ethiopia's Stevie Wonder if he's not bloody well blind? I mean, how the fuck can someone suddenly regain his sight after so long?'

'Hmmm…dunno,' mused Robbie, 'you hear about these things happening sometimes. Did he have a bang on the head?'

'Huh!' snorted Julian as he laughed. 'Either that or he has been eating a lot of carrots, I suppose. Or given up masturbation. Mind you, that seems an unlikely cause of blindness in the first place, judging by how many kids he has.'

'It's amazing, though. What must it be like to see your wife and kids for the first time in your life?'

'Unbelievable. I hope it's not just a temporary thing, for his sake. Maybe it is to do with his diet, he might have been deficient in some vitamin or mineral before. He has been looking well, eating a lot better in the last few years, since the money started coming in from his records. When I first met him he was playing live every night and living on tella, home-brewed beer, giving what little money he was paid to his wife to feed the kids.'

'It's incredible. I'm glad I bumped into you. I'll never forget that. I hope he goes on to be an international star. Thanks very much for introducing me,' said Robbie, as the taxi slowed down and he saw the sign for the hotel.

'That's alright. You can buy me a drink later. I'll show you around some more, if you like, meet some more people?'

'No, I can't stay. I've got to get a train to Dire Dawa tomorrow,' said Robbie, although he was briefly tempted to abandon his original plan, something inside him told him he had to keep on moving until he got to Harar, birthplace of Haile Selassie.

20. THIS TRAIN

Robbie felt like a floppy-eared spaniel that had never been in a car before, dribbling open-mouthed in the breeze of an open window. He could not take his eyes off the view as it flashed by, taking in every scene as if he was watching a film on fast forward. The train had trundled its way out of Addis Ababa and through ever changing scenery, as urban sprawl gave way to open country. A spectacular mountain backdrop rose and fell in the distance to his right, seeming never to get any nearer or further away as the train travelled. On the left, the land stretched out to the horizon, lush forests suddenly turning into sparse savannah scrubland, interrupted by the occasional hut, farmyard, and track. Herds of antelope scattered nervously, and clouds of brightly coloured birds took to the air as the train cut through the early morning tranquillity. Men hacked at stubborn crops in the dirt, women walked casually carrying water and bundles of firewood on their heads, children ran waving alongside the train. A station arrived suddenly in the middle of nowhere and vendors crowded onto the tracks, reaching up to the windows with boiling pots of coffee, cold bottles of soda, plates of food, biscuits, fruit, trays of boiled eggs, newspapers and even souvenirs for tourists. As the train slowed to a stop, the gentle breeze that had floated through the windows with the scent of jasmine and acacia trees dropped and the carriage was flooded with the scent of fresh coffee and boiled rice, which was just enough to mask the stench of the toilet facilities. The other travellers in the first-class compartment barely looked up from the Ethiopian Herald at these scenes of everyday life, but Robbie was filled with inexplicable excitement. He could not believe that he was here in the heart of Africa, watching everyday people getting on with ordinary lives, the thought of it filled him with a strange feeling of joy in humanity. The sights, sounds and smells were so different from London, but in some ways, he felt things were just the same, people working, travelling, buying, selling. It was not that he had actually been expecting a scene of biblical famine or a war zone, but these were the only images of Africa he had known. The thought had not really crossed his mind that the majority of people had to be carrying on with the basics of life, same as anywhere else. Obviously, things were on a much poorer scale financially, he thought to himself, but the people were rich in spirit. Robbie realised he had slipped into a romantic cliché, checked himself and bought a packet of biscuits from a skinny child in a tatty Def Leppard T-shirt. He briefly constructed a history of the garment, from its original purchase at a Villa Park concert, through many cider-stained nights on a teenage rock fan to eventually being discarded to a charity shop went its owner grew out of it. The young biscuit vendor noticed Robbie admiring his T-shirt and waved at him, pleased to have found another fan of eighties British soft rock.

Eight hours later, Robbie was hot, sweaty, tired, and uncomfortable. The train had apparently encountered the wrong kind of leaves on the tracks or some comparable technical hitch. As far as he could tell, they were not far from his destination, Dire Dawa, from where he had planned to get a bus to Harar, but the train had not moved for about forty-five minutes. Grateful as he was for the buffet service provided by the team of vendors who had walked for miles to offer water and snacks outside the train, he did not want to risk eating or drinking anything, as he was in need of emptying his bowels. This had been an alarming enough prospect when the train was moving. He had opened the door between the carriages marked 'WC', to find a hole in the train floor opening onto the tracks speeding beneath. Although this was basically the same principle as British trains, cutting out the middle man, he had decided to wait until he got to a station.

Now he had got off the train to stretch his legs and could see nothing but flat open land for miles around. The train was full and his fellow travellers looked on from the windows or lined the outside of the train, casually waiting for the engine to rumble and the wheels to grind into action. There was not even a bush to hide behind, but this was probably a blessing in disguise, as the train would inevitably begin its movement at the same time as Robbie. He looked up at the cloudless blue sky, which seemed so much higher and wider than sky at home, and wondered what the hell he was doing here. Suddenly remembering why he had never been travelling before, he felt that he was not cut out for this kind of lifestyle, and missed the comforts of home too much, such as a decent toilet and a functioning transport system. On reflection, however, he thought if these were measures of civilisation, London was lagging far behind. It was deeper than that – a hollow sensation in his stomach, fortunately nothing to do with his sphincter – it was homesickness. After only a couple of days, he missed the family and friends he had left behind, and how he had always been able to pick up the phone or hop on a bus to feel safe and secure. He knew that he was lucky, not least because he could count on a precious few people around him who genuinely liked and cared about him. A fear nagged at him that he was putting this stability at risk, and like an idiot on an airbed in a stormy sea, he would not be able to find his way back to the harbour. But then he looked up at the boundless layers of blue in the empty sky above him, felt the return of sheer elation just to be under it and that he had to find out if there was more to himself and the world he had grown up knowing beyond Shepherds Bush.

'Ten minutes! We shall have locomotion in ten minutes!' announced the man who had been sitting opposite Robbie, cheerfully returning from walking the length of the train to talk to the driver.

No one else paid him any attention, so Robbie felt it was only polite to show some interest, although even he knew train announcements could not be trusted.

'What's the problem?' he asked.

'There is flooding in Addis Ababa.'

'Oh.' Robbie thought about this for a few seconds, unsure if he had understood correctly. 'But why is that stopping us moving? We've just come from there.'

'You see the track here is a single line only. We were waiting to circumvent another train, but it will have to turn back if the tracks are flooded further up the line. Fortunately, the driver informs me that we will shortly be able to proceed.'

The man had the look of a commuter on the 8.15 to Paddington, immaculately turned out in a spotless white shirt, crested tie and crisp beige trousers, rather than someone who had been crumpled on a grubby carriage in an old diesel train for most of the day. His excellent command of English was self-evident, relieving Robbie of the need to attempt his faltering few words of Amharic or simply shout at him in the traditional manner.

'Flooding? I thought it was the dry season. Is that normal?' enquired Robbie, unintentionally falling back on another classic of British conversation, the weather.

'It is unheard of. We have not had any heavy precipitation in this area for several years. At last the drought is over. It is very welcome, as long as the conurbations do not become inundated. Come, we may board the train in readiness.'

Following obediently, Robbie found that working out what this guy was talking about helped to take his mind off his bowels and engaged in conversation for the next ten minutes until the train moved as predicted. The commuter turned out to be a teacher who had studied at Aberdeen University and was very disappointed that Robbie was not familiar with the Granite City. It soon also transpired that he was a born-again Christian and was even more disappointed that Robbie was not familiar with the love of Jesus. At this point, Robbie decided to politely excuse himself and take his chances in the train toilet.

Arriving in Dire Dawa as the sun began to set, Robbie donned his rucksack and strode confidently out of the station. Having memorised the sketch map from the guidebook, he immediately started walking down the road that looked the most likely to lead to the bus station. He waved away the taxi drivers, hustlers and guides who offered to help him and continued straight-ahead, refusing to stop for directions or even to consult the map again. After a few hundred yards he found himself at the edge of the town, looking out over a patchwork of fields towards the dusky blue shadows of the mountains in the distance. Casually he stood for a few seconds, nodding as if this was what he expected to find, and turned back the way he came. Passing the crowd at the train station, he became aware of a ripple of laughter.

'Enjoy the view?' a shout stood out from the murmur of amused Amharic.

Robbie kept walking but could not help himself from looking a bit lost and was sweating slightly with the weight of his rucksack.

'The bus station is straight ahead, over the river, just before the market,' came the same voice.

'Oh thanks mate, cheers.' Robbie said and turned round to see one of the hustlers give him the thumbs-up. He cursed the guidebook writer for drawing his maps upside down and kept going. It was getting dark, but he dismissed the instinctive fear that he was about to be followed, robbed, and chucked in the river. Statistically he knew this was much less likely to happen here than in London, and reminded himself that being a thief was an extremely dangerous and short-lived profession in Africa, as according to his guidebook getting beaten to death was an occupational hazard. To his relief, when he crossed the river, he soon saw a square lit up with the glare of headlights and heard the shouting, beeping and revving of engines of the bus station. The next challenge, to try to find which one was going to Harar, was made much more difficult by the fact that that every bus seemed to double as a mobile disco. A group of young men danced around the doors of the nearest bus, occasionally handing out a ticket or hurling some luggage onto the roof, but mainly perfecting an intricate synchronised dance routine to the infectious zoukous beat coming from a tinny radio.

'Harar?' Robbie asked them, pointing at the front of the bus.

Dire Dawa's version of the Temptations barely adjusted their steps, shaking their heads in unison and incorporating a pointing finger into their moves, directing him across the square to another bus. Dodging pedestrians and bicycles, Robbie crossed over the square and approached the bus, which was rapidly filling up.

'Harar?' he shouted. The driver nodded and revved the accelerator.

'Thanks. Can I have a ticket please? One way,' asked Robbie. The driver shook his head and pointed across the square.

'But…this is the bus for Harar?' asked Robbie. The driver nodded and revved the accelerator.

'That is the ticket office,' shouted the driver after a pause, 'this bus leaves in two minutes.'

Robbie sprinted across the square as best he could with a rucksack on his back and bicycles, pedestrians and dogs appearing from nowhere in the darkness in front of him.

'Ticket for that bus to Harar, please!' shouted Robbie as he approached the office, which was a shed with a light bulb dangling from a window.

'Single or return?' asked the elderly gentleman, peering down his glasses.

'Single. Can you hurry please, it's leaving in a minute,' he gasped, sweating and panting at the window. The man fixed him with a cold stare for a few seconds, and then returned to methodically leafing through his ticket book, before slowly tearing one out and stamping it. Robbie gratefully handed over some money, grabbed the ticket and ran back across the square, just in time to see the bus pull away. He slowed down, ready to collapse backwards onto his rucksack and lie on the ground like an upturned beetle all night, when he noticed the doors were still open and the driver was beckoning for him to jump on. With one last burst of energy, he leapt onto the slowly moving bus, showed the driver his ticket as requested and gratefully accepted a seat which an old lady gave up for him. He turned round to see her take a seat at the back, and realised he had paid extra for a luxury all-seater bus with the added attractions of air conditioning and a TV screen. The old lady may have known something he didn't, as the television above his seat suddenly burst into top volume, showing an African music video of women dancing around a fat man in a gold suit. This kept Robbie entertained, or at least awake, for the hour's journey and by the time the bus pulled into Harar he had seen the same video about six times and knew every beat and shuffle off by heart. Stepping off the bus into the darkness of the small old town, lit only by a few roadside stalls with kerosene lamps, Robbie abandoned his former independent traveller attitude and gratefully accepted the help of the first person who offered to show him to a guesthouse. A few minutes later he was fast asleep in the comfort of a thin mattress and a lumpy pillow, enshrouded by a holy mosquito net.

21. IN MY FATHER'S HOUSE

Ras Tafari House. Robbie inspected the sign and looked down at his guidebook, which both indicated it was open for visitors. While he waited, he noticed the incongruous sight of carvings of curvy Indian goddesses decorating the closed wooden doors, wondered if he had the right house and knocked lightly again. Admittedly, it was perhaps a little early. Exhausted by his journey, he had slept soundly, but had woken at dawn, excited that he was so near to reaching his destination and finding out whether he was the grandson of Haile Selassie or just the grandson of a compulsive liar. He was not really expecting to find long lost cousins here and kept laughing to himself at the thought of it, but nevertheless something inside was calling him. When he saw the dawn and looked out of his first-floor window at the old walled city, with its ancient gates, winding alleyways and countless mosques and shrines, he felt as if he had been here before. Walking out into the early morning sunshine and fresh mountain air after a breakfast of pancakes and coffee, he felt as if the smiles and waves of welcome from the local people were especially for him, as if they recognised him, a sort of homecoming. Robbie smiled and waved back, nodding to the rhythm in his head and the spring in his step, as the lyrics of various tunes he had been listening to for years came back to him. Stepping out of Babylon, back to Africa, forward on to Zion, fly away home. Although these tunes had always meant a lot to him, this was the first time he felt they were actually about him. From behind the door of Ras Tafari House there came a muttering and a clattering, followed by the sound of bolts being undone and the creak of the door opening to reveal a bare chest and a bleary-eyed face peering through the narrow gap at Robbie.

'Teanastellen!' ventured Robbie with a smile, remembering his manners and one of the few words of Amharic he had learnt. He was fairly certain he had pronounced the greeting correctly, but it did not bring the accustomed response, as the door slammed shut in his face. Robbie looked around him nervously. A couple of kids were sitting under a tree playing, a man on a bicycle waved at him as he wobbled along the dusty uneven road and an elderly woman selling tiny packets of peanuts stared back at him from her stall opposite. From inside Ras Tafari House there was a frantic commotion, a man and a woman arguing in loud whispers, the sound of furniture being moved around and the crash of pots and pans. Robbie was about to leave when the door opened fully to reveal the same face, this time with smiling eyes behind a pair of glasses, and a shirt and tie.

'Teanastellen. Dehna not?'

'Tenner stealin…' Robbie tried again and hesitated, as the only other Amharic word thought he knew was 'aswad', meaning 'black', but he did not see how this would help at the moment. '…Er, do you speak English?'

'Yes of course. Welcome to Ras Tafari House, the original home of the Emperor Haile Selassie the first. Would you like the full guided tour?'

'Yes, please. Thank you.'

'Good. I am Michael Gebreselassie, proprietor of the museum.'

'My name's Robbie, tourist.'

They shook hands and Robbie handed over the stated admission fee, to be presented with a ticket, which he then handed back to Mr Gebreselassie, to be stamped and returned to him.

'Thank you, sir. These are the humble beginnings of an icon of the twentieth century, the last ruler of one of the world's oldest imperial dynasties. His majesty was born in 1892 during the reign of Emperor Menelik II, and spent his early childhood in this house. His father was Ras Makonnen, governor of the Harar region and cousin of the emperor at the time. Through his grandmother, Selassie could trace his royal ancestry through the line of David all the way back to King Solomon, from the bible. As you can see from these modest surroundings, Tafari was brought up as one of the people. It was in this very yard that he would play games with local children.' Mr Gebreselassie gestured with his hand as he walked through the dingy rooms of the single storey building and into a small overgrown garden. 'The house was built over a hundred years ago by a trader from India, as you can see from the original Hindu figures on the door. Tafari left here at the age of thirteen when he became provincial governor, but the house has retained some of the original pieces from his time, as well as building up a collection of photos and relics, which you are welcome to peruse at your leisure. Feel free to ask if you have any questions. The museum café and shop will open in five minutes.'

Mr Gebreselassie stepped back and left Robbie to admire musty items of furniture and black and white photos of the emperor in his later days. A huge oil painting on an unframed canvas dominated one wall, depicting Haile Selassie in battle against the Italians. In intricate detail, it showed rows of bold Ethiopian soldiers, both eyes pointing in cartoon style facing up to legions of Italian troops, faces in profile, each with a cold eye focused on the machine guns and gas bombs they held. Robbie instantly recognised the traditional stylised form of painting from the inside of Bob Marley's Confrontation album. In fact, looking around him, he could probably have come up with a comparable display by cutting out pictures of Haile Selassie from his record collection at home. Pride of place in the corner of one room was a child's bed with dusty faded covers and a handwritten sign authoritatively claiming 'Ras Tafari slept here'. On closer inspection, however, it looked more recently to have been used by a moulting, flea-ridden cat. Robbie was not sure what he had been expecting to find, perhaps some surviving relatives or a family history, but he could not help feeling a bit disappointed. After waiting a polite few minutes, which was more than enough to examine all the exhibits very closely, he wandered back into the front room to see if he could find out anything more from the proprietor. Robbie was not surprised to see Mr Gebreselassie's desk was being transformed into the museum café and shop, as his wife put a pot on to boil and he produced a collection of mugs, badges and T-shirts from a drawer.

'Fascinating. Thank you.'

'My pleasure. Of course, most of the valuable imperial treasures are kept in the National Museum in Addis Ababa, but here we can offer the visitor a unique insight into the origins of the emperor before he assumed the throne. Coffee?'

Mr Gebreselassie offered Robbie the seat on the other side of his desk and wiped the dust off two Haile Selassie mugs.

'Yes please. Thanks.'

'Where are you from?'

'London.'

'Ah…my favourite city. I studied in London for a few months, years ago now, back in the seventies. I used to spend a lot of time at the British Museum – amazing. I lived in Camtown. Do you know it?' asked Mr Gebreselassie excitedly.

'Er…not sure. I have been to the British Museum though, on a school trip.'

'No, Dentown. In north London.'

'Camden Town?' ventured Robbie.

'Yes – that is it! Cam Den Town. I remember it very well,' a sigh of nostalgia came over him and he went quiet for a few seconds as he reminisced about long summer evenings drinking warm beer outside by the canal and explaining ancient Ethiopian history to a charming young woman with a safety pin through her nose.

'Oh yes, the markets and the canal, it hasn't changed a bit. So how long have you been here?'

'Well…a few years now. We only recently opened to the public as a museum, but it has been difficult to attract visitors. Do you mind me asking, how did you hear about us?'

'Erm…I'm very interested in Haile Selassie, so I came here as I know this is where he is from, and I saw in the guidebook that his house is open to the public.'

'Ah yes, of course, the guidebook. As you can see, it gives most people the impression it is not worth coming here. What I would give for a good review in that – every European traveller has it under their arm. Please, write to them and tell them you had a fascinating visit, and the proprietor is a great guy!' Mr Gebreselassie chuckled away at this, and poured two cups of thick, strong, coffee.

'Thank you.' said Robbie, taking a sip of the bitter, scolding tar. 'So…are you related to Haile Selassie then, I mean, with your name…?'

'Oh, no. Gebre just means subject or servant, and Selassie means trinity – Tafari took the name when he was crowned emperor. So I am servant of trinity, it is a very common name. But, please, call me Michael.'

'OK, Michael. Are there any of the emperor's relatives left around here then?'

'No, no, they all went into exile after the revolution in 1974. I think most of the family are still in New York. Some were in London for a while.'

Robbie felt a bit annoyed at this, and wondered if he should have just started his search for his roots by looking in the phone book under 'S'. The sun was beginning to shed some light into the dingy museum, and Robbie was struck by a flicker of sympathy for Mr Gebreselassie's efforts, as he was obviously trying to make the best out of bare materials. Behind his desk, there were shelves full of newspaper cuttings and old photos, in the process of being catalogued and made into an orderly display.

'Haile Selassie went into exile in Britain himself, didn't he?' asked Robbie casually.

'Yes, in 1936 when the Italians invaded. He stayed there until the British restored him on the throne in 1941.'

'Do you know much about what he did when he was there?'

'Well, he lived in Bath and started writing his autobiography. That's about it, as far as anyone knows.'

'Have you got any stuff from his time there, any old photos or cuttings?'

'Hmmm…probably somewhere. I am working on an extensive collection of photos. Let me have a look.'

Mr Gebreselassie stood up and leafed through the folders and albums on the shelves. After a few minutes, he unearthed two tattered black and white photos and placed them on the desk in front of Robbie.

'This one is a ceremony in Bath – I think he was presented with the freedom of the city or some such honour.'

Robbie inspected the tattered, grainy image. The emperor in a heavy robe tied tightly under his chin, hunched slightly to keep out the cold, walking along what must have been a red carpet, lined by a crowd of men in top hats and formal suits, and women in long flowing dresses and elaborate headgear, looking on in fascination.

'And this one is of the emperor, his family and staff outside the house he bought in Bath,' said Mr Gebreselassie nonchalantly.

Robbie's heart quickened and he held his breath involuntarily. This appeared to be a large original print with a white border, yellowing slightly but much better quality. The emperor posed with his wife and children in the centre of the picture. Lined up behind the royal family on the steps of the house was a row of white faces in butlers' and maids' uniforms. Leaning in closely, there was no mistaking the mischievous, childlike twinkle in the eyes and the crooked smile that had been passed down to his mother and himself. Robbie choked and gasped, pointing at the picture, struggling for words.

'That's.... that's...my gran,' he whispered.

'I beg your pardon?' asked Mr Gebreselassie.

'Its...Do you know the name of the house?'

'Erm...Fairfax...no, Fairfield House, I believe. I can check for you if you like.'

'My grandmother worked there in the late thirties...she said she met Haile Selassie.'

'Oh right, well it is possible. So that's why you came here?'

'Sort of...but she also said that he's my grandfather,' blurted out Robbie, still in shock at seeing the photo, he had not thought through what to say next. Unfortunately, this drew the usual response, and Mr Gebreselassie spent the next few minutes laughing hysterically. He called out to his wife, who had been sitting outside, and told her in Amharic, pointing at Robbie, and she too burst out laughing.

'I am sorry. Let me explain. Haile Selassie visited Jamaica in 1966. Ever since I have been here, I have had a steady stream of Jamaicans who swear that their mothers slept with his majesty on that short visit, and they are the true son and heir to the Ethiopian throne. I know for a fact, as I know someone who was part of the entourage, that the emperor was never left alone for as much as five minutes on any state visit. And he would really have to be a god to have got round all these women and produced so many offspring! Anyway, I've got to hand it to you, most of the others are black!' He fell about laughing again.

'I know it sounds ridiculous; I laughed when I first heard it. I thought she was making the whole thing up, but there she is, my grandmother, in the photo.'

Robbie pointed at the smiling face in the background, and Mr Gebreselassie paused from his laughter for a few seconds to study it.

'Hmm…if you say so. But that does not mean it is true. My father served Haile Selassie for thirty years and told me everything there is to know about him. The emperor was a very chaste, pious man. He loved his wife and children dearly and he was never known as a womaniser. He took himself and his royal duties far too seriously for that. But he was also very charismatic and charming, it is easy to see how a young girl could become infatuated with him, and perhaps make up a fantasy about an exotic African king. Please, I am very glad that you came all this way to visit our museum, but you will not find anything here to corroborate your story.'

Robbie nodded in acknowledgement and then remembered something. He reached inside his shirt to get to his holster style travel wallet and unzipped the small side pocket.

'I know…but she gave me this – what do you make of it?'

Robbie placed the large gold ring in Mr Gebreselassie's hand. At the same moment the sun streamed in through the door and flashed reflections of gold around the room. Mr Gebreselassie squinted slightly and moved it out of the light, inspecting the royal crest, depicting the familiar lion of Judah. He nodded gravely and handed it back to Robbie, who put it back in his pocket. Mr Gebreselassie leant back in his chair for a few seconds and smiled. He then leant forward and whispered to Robbie:

'Now let me show you something,' he opened the drawer of his desk and reached deep into the back of it. His hand emerged with a plastic bag, which he emptied on to the desk. Twenty gold rings tinkled and span across the top of the desk. As Robbie followed one with his eyes as it rolled to a stop, he could see a black crest depicting the lion of Judah. Each one was identical, and apparently exactly the same as the one he had carried preciously close to his heart all the way from London since his grandmother had given it to him on the eve of her death.

'Five birr each, about fifty English pence. They were mass-produced on the black market in the seventies and eighties to cash in on the Rasta and reggae tourists, along with chains, bracelets, and these badges. They are not real gold of course, but feel quite heavy.'

'Oh…' said Robbie, picking up one of the rings to check.

'I am afraid you may have been the victim of some sort of practical joke. But don't worry, like I say, we get a lot of these tourists who get caught up in the whole Bob Marley Rastafarian thing. Personally, I think it is a negative, mystical image of our country that we should no longer encourage. Ethiopia is a modern nation. In the past few years, we have moved towards economic growth and democracy. My idea for this museum is it should cover all our twentieth century history. The emperor is part of our past, but we no longer wish to be closely associated with a despotic feudal monarch.'

'Right, yeah. I know what you mean. I was just curious. Didn't take it seriously,' muttered Robbie, but he was unable to hide his deflation.

'There is so much more to our country. Here the ancient walled city of Harar is well worth visiting. And if you have time, I recommend you head up north to Aksum – one of the wonders of the world. But please, do not waste any more time thinking about Haile Selassie. He is an irrelevance now to our modern way of life. We Ethiopians are embarrassed by the way these Rastas believe he was God – we never even thought that for a second. We are proud of our history of independence, free from colonialism, but we and the rest of Africa must move on.'

'Yeah. Thanks very much anyway. It was very interesting,' said Robbie, getting up and heading for the door.

'Thank you. And remember – send a good review to the guidebook!' called Mr Gebreselassie after him, waving in the doorway as Robbie trudged off into the midday sun.

22. ZION IN A VISION

What an idiot. Robbie kicked a stone along the dusty road and tormented himself thinking about how stupid he had been to think for a second that he could be related to Haile Selassie. It was clearly true what everyone else had been telling him for years; he had been listening to too much reggae. The imagery and romance of the emperor and the music he inspired had gone to his head. Obviously, his grandmother had come across the ring in a jumble sale or something, and it had reminded her of a claim to fame when she was young. Her illness had detached her from reality, and she had imagined the story, probably with a lot of help from Charlotte Bronte, as his mother had pointed out. A nagging voice in his head kept telling him the bare facts were true, but he kept telling it to shut up, there was no more to it than that. Haile Selassie had lived at Fairfield House outside Bath from October 1936 to January 1941. His grandmother had worked there at the same time. But that was not enough to prove anything else. He supposed it was always a bit far-fetched to think something could have happened between them. The truth was he would probably never know the identity of his real grandfather, or even his nationality. His mother was right; the only person that mattered was the grandfather he had always known. There was no romantic story, no lost history; Robbie was white, his parents were Welsh, and he had been brought up in London.

So, Robbie sighed to himself, he had become the kind of person he had always despised, another rich western traveller finding himself amid the poverty of the third world. It would not be long before he was wearing brightly coloured trousers and wooden jewellery, showing off about all the places he had been. Still, there were worse things and places to be; the sun was shining, there was a cool breeze and he was in the middle of a beautiful country with enough money to keep going in comfort for a couple of months. In a way he was glad he had got that little bit of business out of the way and now he was free to forget his preconceptions and explore anywhere he liked. He had not really appreciated the opportunity before, obsessed by his quest for a holy granddad and passing through spectacular sights and scenes without really taking them in. Ethiopia was an exciting place and the people he met had been very friendly, he had to make the best of it. Deciding to take Mr Gebreselassie's advice, he took out his guidebook as he walked and planned a route weaving up to Aksum in the north, trekking round the lakes and mountains of the Ethiopian highlands and stopping off in villages dotted with ancient castles, palaces and churches.

Looking up, Robbie noticed that he had walked miles out of the town without looking where he was going, preoccupied with his thoughts. He had followed the road towards the foot of the Chercher Mountains for about an hour and found himself in a barren rocky landscape with not a building in sight. A sudden wave of panic hit him, as he had broken the golden rule of travelling. Here he was, in the middle of nowhere at the hottest part of the day, without a bottle of water. All he had drunk all day was coffee, which he remembered to be a cause of dehydration, although how something containing water could do this he had never understood. Now he was up in the higher altitude where the air was thin, which he also thought was probably linked to dehydration. Suddenly in the grip of an entirely psychosomatic raging thirst, he knew he could turn back and would eventually find himself back in Harar, but was worried he would not make it. The road ahead sloped up to the brow of a hill, so he could not see what might be just ahead of him. Picturing himself fainting of thirst and being eaten by vultures, Robbie decided to gamble on keeping going in the hope that he could see signs of civilisation from the top of the hill.

Breathless and sweating, Robbie was relieved to see a little village on the other side of the hill where a dirt track crossed the main road. Although it hardly constituted a village, consisting of a handful of houses clustered round an old church. Most importantly, there was a roadside stall with a Coca-Cola sign. He blinked and looked again, to make sure it was not a mirage. Thank god, thought Robbie as he jogged casually down the hill, feelings of exhaustion on the verge of collapse miraculously lifted. Cheerfully he greeted the stallholder and was amazed to find he was equipped with a mini-generator and ice-cold fridge. Robbie sat by the side of the road and sipped from the bottle, soaking up the sunshine and admiring the view of the mountains stretching up into the blue sky all around him.

'Where you from?' asked the stallholder.

'London.'

'London…' he repeated it uncertainly and considered it for a few seconds. 'Why you come here?'

'Er…' Robbie was a little taken aback by this direct line of questioning. He looked around him and pointed up vaguely. '…to see the mountains.'

'Oh.' The stallholder looked up at the mountains and nodded. 'Beautiful. You walk from Harar?'

'Yeah, nice day for it, eh?'

'Yes. Nice day. But rain is coming. My name is Tesfay.'

'Pleased to meet you. My name is Robbie.'

'Robbie. I like to go London. To speak more English.' Tesfay was clearly keen to make the most of an opportunity to practice now.

'OK. Good luck.'

'But I am poor. I need to sell more.' Tesfay gestured at the shelves of his tiny stall, crammed full of fresh fruit and vegetables, tins and packets of everything you could ever need for a handful of houses at a crossroads halfway up some mountains. 'But we have more seller than buyer. You know I-M-F?'

'Er, yeah.'

'They set market prices. We cannot get rich.'

'Oh, sorry,' said Robbie, taking personal responsibility for the inequities of global trade.

'Long walk back to Harar. There is a bus. Here in one hour.'

'Thanks.'

'You stay in Harar?'

'Yes.'

'Good. But you stay for a week. Rain very bad back all the way to Addis.

Roads flooded.'

'Oh dear. Well, I had better make the most of it while I am here.'

'See church. It is also beautiful. Very old. You can go inside,' said Tesfay.

'Oh, thanks. Great.' Robbie returned the empty soda bottle and got up, although he was tempted to stay and listen to Tesfay's global economic news, travel advice, weather report and tourist guide all day.

The interior of the church felt cool and damp, the air heavy with incense. A few shafts of light crept in from the portholes in the ancient sandstone, and hundreds of candles flickered around a shrine at one end. Robbie stepped forward, letting the heavy wooden doors creak to a close behind him. He looked around uneasily to see if he was interrupting prayers or a ceremony, but the whole place appeared to be deserted. Whoever had lit the candles seemed to have disappeared into the silent gloom, neglecting basic fire safety rules. From outside, the church looked like a ruined cave dwelling, but once through the doors it was a spectacular feat of architecture, perfectly preserved. The walls had been chiselled from the mountain in perfect symmetry, with sculpted pillars and elaborately carved ceiling. The walls were covered in faint, fading murals depicting scenes of saints doing battle with various devils and animals. Robbie had read about ancient rock-hewn churches in the guidebook, but he thought they were all in the north, near Aksum, and he was certain it had not mentioned anything like this around Harar. He suddenly felt guilty for intruding on this historic religious monument, and worried that his footsteps were causing irreparable structural damage. Edging back towards the door, he was about to leave when his eyes, getting accustomed to the dim light, made out a dark figure at the far end of the church, partially obscured by the hazy glow from the candles. A tall man in long black robes was pointing right at him. Robbie froze. His stomach gurgled and he was suddenly conscious of his own heartbeat, which seemed to echo against the silent cold stone. Knowing they take religion very seriously in this country, he thought he was probably trespassing in the church without permission and would at best be arrested and fined. After the initial shock had subsided, Robbie felt in his pocket to see if he had any money and took a few steps deeper into the church, deciding to break the ice with a donation.

'Hello... Teanastellen...Er...I'm sorry...I...'

The figure had not moved as he approached and continued to fix him with an outstretched hand and a cold stare. Robbie let out a half-sigh, half-laugh. It was a statue. He carried on walking slowly forward in a trance, hypnotised by its life-like beauty. It appeared to be made of a smooth black stone, reflecting the candlelight in a rich ebony sheen. The statue was about seven foot tall, standing on a pedestal with the right hand semi-raised, as if he was about to pat a small child on the head. Robbie guessed it must be Jesus, as he knew this to be a popular character in most churches, but it was unlike any image of the Son of God that he had ever seen before. The facial features were unmistakeably African, and the flowing hair looked suspiciously like dreadlocks. Amazed, Robbie searched in vain for a notice giving the history and age of the statue, but there was nothing to mark its existence at all. Stepping back to admire it, he took his hands out of his pockets and realised he was holding the ring his grandmother had given him in his fist. He glanced down and looked at it, turning it over in his fingers and remembering what Mr Gebreselassie had told him.

Feeling inspired by the power and beauty of the statue, Robbie felt that he had reached a turning point in his life. This was his chance to do something decisive, to stop hanging on to adolescent dreams that had been holding him back. He had been wasting all those years, waiting in vain for something exciting to happen to him. Now it had happened, and it turned out to be a wild granddad chase. Nearly a quarter of a century and he had done nothing with his life, except listen to a hell of a lot of reggae. Sitting in limbo had stopped him knuckling down to a proper career or making a real commitment to Angela. He realised that he sounded like his parents but for once in his life he thought maybe they were right. Robbie knew he had to accept that the reality of his life had been right outside his door all along, not within a seven-inch piece of vinyl from Jamaica, or halfway across the world on the trail of a dead emperor. Another month or so travelling, then he would go back home a changed person. Make himself a plan, try to do something worthwhile that led somewhere. Angela – he would patch things up with her, instead of hedging his bets and waiting around to see if someone more perfect was going to turn up. That's if she would have him back. Typical, he thought, you never miss your water 'til your well runs dry, or in his case, when you are wandering around Ethiopia without a bottle of water. It hit him like a Sly Dunbar drum-roll; he had to hold on to what he had and stop dreaming his life away.

Shit, this must be what is meant by travelling the world and discovering yourself, thought Robbie. And it had happened after only a week without him even trying. No near-death experiences, no malaria-induced hallucinations, not even a mystical guru. The people he met had taught him something, but it was mainly that they were ordinary people trying to get on with their lives, and so should he. London was where he belonged, and for the first time in his life he felt British. Not that he loved the Queen and missed Eastenders, but that he was suddenly, painfully aware of the forces that had shaped him, and how much he needed to keep them close. Travelling was good fun for a while, but it would take too much time and effort to learn a whole new culture, even a language was a bit much for him. To the people he met here, he would always be a foreigner, a symbol of the wealth and power of the west, and he lacked the dedication and charisma to get beyond that. It was a sensation that made him uncomfortable, and on balance he preferred to be where he fitted in, where he could walk the streets unnoticed and quietly get on with making the best of the life he led. This is what he would do when he got back home.

Robbie looked up at the statue and then at the gold ring in his palm. Checking over his shoulder to see if anyone was emerging from the gloom to tell him off for touching a religious artefact, he reached out and placed the ring on the little finger of the statue's outstretched right hand. A perfect fit, it held fast immediately, before he had a chance to decide whether he was just messing about. He was surprised to find that instead of the cool marble-like stone he had been expecting, the statue felt warm to his touch. It was as if it had somehow absorbed the heat from the surrounding candles, or on closer inspection, perhaps it was actually made of ebony or some other substance. Robbie removed his hand and shrugged. Well, it was a worthless souvenir anyway, according to Mr Gebreselassie. And his grandmother had asked him to return it to its rightful owner, and he figured this was about as near as he would ever get. Turning and walking out of the church without looking back, Robbie emerged blinking into the brilliant sunshine and oppressive heat of the afternoon. From his stall across the road, Tesfay waved at him enthusiastically and pointed at his watch to let him know he was just in time for the bus back to Harar.

23. AFRICAN TEARS

Malaika pulled the worn, grubby sheet over her mother's charcoal grey face and sighed. She mumbled a simple prayer that she half-remembered from school, back in the days before she had to give it up to work the field and look after her parents. From the other side of the tiny round hut they shared, there was an unnerving silence. Her brother, Baraka, briefly stopped crying for the first time in what seemed like days, as if he knew this was the time to pay his respects, because he had just become an orphan. Suddenly, Malaika realised she was totally alone in the world, save for her baby brother, who was too young to understand what was going on. A gurgle and a hiccup were followed by renewed screams to distract her from any further chance of reflection, and she went over to try to comfort him. Picking him up easily, he still weighed as much as a healthy newborn baby should, even though he was two years old, his helplessness comforted her and she managed to gently rock him to sleep.

The dirt was tough, but fairly loose after hacking through the outer crust with the rusty old hoe. Malaika knew this because she had helped her mother dig a similar sized hole for her father a couple of months ago. It had not rained much since then and it took her twice as long on her own, even though her mother had been very weak at the time. Sweating in the morning sun, her arms began to ache and she felt that the ancient implement she was using was about to give way. She paused from scraping at the parched ground for a few seconds, just long enough for Baraka to wake up and his cries to fill the silence. Looking out onto the dying crops on their small plot of land, Malaika shrugged, thinking the hoe would not be much use anymore for what she had planned. After a couple of hours, there was a shallow grave about five feet by one, alongside the mound of earth where her father lay. Back inside the gloomy hut, already smelling of death, Malaika weighed up the situation. It would be difficult, but she had helped to drag her father's body outside, and her mother was surely much lighter after wasting away for the past few months. She pulled at the lifeless form, finding it hard to tell where the thin sheet ended, and her mother's saggy skin began. Sliding the body off the mattress and onto the floor was easy, then she managed to roll her over so that the sheet wrapped around her. This gave a good leverage, so she could twist the end of the sheet and drag the body a few feet at a time, resting in between.

Scraping the dirt back over her mother's body was easy. Malaika then collected as many rocks as she could find to pile up over the burial mound to stop wild dogs digging it up. She knew the village elders would probably not approve of her makeshift funeral, but she did not have much choice. If she announced her mother's death to her relatives, her family's meagre possessions would be divided up between them. This would inevitably include herself, and she would be taken in by her father's cousin as his future wife. Not a bad fate for herself, as she would be guaranteed food and a roof over her head, but she was worried about what would become of Baraka. He needed medicine and if they stayed in the village, he would be just another crying hungry mouth, without a hope, waiting to join his parents. Malaika found two sticks, fashioned them into a rough cross with a bit of string and pushed it into the ground at the head of her mother's grave. She murmured a few words of farewell and went back inside. Baraka went quiet again, grateful for the warmth and attention as she picked him up and tied him onto her back with a kanga. Her mother had always saved a little money in a tin by her bed in case of emergencies. Malaika considered this to be such an occasion and wrapped the few notes inside the waistline of her skirt. Without looking back at the only home she had ever known and the graves of her parents, she set off for the neighbouring village health centre. The eight miles would be easy enough to cover before it started getting dark, even for an eleven-year-old girl carrying a baby.

24. AMBUSH IN THE NIGHT

Over the hills to the north lay Eritrea and the Red Sea. Robbie had travelled up through the mountainous spine of Ethiopia, taking in spectacular peaks and gorges, visiting ancient castles and palaces, and seeking out two thousand years and more of historical ruins hidden away in the countryside. It had taken him a lot longer than he had thought, as he was delayed in Harar due to unseasonal downpours making the roads impassable. Fortunately, the rain had eased off before any serious flooding, but once he had got going, he had underestimated the time it would take to cover the distance along winding, bumpy roads weaving through highland villages. It was over two months since he had left London and he had spent most of his money, although the cost of living was negligible. In the past few weeks, he had ticked off all the essential sights mentioned in the guidebook, including more rock-hewn churches in Tigray, the tombs of Aksum, the battlefield at Adowa and now he found himself at what seemed literally like the end of the road. Strolling on out of the peaceful little village to admire the sunset, Robbie discovered that the mountains rose to an abrupt halt ahead of him, giving way to a deep ravine with no sign of life for miles. Grateful that he had brought his personal stereo with him, he sat down and nodded his head to the perfect accompaniment for these surroundings. As the sun melted into the horizon and the road disintegrated into a dirt track, he was satisfied that this was symbolic of the end of his journey, even though the sun went down every day without fail and a dead end was clearly indicated on the map, and decided it was time to turn around and go back home to London.

The truck came bouncing over the hills at high speed, tearing through the tranquil evening air with a cloud of dust rising up in its wake. Robbie was dimly aware of the roar of an engine interrupting his meditations just before the vehicle shot out of the dirt track to his left, masked by the glare of the setting sun. Thinking the driver was in no mood to give way to pedestrians, Robbie scrambled to his feet and onto a barren field off the road. Shielding his eyes from the sun with his hand, he looked up in horror to see the truck swerve off the track and head straight for him. Instead of his life flashing before his eyes, he took these precious few moments to notice that the driver was wearing shades, and he thought to himself that this greatly reduced his chances of being seen in the fading light, even if the driver had been looking in his direction. With one hand casually on the steering wheel and a foot firmly on the accelerator, the driver was turning round to remonstrate with a passenger who seemed to be making a point about the road ahead. Instinctively, Robbie closed his eyes and dived for cover, as the sound of screeching brakes and skidding tyres echoed around the mountains. He could feel the heat of the engine and the weight of displaced air hit him as he was thrown onto his front, putting out his hands to protect himself. Not sure if he had been hit or not, and not even sure if he had hit the ground, he opened his eyes. Total darkness had replaced the twilight and he had a sudden feeling of vertigo, as if he was still moving. He turned around and sat up, steadying himself against the floor, which was definitely bouncing up and down in a disorientating fashion. Opening his eyes, the relief at not being knocked over barely materialised before it was replaced by a deeper sense of dread and fear. To his right he could see the road and countryside flashing by through a hole in the floor. At his back he felt the metal bars of the sides of the truck. To his left, as his eyes adjusted to the darkness inside the flapping canvas cover, he could make out the two shadowy figures who had bundled him into the swerving vehicle as he fell. They were both wearing scarves wrapped around their faces, and dark glasses. Between them was a huge pile of guns.

'Shit,' breathed Robbie, before realising this was probably not the best way to open negotiations with his kidnappers. He decided it was best not to let them see his fear, as if being snatched into the back of a truck was the sort of thing that happened to him all the time.

'Teanastellen?' he offered, remembering his manners and basic grasp of Amharic. They both sat facing him without moving. Robbie started thinking fast. He wondered how far he was from the Somali border, as he had been warned about gangs of terrorists taking westerners hostage in that area. No wonder they did not respond to the traditional Ethiopian greeting, he cursed himself for not having mastered any other regional languages, until a sudden brainwave hit him.

'Allah akbar!' he shouted, and smiled, giving them the thumbs up. They turned and looked at each other, and Robbie was satisfied this stroke of brilliance had convinced them they were in the company of another Muslim brother. However, his captors remained silent, so he persevered.

'Me Welsh. Not English. Not American. Me also victim of colonialism. Down with imperialism!' he raised his fist in a gesture of international solidarity. This clearly had the desired effect, as one of the terrorists took off the glasses and started unravelling the scarf. The truck lurched uphill and a shaft of light from the setting sun beamed through a gap in the canvas. Robbie was surprised to see the scarf slowly reveal a pair of soft brown eyes and dark long eyelashes, followed by long black hair and a strikingly beautiful face. It was at this point that he also noticed the bumps in the sweatshirt. Despite the danger or perhaps because of it, he felt a faint stirring in his trousers. Or maybe it was just the movement of the truck, not unlike being on the top deck of a bus.

'What the fuck are you crapping on about?' she asked, in a west London accent.

'Oh...er...sorry,' said Robbie sheepishly.

'I mean, a thank you would be nice. In any language you like.'

'Right. Thanks... for kidnapping me,'

'We ain't *kidnapping* anyone,' she snorted derisively.

'OK, that's good. Would you mind just letting me out here then?'

'No problem. We can drop you to your door if you like...' his captor seemed genuinely disinterested about his fate, which was a worrying sign, '...But I wouldn't recommend it.'

Robbie had visibly relaxed for a few seconds at the sound of a familiar accent but tensed at the way she coldly uttered these last ominous words. She looked sweet and kind, but she was probably a nice middle class suburban girl brainwashed into an even more dangerous than average brand of international terrorist. He looked around and weighed up his chances if he dived out of the back of the truck. The other one was facing the other way, leaning towards the driver, who was still paying insufficient attention to the road, but they both had shades and scarves on, so it was hard to tell whether they had their eyes on him or not. It would take them a few seconds to grab their guns, but they were careering through open country so they would easily catch him in the truck. And an escape attempt this early in the proceedings would only anger them. He decided his best bet was to try to befriend them and express sympathy with their cause, whatever it was.

'Oh…why not?' he squeaked, casually.

'Have you any idea where you are?' she asked him.

'Yes of course, northern Ethiopia, near the border with Eritrea.'

'Don't you know what's going on?'

'Well, I haven't caught the news lately. Has someone famous died? That always happens when I go on holiday.' Robbie thought better at this attempt at humour.

'There's a fucking war breaking out, you dickhead. We just saved your arse from wandering into an area covered in landmines back there. And if we drop you back into the village that we've just helped to evacuate, you'll find a fuckload of shells dropping on your head in about ten minutes.'

'What here? But there's nothing for miles except rocks. I mean…thanks a lot all the same. Seriously.' Robbie breathed a little more easily and leaned back against the side of the truck, before being thrown forward suddenly as a deafening boom shook the road and an explosion lit up the dusky sky behind them.

'Oops. They're early,' the woman looked at her watch and then banged on the back of the driver's seat, encouraging him to press down on the accelerator. After his ears had stopped ringing, Robbie felt heartened by this dramatic confirmation of her story and relatively safe, as his companions paid him scant attention, and were obviously more concerned with escaping a war zone. But there was still something bothering him, aside from the fact that he was escaping a war zone. That was it, the huge pile of guns on the floor at the other end of the truck. He sat for a while in silence, contemplating his fate and waiting to see if they made the next move. He gave up.

'Where are we going?'

'Somewhere safe. Relax.'

'What about my stuff? It's in a guest house in the village.'

'Oh, well. If it has not been burnt the looters will have got it. Think of it as redistribution of wealth.'

Robbie mourned the loss of his bright orange rucksack. It had served him well and become a worthy friend during his travels. True, it was mostly full of dirty T-shirts and souvenirs by now, but he could not help feeling he would probably need something other than the clothes he was standing in before he got home, if he ever did. He touched the inside of his shirt and was relieved to find that he still had his security wallet on him, containing passport, ticket home and money, although he simultaneously worried how long it would be before this too would be redistributed.

'So, what's with the scarves over your faces then, if you're not terrorists?'

'It is fucking windy and dusty out there,'

'Right…so are you with the army ?' asked Robbie.

'No.'

'Who are you then?'

'I'm Sarita. This is Saleh.' She gestured at the big, burly guy next to her, who had taken most of his weight when they bundled him into the truck. 'The driver is David.' Saleh nodded from behind his shades and David waved a hand cheerfully as he wrenched the steering wheel about with the other.

'Hi. I'm Robbie, pleased to meet you. So, where are you from?'

'Hi Robbie, man.' shouted David above the roar of the engine, 'I'm Eritrean. No, hang on, I'm Ethiopian. Wait, my younger brother is Eritrean…' he looked down for a few seconds, pondering this puzzle, as if he was about to abandon the steering wheel altogether and search for clues under the seat.

'We are Africans.' Sarita interrupted, as the truck veered alarmingly off the road and back again.

Robbie remembered Trevor's mock solemnity on the plane and chuckled casually, thinking she too was testing his level of white liberal guilt. Sarita remained deadly solemn.

'Sorry…it's just you sound like you are from London, and you look Indian,' he said plainly.

'I was born in Nairobi, I'm African Asian. My parents moved to Britain when I was six. I came back here when I was twenty-two for a holiday. I was just planning on visiting relatives and going on a safari, but I never left. That was three years ago.'

'Where did you live in Britain then, west London, innit?'

'Hounslow.'

'For real? I don't believe it. I'm from Acton!' Robbie laughed at this revelation of common ground and expected her to embrace him as a long-lost brother. Sarita was not impressed, but he persevered. 'We must be about the same age! What high school did you go to? Let me think, who do I know from Hounslow…Do you know a bloke called Helly? Long hair, always wore a shell suit.'

'I'm not having this conversation. For fuck's sake, I'm an African freedom fighter, this is a revolution, not a fucking school reunion.' Sarita suddenly looked quite fierce, and although he was tempted to tell her that she was even more beautiful when she was angry, Robbie was reminded of the big pile of guns next to her and decided to shut up. After another half hour hurtling through the hills and night, Robbie ventured another line of questioning.

'So, whose side are you on in the war then?'

'No one's. We are on the side of the people,' replied Sarita.

'Good. So am I.'

'Look, I'm tired and I'm not in the mood for making chit-chat with tourists, so just shut up and try to get some sleep. We mean you no harm – like I said, we already saved your life once and are now escorting you from a war zone. We've got some business to take care of, but we can leave you in Aksum in a couple of days, where you can get a train to Addis. I suggest you fly away home before things get out of hand here.'

Robbie took the hint and sat back, trying to make himself comfortable on the bouncing floor of the truck. As he had travelled north towards the semi-desert region, it had got a lot hotter, but the temperature dropped suddenly as the night fell, and Sarita threw him an old sack for a blanket.

25. HOW CAN WE EASE THE PAIN

The doctor shook his head and waved Malaika away. She had been queuing for two hours with her sick baby brother asleep wrapped up on her back. Although he was not very heavy, she was bent almost double with his weight and exhausted after walking for miles. Undaunted, she stood her ground and looked up at the doctor who was towering over her.

'Why?' she asked, in Swahili.

'We have no medication for these little ones. The virus is too far gone. We can only help the stronger ones. Go back to your mother.'

'My mother is dead.'

The doctor did not hear her and had already moved on to the next patient. Malaika went outside and sat on the steps of the health centre porch. She felt like crying but had forgotten how to, knowing it would not help her anyway. There were family friends in this village that she could try to find, but she did not want to burden them, as they were barely able to feed their own children. Taking some money out of her waist, she called to a nearby vendor, a boy about her age. She bought a cup of water, a little packet of biscuits and a banana, which she shared with Baraka while contemplating the long journey back to her village. It was getting dark already and she was scared to walk home on her own at night, in case lions or hyenas attacked her. Sitting on the steps, she listened to the conversation of the women gathered outside the health centre.

'These doctors know nothing.'

'It is not Dr Mbombo's fault. The government cannot afford the drugs.'

'But I have heard there is a bush doctor in Tabora region who can cure this disease.'

     'That is nonsense. All those charlatans relieve you of is your money. Our only hope is the almighty.'

     'That is true...'

     Malaika stopped listening as the rhythms of the voices reminded her of her mother, and she started drifting half-asleep into a dream, her head resting against a post. She saw her mother and father waving at her from their house. It was a bright sunny day, and they were both fit and healthy, faces shining and animated, how she remembered them when she was younger. They knew she was going away with Baraka, but they were smiling and wishing her good luck. Suddenly she awoke with a start, as something one of the women said became lodged in her consciousness. The way the words entered her dream it was as if her mother was calling them to her. It might have been another nonsense story, but she believed it was a sign and she was desperate to follow any thread of hope. Malaika got to her feet and headed for the marketplace. It was noisy with vendors selling the last of their wares as the day drew to a close. Trucks, cars, scooters, bikes, and handcarts were being frantically loaded up and heading out of the village. She had been here a few times before and knew there was a bus to the district capital. As she wandered through the crowds, she heard a woman ask a bus-driver if he was headed for the city. He was, but it would take a whole night's journey. Unnoticed, Malaika followed the woman onto the bus and fell asleep in a back corner seat with Baraka on her lap.

26. RUB-A-DUB SOLDIER

Woken by the flapping noise of Sarita pulling up the canvas at the back of the truck, Robbie opened his eyes and squinted against the morning sun. For a moment, childhood memories of camping in a musty old tent in Ravi's back garden came back to him, and he briefly expected Mrs Patel to appear with a cup of tea and a plate of scrambled eggs. But then a figure loomed large into his vision, wearing the matching black fatigues, shades and scarf that were so popular with his companions and he remembered the events of the night before. The watchman waved them through the gates into some kind of compound, exchanging greetings and sharing a joke that Robbie did not catch, but had a distinct feeling was at his expense. The truck rumbled along a narrow road, overtaking a boy riding a very strange looking tricycle. It didn't appear to have any handlebars, and he was sitting very low on the frame welded from long metal pipes, and crouched down, furiously turning the pedals with his hands beneath his seat. Looking up, he smiled and waved, freewheeling for a few seconds, allowing the truck to pass him. Waving back, Robbie noticed the boy had no legs. In the distance he heard a chorus of 'Good morning teacher' and turned to see a man in shirtsleeves standing in front of a group of children sitting under the porch of a small building. They passed neat fields of healthy crops and the occasional goat and chicken. Another building appeared, with a line of children, many of them missing various limbs, queuing to see a smiling woman in a white coat. The truck trundled to a stop and Sarita gestured for Robbie to get out, and then tutted as he jumped down into the path of another two children riding tricycles, swerving and laughing as they avoided him.

'Wait here. What do you want for breakfast?' she asked him.

'Scrambled eggs on toast would be nice,' joked Robbie.

Sarita followed Saleh and David into the building, leaving Robbie sitting on the porch taking in his surroundings. He could just make out the gate and the perimeter fence in the distance, inside which were a handful of buildings dotted around a flat area of about one square mile, protected on all sides by rugged mountains. Besides what he assumed was a school and a health centre, there was a low brick building with piles of scrap metal outside and a steady plume of smoke emerging from a chimney. There were rows of little huts that put him in mind of holiday chalets at Butlins, washing lines outside decorating the slightly formal, military atmosphere with brightly coloured material. Behind him he assumed was some sort of kitchen or cafeteria, as he could smell food and there were lots of people coming and going. To his surprise, Sarita appeared next to him with two plates of scrambled eggs on toast.

'Wow, thanks...I didn't mean it.'

'Don't you want it?' teased Sarita, whisking the plate away from him.

'No, yes please, it looks lovely. I just mean, where did you get it...what is this place anyway?' asked Robbie.

'Eat first, then talk.'

Robbie obeyed and tucked into his breakfast enthusiastically, as he had missed a meal the evening before, what with all the excitement. Saleh appeared before them with a tall pot and poured then each a small cup of sweet milky tea, steaming with an aroma of cardamom and cloves.

'Thanks,' said Robbie, through a mouthful of toast. Saleh nodded and went back inside the building. 'Doesn't say much does he, your mate?' Robbie said to Sarita.

'He's deaf.'

'Oh.'

'Ear drums burst as a child by a bomb blast in Angola. He lip-reads English quite well and uses signs.'

Robbie nodded and finished eating. 'That was lovely, thanks. So, are you going to tell me what you all do here then?'

'Come on, I will show you while we work, now you must earn your breakfast.'

Sarita took his plate and cup and disappeared into the building, re-emerging a few seconds later with Saleh and David behind her.

'Don't worry, it's our turn to wash up tonight. Right now, we have got to get this truck unloaded,' Sarita pointed at the big pile of guns.

Saleh jumped up into the truck and started handing down pairs of rifles and machine guns.

'Hang on, I don't know about this,' said Robbie anxiously. 'I've never handled a gun before, I'm sorry, but I don't want to get involved in anything like this.'

David and Sarita laughed and made signs at Saleh, who joined in as he held a machine gun out towards Robbie, barrel first. It occurred to him that he was actually looking down the barrel of a gun and did not have much choice about what he would be asked to do. For all Sarita's kind manner and tasty scrambled eggs, his first suspicions were right. They were obviously some sort of bloodthirsty mercenaries who would make him kill or be killed for their cause.

'Don't look so frightened,' Sarita suppressed her laughter. 'Look, they're not loaded and they're rusty and broken. They have all been decommissioned. We are just recycling the metal. Come on, we are taking them over to the factory. I told you I will explain, just make yourself useful.'

Although he had made a snap decision that he would kill rather than be killed, Robbie breathed a sigh of relief that this would not now be necessary. He grabbed the gun, which was indeed rusty but still a lot heavier than they look in films. Saleh showed him how to carry it with his arms outstretched and dropped another one on top. The three of them were loaded up and walked across the compound to the low brick building with the chimney.

'We are trying to get the guns out of Africa,' explained Sarita, 'We travel around the villages persuading local warlords and disbanded soldiers to give up their arms. In exchange for education, healthcare, tools, seeds…an alternative basically. There are people who have grown up seeing a gun as their only means of survival, but we show them another way. You might say this is just a drop in the ocean, as new supplies are pouring in every day, but it's a start.'

'Oh, yeah, I thought it was something like that. Sounds brilliant. What do you do with them?'

'This is Kwami – he is in charge of the metalworks here,' she introduced him to a dread with his face obscured by a thick visor. He mumbled something and took the guns from them and inside the building, where they could feel the heat from the furnace.

'He makes the tricycles that you nearly knocked over earlier on. A Kalashnikov melts down quite nicely into a child's bicycle frame, apparently. Also hoes, spades that sort of thing, swords into ploughshares, basically.' She lowered her voice into a whisper and indicated a figure inside the building. 'But Tinga makes the real clever stuff – he is quite a famous artist from South Africa. That's him inside – don't interrupt him while he is working. He makes sculptures out of guns, mines, shells, you name it – they sell for thousands in Europe. There is a huge metal dove in Stockholm railway station, have you seen it? That is one of his. Financed the schoolhouse and health centre here.'

'Wow. That is amazing. So, whose are all the children here?'

'They are all orphans. Found wandering around warzones from Somalia to Sierra Leone, some injured by landmines, parents killed. We give them shelter, medical help and education. Hopefully when they get older, they will go back to their countries and make some real changes.'

'What, you really travel all around Africa in that truck?'

'Yeah, that's the idea, when it's working.'

'Sort of like the A-Team?'

'Ha fucking ha. I like to think of us as more like the Black Panthers. Not just three, there's a few hundred people based here, with thirty vehicles, although about half of them are broken down at the moment. People from all over Africa, drawn together to help ourselves.'

'Sorry, seriously that sounds brilliant. Are you part of some religious group then?' asked Robbie, thinking it must be a cult.

'No, we have people of all religions here. And we are not aligned with any political party. We just believe it is up to us Africans to sort our problems out, for which we first need peace, then self-sufficiency and real independence will follow.'

'Wow, so how did you get involved then, from Hounslow?'

'I just woke up one morning and realised everything we consume in the west is adding to the oppression of the poor world. Drink a cup of coffee, even the milk – you know how much land in Africa is used to feed cattle for the west? You have a mobile phone – you know the war in the Congo has been fought over the mining rights for a mineral used in them? Same with diamonds, funding the Angolan civil war for two decades and don't even get me started on oil and the Ogoni people in Nigeria.'

'Well, I know what you mean, but I drink fair trade coffee, I don't have a car and I don't use diamonds on a daily basis.'

'You have a record player?'

'Diamond stylus. Shit. Fair enough. Anything I can do to help?'

'Yeah, you can teach English, can't you?'

Robbie looked uncertain.

'Well, you can speak it anyway, that will do. Come on, let's go and help at the school.' Sarita clapped her hands and strode off boldly. Robbie followed, thinking about the challenging, revolutionary ideas she had introduced to his understanding of global development, and also what a nice arse she had.

27. RAGGAMUFFIN GIRL

A few days turned into a week, and Robbie was finding it difficult to leave. He acted casual when Sarita asked him if he wanted to get a lift with another truck to Aksum, saying he preferred to wait until David could take him direct to Addis Ababa as he felt safer with his driving. Sarita was not remotely convinced by this argument as everyone who had driven with David kissed the ground when they got out alive, but she was enjoying his company and so were the kids. Robbie had done very well as a school assistant and taught them all some nice songs. She had reservations about the teaching of English as she felt it reinforced the cultural imperialism of America, but she had given up this argument to be pragmatic. He had also made himself useful around the camp, helping out with the cooking and fitting in well with everyone else. She had been quite worried about bringing him in, because he was the first European who had been there. But she felt it would be a good test of everyone's non-racist principles, and despite some initial trepidation, there had been no problems. For her, it helped that she found Robbie quite attractive, despite or perhaps because she had a major thing about one of the other guys in the group. However, she had a strict rule not to get involved with anyone in the camp, but she felt this would not matter with Robbie because he would not be staying around that long. She also liked the way he did everything she asked.

'Robbie, come with me in the truck, we have to go to the village to get some supplies.'

Robbie hopped into the passenger seat and Sarita revved the engine.

'Hey, be careful with that, she is very gentle,' shouted David, who did not like anyone else driving his truck, but he was taking an afternoon nap and could not be bothered to go with them.

'Don't worry, I will,' she waved as she turned the truck around and eased slowly along the track out of the compound.

On the way back from the village, which was about two hours' drive, Robbie continued his tentative efforts to get to know her better.

'So, don't you miss London then?'

'Not really, there is too much going on here. I used to get homesick but I still keep in touch with my family.'

'Yeah, I felt homesick after one week, but I haven't thought about it lately.'

'Actually, the one thing I really miss is music. This truck has no stereo and we can hardly pick up any radio stations up here because of the mountains.'

'Yeah, what kind of stuff are you into?' asked Robbie, a question he was always dying to ask straight away whenever he met someone, but felt embarrassed to do so.

'Mainly seventies and eighties funk, a bit of hip-hop and ragga.'

Robbie nodded at this last one with satisfaction. He thought for a while and checked the pocket of his one pair of combat trousers.

'Tell you what, you can have my walkman CD player if you like. I've only got one CD since I lost my rucksack. There's some dancehall on there, but I'm getting a bit bored of it now and I'd better be going home soon anyway.'

'Oh no, I couldn't possibly…alright then, if you insist,' said Sarita quickly, before Robbie had a chance to insist. He held out the thin round personal CD player and she tucked it away in the inside pocket of her jacket without taking her other hand off the steering wheel. 'Thanks Robbie, you're not so bad you know.'

He smiled to himself as they carried on in silence, heading into the setting sun. As the truck jerked and rocked over the mountain roads, suddenly the engine started making an alarming hissing noise, and thick steam was belching out of the bonnet.

'Shit! It's fucking blown. That fucker David was supposed to check it,' shouted Sarita as she slammed on the brakes. They got out and she opened up the bonnet to try and cool it down. She was fuming almost as much as the engine, and kicked the tyres. 'Fucking fucker's fucked! This is always fucking happening! What

I wouldn't give for a decent fucking mechanic in this country!'

'What are we going to do?' asked Robbie.

'There's nothing else for it, we're miles from the village or the camp. We'll just have to wait here and hope someone comes past, or see if it works again in a while. Bollocks!' she sat down on a rock by the side of the road and folded her arms.

Robbie walked up and down, with a concerned expression on his face. He looked around, they had come to a stop on a small ridge, but the rise and fall of the mountains were unbroken by any sign of life and was looking increasingly like a desert. Long shadows were creeping across the hills, merging the road ahead into darkness.

'But it's going to be dark soon,' he said, and then realising how pathetic he sounded, added in an effort to emulate Sarita's compulsive swearing, 'fucking dark.'

'Yeah. We might have to camp out here for the night. You're not scared of snakes and scorpions, are you?'

'Me? Nah,' said Robbie, just managing to stop himself putting his hands in his pockets and whistling to convey the impression of a relaxed, laid back attitude to poisonous reptiles, not that he had encountered any as yet.

'Good, cos I hate the little fuckers, so you can deal with them. At least we won't starve with all the supplies. Come on, let's go and explore.' Sarita started walking off the road and up a hill.

'What about the truck, is it locked?' asked Robbie as he trotted after her.

'Robbie, we are in the middle of fucking nowhere, not the Uxbridge Road. The truck is fucked, and if anyone wants to steal our supplies, they would probably come armed round here, so we would just let them. In fact, we would be really nice and help them.'

'Yeah, course. Where are we exactly then?'

'Bandit country. Desert between Eritrea, Ethiopia and Sudan. There is no border or real government authority in this area, just roaming gangs. Most of them tolerate our camp because we bring some medicines to the villages. But some of the local warlords are finding us a bit of an irritation since we've been encouraging their followers to disarm.'

They wandered up to the crest of the ridge and stopped to admire the view.

It was as if they were standing on top of the setting sun, and the rays were flooding over hills and valleys beneath them, making the dips and bumps in the desert seem like a rolling ocean. A gentle breeze fluttered into their faces, bringing a fine dust scented with wood and spice from distant, unseen fires.

'Beautiful,' said Sarita, looking out toward the horizon.

'Yeah, beautiful,' said Robbie, looking out of the corner of his eye at Sarita's face set against the sunset as the wind rippled through her hair. Instinctively, he leaned closer to her, like a moth to a light bulb, except he avoided repeatedly banging his head against her. He was dimly aware of a sharp crack echoing around the hills, felt something wizz through the air past him and suddenly Sarita fell to the ground. Robbie crouched down next to her and wracked his brains for basic first aid.

'Shit! Stray bullet.' gasped Sarita, lifting her head up as she lay on her back and held her right hand over her chest. 'Fuck, I felt the impact right here, by my heart.'

Robbie's hand hovered over the area as she lay on her back, but he could not see any blood. 'Are you alright?'

'I don't know, I think I've gone numb. Hang on, help me take my jacket off.'

Robbie carefully eased the sleeves off her arms and whispered, 'Don't move, the bullet might be lodged in your ribcage,' something he remembered happening on an episode of ER once. He placed his hand gently beneath her left breast, feeling the warmth of her body, but strangely still no warm sticky liquid. Meanwhile Sarita patted the ground around her, feeling for her jacket, and reaching for the inside pocket. Robbie was concentrating on the matter in hand, and slowly moved his hand inside her cleavage and around the top of her nipple, which even at a time of life and death such as this he could not help but notice, stiffening and rising through her T-shirt.

As he felt in vain for the wound, he noticed Sarita smirking and looking at him. Poor girl was probably getting hysterical with the shock.

'Having fun?' she asked.

'I'm sorry, I can't find where you were hit. Where do you feel the pain?'

'Right here,' she said, nodding towards her outstretched hand. She was holding up his personal stereo, complete with a big dent and a bullet lodged in the CD player.

'Ah!' Robbie yelped and whipped his hand away from Sarita's breast as if he had been burnt. 'Sorry. Thank fuck for that. You're OK, then?'

'Mmm…fine thanks.' Sarita started giggling and Robbie joined in, relieved and pleasantly aroused that she had not slapped his face. Suddenly another shot rang out in the distance and interrupted their mirth. Robbie leapt on top of Sarita, ostensibly for her protection. She squirmed beneath him, turning and flipping him over with surprising strength.

'Don't fucking move,' she hissed.

'Call me old-fashioned, but I should be on top of you, I'm being a gentleman,' whispered Robbie, struggling as he rolled them over and down the slope, into a more sheltered position.

'You're being a prat. If an innocent British tourist is killed out here it will cause a whole lot of trouble for us. The last thing we need is a media circus and international intervention.' Sarita bent his arm behind his back and turned him over, pinning him to the ground. 'So just shut up and lie still. Wait until it gets dark, a sniper might be watching us. Hopefully it was just someone celebrating miles away.'

They lay still on the ground in silence, waiting to make sure there were no signs of any activity. The sun sank behind the jagged mountains to the west and streaks of red and gold were wiped out by the encroaching blackness. Looking up as the stars popped out suddenly, they seemed a lot nearer and brighter than normal, which prompted Robbie to make a mental note to look up whether this was actually the case because he was nearer the equator. Sarita lay with her head on his chest. Robbie could feel her hair against his face and her breathing slowly on his neck. He was acutely conscious of her heart pumping just a few centimetres away from his own. He felt painfully aware of every line and curve of her body, the weight and warmth of every muscle tensing on top of him. He could not help but visualise the shape of her thighs and breasts as they pressed down against him. They lay together in the encroaching darkness like a petrified couple from Pompeii, caught for all eternity in a moment of heat and passion, waiting for the moment they would be returned to life. Except they both knew they had left it long enough, and could probably get up in safety, as the only stirrings of movement were in the area of Robbie's groin. He felt his heart race and the blood rush to his groin and desperately tried to think of something else to avert the building embarrassment. All he was reminded of was a school disco when he was thirteen, at which he got a huge erection during a slow dance with Cheryl Dunkley, she slapped him round the face and everyone laughed. Since then, Lionel Richie always brought a tear to his eye. This was not helping, and he decided he was going to have to get up. As he prepared to distract Sarita with the old 'oh look, there's a snake' trick, he was surprised to find her hand moving downwards, and slipping inside his trousers. At this moment, a number of thoughts competed for consideration in Robbie's brain.

Robbie was aware of the widespread problem of HIV in Africa. Of course, it was always an issue at home, but according to statistics, a greater risk in sub-Saharan Africa. He briefly considered the geographical issue of exactly where the Sahara was in relation to his current location, but quickly decided this was not the most important factor. Unfortunately, the condoms that he had brought with him on the trip, an optimistic just in case, had remained unopened in his rucksack, which had been lost. Although he had grown to like Sarita in the past week, he did not really know her that well, and was a bit suspicious of her relationship with some of the guys back at the camp. For all he knew, she might travel around the horn of Africa quite literally, bundling men into trucks and kidnapping them for sex all the time. He made a firm decision that unprotected sex was a very bad idea on this point alone.

Robbie also recollected that, according to the guidebook, so it must be true, Ethiopia was a traditional, patriarchal, morally conservative country, and the only women who approached or responded to the advances of strange men were prostitutes. This was becoming a common phenomenon in many poor countries as the number of western tourists seeking excitement or even love increased and exploited the desperation of young women, economically forced to go on the game. Robbie had decided on principle that he would play no part in this, and a sexual relationship in this global context would be inherently unequal. However, Sarita was from Hounslow, and they could in theory have met in a club in Ealing Broadway, so he was confident that in this case, this point was not an issue.

Robbie struggle to remember the exact words when he and Angela had parted, but he was fairly sure she had shouted something to the effect of not expecting her to wait around for him. He had sent her a postcard a month ago, but that was it. For all he knew, she might be seeing someone else, anything could have happened. Earlier in his journey of self-discovery, he had decided that his future belonged with her, but now he was not so sure. He felt perhaps he had found himself a bit too soon, before he had the opportunity of finding someone else. Of course, he was several thousand miles away and surrounded by mountains, desert and darkness, so it occurred to him that she would never know. However, he would know, and he might feel guilty about it at some point in the future.

While these thoughts had been mulling around inside Robbie's mind, Sarita had relieved him of his trousers, socks, trainers and boxer shorts. She had expertly rolled a UN-issue condom onto his twitching erection and had stripped off all her clothes. She sat astride him and stretched up to the night sky. Robbie looked up at her naked skin shining under the moonlight and now that she had taken care of point one, could not remember what the other issues were. At this stage in the proceedings, he concluded, it would be rude not to.

28. BORDER

Malaika closed her eyes as the bus left another strange town and weaved its way along bumpy, pot-holed roads through open scrubland punctuated by trees, shacks and the odd antelope. Progress was slow over hills and valleys, and the excitement of looking out of the window had long passed, as the countryside and villages started to look the same after a while. She found that as long as she tagged along behind an older woman, preferably one with a few children around, no one really troubled her. This had worked further in her favour because the ticket collectors often missed her out when checking tickets, assuming the woman sitting nearby had paid for her and Baraka, without bothering to count. She had been able to save what little money she had for food, living off snacks from roadside vendors. There had been a very scary moment in the middle of the night at a bus station in a strange city when an old man had tried to grab her as she slept on a bench, but luckily one of the drivers chased him off when she started shouting. The driver felt sorry for her and let her sleep in his bus once she persuaded him she was waiting for her mother to return, and was not a runaway, and it really was not necessary to tell the police. From then on, Malaika stayed wide awake at night by softly singing Baraka to sleep, and keeping one eye on what was going on around her. She tried to make sure she was always on the move at night. She was not sure exactly where she was, just that she was going north, and it was getting hotter. The people started to look different and spoke different languages, but usually understood enough Swahili for her to get by. She was pretty certain she had crossed a border, but no one was interested in her papers.

The brakes squealed suddenly as the bus turned off the main road and onto a steep slope, its own momentum threatening to send it rolling off the road and down the hill into dense forest, from which protruded the rusty remains of crumpled vehicles with less cautious drivers. Holding on to the seat in front, Malaika looked down and over the valley, where the thick green vegetation was broken by a clearing at a crossroads that was home to the weekly market. The late afternoon sun picked out the bright colours of huge piles of tomatoes, aubergines, bananas and other fresh fruit and vegetables laid out on the ground in front of the vendors, competing for the attention of the few potential customers walking up and down in their loud patterned market day best. From a distance the scene looked like a row of exotic flowers trying to attract some unusual bees. As the bus approached the movement of the crowd increased, frantically completing sales, packing bags and loading them on to heads and backs. Before the bus had even come to a stop, the brave or foolish jumped onto the back, hanging on to a rail or climbing onto the roof. Malaika felt the weight of dozens of people suddenly jumping on board as the suspension creaked and the bus seemed to sink into the ground. Every seat, rail and aisle was suddenly filled with pressing bodies, bags and boxes. The woman next to her moved up and squashed Malaika in by the window. A stinking bag of little dried fish was thrust onto her lap, and she struggled to lift Baraka up so that he lay on top of it. The gears groaned and the bus lurched forward reluctantly.

A wave of fear and panic suddenly swept over Malaika. It hit her out of the blue that she had no idea where she was or where she was going, except she was hundreds of miles from home and heading north on the whim of a half-overheard half-dreamt story. She had hardly any money left and was surrounded by strangers whose language she did not understand. She had hoped that she could help her little brother, but he seemed to be getting weaker in the past few days and was barely moving in her arms. She knew it was a bad sign when sick children became too ill to cry or complain. She suddenly wished she could go back home and thought about fighting her way through the passengers hemming her in and trying to get a bus in the other direction. But she knew this was hopeless, even if she could get off the bus she did not know when there would be a bus going south. It crossed her mind to go to the police at the next town, but she was more scared of what they might do to her than what they might save her from. Just as she was thinking of giving up, through the competing conversations, shouts, a blaring transistor radio and the roar of the engine, there came a familiar sound. Her ears strained as she tried to filter out the background noise and she picked up the conversation of two people further down the bus speaking in Swahili.

'This rumour has been spreading through the villages like wildfire. I heard people have come all the way from Tabora region.'

'What? I thought we had travelled far enough. This had better not be a joke, I don't think my legs can take much more of this.'

'You must have faith, brother, if you do not believe, you cannot be healed.'

'Yes sister, I have faith, but we must also beware the false prophets.'

'Well, with my eyes and your legs, I think we have nothing to lose.'

Malaika bobbed her head up over the back of the seat and down to the floor, around heads and between arms and legs to try to see who was speaking. She caught a glimpse of an elderly couple sitting near the front. One of them appeared to be blind and the other held two walking sticks. She did not recognise them, but she resolved to follow them from now on, as they had to be heading to the same place.

29. POLICE AND THIEVES

'**W**hen will I see you again?'

    'Probably never.'

    'I never can say goodbye,'

    'Try it. Do you always speak in song lyrics? Look, don't start getting all fucking sentimental on me, Robbie. It's been fun, but I've got work to do. You had better get home to your family, they'll be worried about you.'

    'But I could come back and help.'

    'Well, like I say, you are welcome to, but I don't think you're cut out for it.'

    'Why not, Sarita?'

    'No offence, but you're not serious enough, you're not a revolutionary. Somehow, I don't think you are prepared to put your life on the line to liberate the African continent from poverty.'

    'I might be...depends.'

    'See what I mean? We need firm commitment, people we can rely on in a crisis. You would be better off volunteering in Oxfam in Ealing Broadway, every little helps.'

    'I thought you were against aid agencies as they prolonged the status quo.'

    'Yes, but they are handy in an emergency. Well, you could campaign against multinational criminals in Britain, organise boycotts and demos, we would really appreciate that,' suggested Sarita, although Robbie was fairly certain she was taking the piss.

    After their night in the desert, the truck had mysteriously started working again the next morning. They had spent a few more days together at the camp, sneaking off on regular supply runs until David pointed out that they would not need petrol so often if she did not keep driving off to get it. Earlier that morning Sarita informed Robbie that her team were going on a mission into southern Ethiopia near the Kenyan border, and he had three options. He could come with them, stay at the camp, or catch a lift to the nearest city with a bus connection to Addis Ababa. Robbie had chosen the latter, aware that his visa and return air ticket had nearly expired, and that his homesickness had only gone into temporary remission. On reflection, he could see how this might not appear very revolutionary, but when he told Sarita he had quite a few ties in London, he thought it was a bit unnecessary for her to point out that he did not even own a shirt. Half of him wanted to let himself go and tell her how he felt about her, and dedicate his life to the struggle. The other half was not sure how she felt about him, or that it was his struggle. He was not even sure that this was his real life, not some malaria-induced hallucination, from which he would wake up sweating and delirious in the London Hospital for Tropical Diseases. It was too late to turn back now, as they were approaching the city centre bus station, and the length of the traffic jam was all the time they had left.

The truck stopped again and an orchestra of beeping horns started up, conducted by the occasional hand gesture and opening of a car door accompanied with swearing and shouting. No one was actually sure what the hold-up was, but there seemed to be an unusual degree of congestion for the time of day. From their vantage point in the front of the truck, David and Saleh peered up the road at the commotion ahead. Saleh tapped David's arm and pointed, a look of alarm on his face.

'Police,' said David.

The news interrupted Robbie and Sarita's emotional farewell in the back of the truck.

'Shit,' said Sarita, leaning over between the front seats. 'What are they up to?'

'Looks like they've stopped to grab someone,' observed David as he eased the truck another few feet forward.

Saleh made a sign moving his fist against his forehead, which Robbie interpreted as meaning 'bunch of dickheads'.

'A guy with dreadlocks?' Sarita enunciated clearly.

Saleh nodded.

'Typical police harassment,' said Robbie, leaning over Saleh's shoulder.

The truck moved nearer to the police car that was causing the hold-up. One policeman tried to direct traffic around the vehicle, while three of his uniformed colleagues wrestled with the dread, who was holding his hands up and offering little resistance as they pushed him down on the pavement, batons and guns drawn.

'We'd better keep our heads down. Some of the police have got it in for us as well. If they recognise us, we could be in trouble,' said Sarita.

'Hang on a minute,' said Robbie, opening the canvas and climbing out of the back of the truck. He walked along the side of the road, ignoring Sarita's hissed threats and the beeping and shouting of other cars and drivers all around him. Robbie walked up to the policemen and bent down slightly to get a good look at the face of the person they were holding. Thinner and more haggard than the last time they met, but there was no mistaking him.

'Trevor!'

'Oh, alright, our kid! From the plane... Robbie, yeah?' said Trevor through gritted teeth and a policeman's arm around his neck.

'Yeah, how are you?'

'Oh, not so bad. Spot of bother at the moment.'

'So I see, can I help at all?'

Noticing a scruffy white Englishman in their presence, the policemen sheepishly eased off Trevor and allowed him to stand up freely, two holding an arm each.

'Who are you?' one of them asked.

'Friend. From England,' said Robbie.

'England? You also from England?' the senior policeman asked Trevor.

'Yes officer, I can show you my passport if you like.'

'Hmmm...yes, passport,' said the senior policeman, who spoke English well enough.

As the other policemen relaxed their grip, Trevor reached into his inside pocket, causing their hands to twitch nervously over their guns, and produced his passport. The officer inspected it closely, tapping the photo and taking a long hard look at Trevor's face. With a nod, he instructed one of the officers to go through Trevor's pockets. There followed a nervous silence, as Robbie's arrival had transformed the scene from an annoyance to a source of fascination for the other car drivers, who had stopped beeping their horns and shouting, and were now watching with interest.

'In our country, possession of illegal drugs, marijuana, is serious offence, carrying heavy sentence,' warned the policeman. His colleague who had searched Trevor shook his head disappointedly. '…But you clean, you can go.'

The policemen returned to their vehicle and sped off, allowing the traffic to flow freely again. David's truck reached them, and he beckoned Robbie and Trevor to jump in the back.

'Thanks guys, this is Trevor – I met him on the plane, seems like ages ago now. Trevor, these are some people I bumped into – David, Sarita and Saleh.'

Robbie could tell from the look on Sarita's face that she was not happy that he had attracted so much attention. She squeezed into the front seat next to Saleh and turned her back on them.

'Man, Babylon no love the rasta. Same all over the world, even here in Zion.'

'Yeah? It's a good thing they didn't look in my sock,' said Robbie, who had been contributing to the local economy as best he could.

'What? You're joking!' Trevor laughed. 'I wouldn't mind, but I hardly ever smoke, only for meditation.'

'So, how's your trip been?' asked Robbie.

'Oh, interesting, y'know. How about you?'

'Yeah, amazing, I'm on my way home now,'

'Oh right…' Trevor hesitated, as if he was considering this himself, before continuing the conversation. 'So, where have you been?'

'Y'know, pretty much the guidebook tourist route, ticking off the sights. But then I wandered near the Eritrean border – that's where I met this lot and lost my rucksack – they rescued me from the war breaking out.'

'Yeah, that is madness. This country is not what I expected.'

'How do you mean? How did you get on in Shashemene land?'

'Well…It was beautiful, I felt so good when I arrived there. You know the history – His Majesty set aside this piece of the holy land for Rastafarians who want to come home. I just never knew it was so poor. If you really want to know about hard times, you got to try to make a living out of the land. The dirt was tough and the food no nuff, for real. Still, we did get a whole heap of rain in the last few weeks that was desperately needed.'

'Yeah, it's been funny weather here. I seem to have been lucky – it's been really sunny most of the time, I keep just ahead of the rain,' mused Robbie. 'But what happened, I thought you were going to stay there?'

'I'll tell you. There's a few hundred bredren and sistren who have settled there over the years, mostly from Jamaica. Like I say, everything was just irie in the first few weeks. But then, I started to feel like they never really accepted me, like they didn't think I was a true Rasta cos I'm not Jamaican. And some of the elders started going on at me to grow a beard. I have this condition you see, it's like ingrowing hair – if I leave it, it gets really itchy, look.' Trevor tugged at a piece of stubble protruding from the bumpy skin on his cheeks.

'Ooh, looks nasty,' commented Robbie.

'It is – shaving is damned painful, but if I leave it, it's unbearable. But anyway, them never like that, or a lot of other things I man did. Them never let me fit in. And then I started getting some hassle from the authorities – they said my visa had nearly expired and I had no permission to live in this country. I kept telling them I'm an African come home, but they never see it like that, just want me to fill in forms and pay more money.'

'Yeah, red tape, eh? So where are you heading now?'

'Well, to be honest with you, I took some time out from Shashemene to check out more of the country, meet some of the Ethiopian people, but I was thinking of heading back to England soon,' said Trevor with an air of resignation.

They sat in silence for a while as the truck made its way through the bustling streets towards the bus station. Robbie looked at Trevor and then at his three revolutionary friends in the front seat. An idea so obvious and yet so brilliant hit him, he expected to hear a triangle ping or find a light bulb suspended over his head. He realised he could bring together a perfect match and thereby contribute in his own small way to the cause.

'Hang on, I remember you saying that you worked as a mechanic in Manchester, didn't you.'

'Yeah,' said Trevor, a puzzled look on his face.

Robbie could hardly contain his excitement and leaned over the front seat and whispered something to Sarita, who passed it on to David. They both nodded to Robbie and then Sarita mouthed some words and made a sign to Saleh, who gave it the thumbs up.

'These guys are looking for a mechanic. If you want to stick around, they could really use your help. They are like-minded people, trust me,' said Robbie, sitting back in a self-satisfied way as Sarita turned round and started telling Trevor about what they did, to his great interest. Robbie felt so clever at bringing them together, he forgot it was his time to go, and looked a bit confused when the truck stopped at the bus station. He was still congratulating himself as he shook hands with each of them and hugged Sarita, and when he watched the truck disappear into the haze of traffic, before he realised it was too late. A sudden whirlwind blew dust into his eyes. When he opened them again they were gone, taking with them the potential of a whole parallel life that was just developing in his mind. He was alone and going home to his old life.

30. PUSH COME TO SHOVE

The man sitting opposite briefly met Robbie's eye and then started looking at the person sitting next to him instead. Robbie nodded and was about to say hello and tell him where he was from and where he was going. Then he remembered he was on the Piccadilly Line, not a rural Ethiopian bus service. As a lone white traveller off the usual tourist routes in Africa, he had got used to being stared at and the feeling of being a celebrity, of people waving at him, smiling and asking questions all the time. Now he was just an anonymous face in the crowd of millions, and no one was remotely interested in where he was from or where he was going. If he started making conversation with a total stranger, he knew he might as well just call the police himself. The tight lips and expressionless faces crammed against each other in a hot, stuffy tube train suddenly made him feel quite at home. Released from the need to explain himself, he relaxed in his seat and realised this is what he had been missing; the freedom to disappear.

'Alright, Robbie, been on holiday?'

Dez, an old acquaintance from school and former member of the Pull Up Posse, slumped into the seat next to him and punched him on the arm.

'Er...alright, Dez. Yeah. How are you doing?'

'Alright. Where you been?'

'Ethiopia. Just travelling around for a few months.'

'Yeah? I was thinking of doing that myself, maybe Thailand, y'know.'

'Right, well, go for it, mate.'

They sat in silence for a few minutes as the tube rattled through a tunnel, picking up speed and making their ears pop.

'So, you still playing football? Didn't you have trials with Brentford?' asked Robbie.

'Yeah, I was on their books for a while, but it didn't really work out, too busy enjoying myself, then I got a bad injury.'

'Oh, sorry to hear that, mate, you were magic at school. Do you still see much of the old Pull Up Posse?'

'Yeah, of course, we still rolling. You should hook up with us some time. Seeyah around, mate, this is my stop,' said Dez.

Robbie raised his hand and watched Dez go, feeling slightly honoured by this vague invitation and wondering if he had a hallucinatory form of jetlag. It was the last person he expected to see to welcome him home, and he tried to resume his reflections on the city of his birth. The tube emerged above ground and trundled along at rooftop level. Robbie could not help but take the fleeting opportunity to gaze into the windows and gardens that backed onto the line. He had always felt that these high-speed snatches of other people's lives made them seem much more interesting than his, their flats looked cosier and more tastefully decorated, they were having something nicer for tea and having far more sophisticated conversations than he could ever imagine. In fact, very few of them had probably just returned from a trip to Ethiopia in search of their long-lost emperor grandfather, so on this occasion Robbie conceded his own life was more interesting. He still felt a twinge of envy, as he did not know what he would have for tea, but then again, at least he didn't live backing onto the tube line, with nosey bastards staring in the whole time. The tube sped on overlooking the bustling heartlands of west London. Through the window opposite, scenes of sunny streets full of shoppers flashed up, alternating with close-ups of graffitied walls like a very dull slide show. Robbie noticed people were walking about in shorts and t-shirts. This caught him by surprise, as it had been a cold, winter morning when he had left, and he had expected everything to remain frozen just as he had left it, forgetting it was now July in London. Obviously, the months had passed in the same order in Ethiopia, but the time had gone quickly, and it had felt like summer the whole time. Anyway, he had not paid much attention to the calendar, as he had enough trouble working out if the time difference actually meant he could find out football scores before people back home. Now, as he caught glimpses of the people on the pavement below, he remembered this was what he had been missing about London; the freedom enjoyed by beautiful women of all shapes, sizes and colours walking about the streets in mini-skirts and skimpy tops. He really did get a funny feeling inside of him, just walking up and down, but it was usually an erection.

Getting off at Hammersmith, Robbie decided to walk down and through Shepherds Bush Market to his flat instead of taking another couple of stops on the tube. He wondered what he must look like, as he had been wearing the same clothes for weeks, since losing his rucksack. He was vaguely aware that he could do with a shave and a haircut, and that he had lost a bit of weight. Still, he felt he was his old self again and it was good to be back home. Familiar faces from the market seemed to welcome him home, obviously without actually doing so verbally, as this only happened on Eastenders. The sight of yams and plantains on one stall and saris on the next warmed his heart. Nodding to the beat from a record stall, he started getting excited about how much tunes he had to catch up on. He felt that it was here all along, everything he was looking for was here in London, and most importantly, he was part of it. It was more than just ogling sexy women, he reflected, it was the infinite potential around every corner, the fact that you could fall in love with someone new several times on the way to work every morning, someone uniquely beautiful and totally different who could introduce you to a brand-new world. The fact that this had never actually happened to him in twenty-three years did not bother him; it was all still there for the taking, he could always erase and start again. For a few seconds he felt a twinge of regret for having left at all, he felt disloyal and anxious in case he had missed something important. He had sent postcards and there were a couple of letters waiting for him in Addis Ababa but that was all the contact he had had with his family and friends for over three months. What was he thinking of? These were the most important people to him in the world and he had gone half a world away to realise it. A quick call to his mum from Heathrow reassured him that everyone was fine, and he planned on surprising Angela later, but first of all he wanted to find out what Ravi had done to his flat.

Robbie turned the key and bounded up the stairs two at a time. Opening the inside door to his flat, he was relieved to find no signs of major disaster. Fire, flood and earthquakes had all been averted and his belongings had been spared from acts of burglars. Popping his head round the door of his living room, he was pleasantly surprised to see Angela sitting in the armchair reading a magazine.

'Hello, how did you know I was coming home? Hey, is this a surprise welcome home party?'

Angela sat speechless, looking much more surprised than he was. She smiled uncertainly.

'Robbie…we…I… didn't expect you back,'

She looked up and then turned round as Ravi emerged from the bedroom in bare feet. At this point, Robbie noticed Angela was in her dressing gown.

'Hi, Robbie…I'm sorry, man,' said Ravi, looking guilty.

'Shit,' said Robbie, putting one and one together.

'I'm sorry, Robbie, we didn't mean to…' began Angela, as she stood up in front of Ravi.

'How long has this been going on?' asked Robbie, and then reminded himself he would have to do something about this habit of speaking in song lyrics.

'Not long. Mate, you've been away for nearly six months. We haven't heard from you for time.'

'Oh right, so it's my fault?' reacted Robbie angrily.

'You're not going to get all macho and hit me, are you?' asked Ravi.

Robbie shook his head and sat down on the sofa.

'Good,' said Ravi as he stepped out from behind Angela.

The three of them sat in silence for a few seconds, looking at each other in turn.

'Robbie, you are the one who left. And we agreed there was no sense in making promises we couldn't keep,' cajoled Angela softly.

'Right, I made my bed so you two lay in it,' joked Robbie bitterly.

'Yeah, and mate, aren't you pleased she's with me rather than some bloke you don't know?' offered Ravi optimistically.

'Hmmm… I'll have to think about that.'

'Seriously, cos I know I used to go on about pulling loads of different chicks in clubs all the time, but it was mostly bullshit y'know,' confessed Ravi.

'No! Surely not!' remarked Robbie sarcastically.

'Well, y'know we were both quite lonely after you left, and with James and Fiona moved to Liverpool, we were spending a lot of time together.'

'What? James has gone to Liverpool?'

'Yeah, 'fraid so. He got a placement at a barrister's chambers there, started straight after his exams.'

'Great! Bastards. One best friend goes off with my girlfriend, the other buggers off to Liverpool.'

'Ex-girlfriend,' corrected Angela. 'So, how was your holiday? Did you find yourself?'

'No, it was good though. Is everything OK here, I mean with the flat?'

'Yeah, well no, actually,' said Ravi, 'I checked the housing benefit is still being paid into your account like you said, but for some reason your landlord said the standing order stopped a couple of months ago. He said he would wait til you get back.'

'Right, I'll sort it out tomorrow,' murmured Robbie, hardly interested.

'Look, you guys carry on, don't mind me. I'll just take a shower, change my clothes and go for a walk, pop in on my mum and dad.'

31. GOING HOME

Scotch gazed lazily out into the street and thought about closing early. It was a quiet midweek afternoon and it looked like there would be no more customers for one day. He put on one of his favourite records for once, turned the music down to an acceptable level and removed his earplugs. He relaxed and watched the people passing by. They were looking up anxiously at the sky as they hurried home, or sat nervously outside cafes and bars, occasionally holding a hand out to check for the first spots of rain. The forecast had warned that the rare spell of hot sunny weather London had been enjoying would at last break with heavy thunderstorms that evening. As usual, most people had ignored it, and were walking about in shorts and T-shirts, making the most of the sunshine while it lasted. Out of boredom, Scotch found himself thinking about the rainstorms he remembered in Jamaica as a child. How the world smelt so new, all the flowers came out and the night was alive with fireflies. He wished he could go back and just chill in the country, but his time was fully taken up with the music business these days. It was not that he was bored of reggae, of course, that would be impossible; it would be like being bored of the sun rising every day.

Reggae was in his veins, the beat of his heart and every breath he took. He had grown up with it, as his dad had been a friend of Marley and a record producer, one of the first to bring the sound of Rasta drumming down from the hills into ska music in the late fifties. As a teenager, Scotch had rebelled against his strict Rasta upbringing, become a baldhead and ran away to London to make lots of money in the music industry boom of the seventies. He had hardly spoken to his dad since, and desperately wanted to patch things up, as he knew time was running out. Scotch had realised too late that the older Windrush generation who had seemed like boring old farts when he first came to London were dying out fast. It occurred to him recently that he had spoken to someone who had spoken to someone who was born in slavery. His grandmother's generation remembered their own grandparents, who were children in the last days of slavery. Scotch wanted to talk about this to his customers, and their memories of the old people in the country back a yard, maybe write some stuff down. Mostly he just wanted to talk about something other than music. Music was a thing that spoke for itself, he did not see why people felt they had to talk about it the whole time, or worse, over it. He sighed and closed his eyes as the afternoon clouded over.

Robbie pounded the streets, thinking about this unexpected turning upside down of his world. When he had left a few months ago, Angela, Ravi and James were the few people he really trusted, and he felt that they were a constant in his life. A couple of hours ago he thought he knew where he belonged in the world, and that he had sorted out where he was going with his life but now, he did not know anything. Alright, so he had been away a bit longer than he originally intended, but he did not understand how things could change that much in a few months. Everything else seemed the same. His parents acted like he had hardly been away, he caught up on the family news in about ten minutes and he promised to come back when he had got his photos developed. Nothing had changed in their lives, he even thought they were watching the same television programme as when he had last seen them – this was actually true as the series was being repeated. Outside, the streets were the same, the buses were the same colour, and the announcements on the tube had been the same. There were a few new adverts around, but that was about it. Yet when he went into his flat, he felt like a stranger and someone else had taken over his life. It was like a parallel life where Ravi and Angela had been together all along, and he was their friend. He couldn't help thinking about how well they used to all get on, and he felt like the year he had spent with Angela had all been a big joke at his expense.

A large, heavy raindrop hit him on the head. Typical, thought Robbie as he looked up at the darkening sky, realising he had been walking without any idea where he was going. The first few spots of rain appeared and then faded on the hot baked concrete, giving off a fresh vapour. He could feel his hair standing up on end slightly with the electricity in the air and braced himself for the downpour, cursing himself for coming out in just a T-shirt. The rain was actually quite welcome after a fortnight's drought, washing the pavements clean and flushing the gutters and alleyways of the dried vomit, spit, urine and other bodily products that London accumulated. Robbie was getting drenched and to his disappointment all the scantily clad women he had been praising earlier had evacuated the streets. With a sense of relief, he realised he was round the corner from his favourite record shop, and was pleased to find that at least something that was important to him was still there how he left it, and had not been turned into an internet café or a mobile phone shop. This was an ideal time to catch up on the tunes he had missed, and to take shelter from the rain.

Robbie pushed open the door and was reassured to find one of his favourite records playing at a surprisingly gentle volume. He nodded to Scotch and continued nodding in time to the music as he flicked through the new releases. After a couple of minutes, the tune faded and an unaccustomed quietness filled the shop, except for the sound of the rain bouncing off the pavement outside. Thinking perhaps something was wrong or the shop was about to close, Robbie looked up uncertainly.

'Alright, boss. Me nah seen you round for a while,' said Scotch as he put the record back in its sleeve.

'Alright, yeah. I've been away for a few months. Missed out on some good tunes by the look of things.'

'Yeah, yeah, it's been busy…so where you been?'

'Oh, me…I went to Ethiopia as it happens,' said Robbie a little sheepishly, as he did not want to look like he was obsessed with reggae or anything.

'Yeah? Nice one, for real. What you doing out deh?' Scotch raised his eyebrows animatedly.

'Well, just travelling around, then I linked up with a sort of charity project, y'know, helping in schools and stuff,' said Robbie, slightly misrepresenting Sarita's motives, but he felt he needed something to show he was not a white Rasta on a pilgrimage or anything foolish like that.

'Wow, so what it like out deh - you enjoy it?'

'Yeah, it was brilliant. Lots of beautiful scenery, ancient monuments, and the people are really friendly,' Robbie trailed off, feeling like a holiday programme.

'Yeah, man. I spent some time in Africa a few years ago, over the other side, Gambia, y'know? It was beautiful, always wanted to go back, but due to certain tings...'

'Yeah...that would be nice...Are these two for twenty quid?' Robbie slid the two CDs he was holding across the counter.

Scotch nodded and put them into a bag as Robbie handed over the money.

'There you go, boss,' said Scotch, smiling.

'Thanks a lot, mate, cheers,' said Robbie as he reached for the bag. Scotch held onto it for a moment and looked him in the eye.

'You should go back,' said Scotch seriously.

'Well, you never know...Seeyah around,' said Robbie with a chuckle.

'Laters,' said Scotch as he took the next tune out of its sleeve.

Robbie turned and walked towards the door. As the turntable crackled, he opened the door and looked round to give the final respectful nod.

'Bye'

'You should go back.' Scotch repeated, as the drum rolled and the bassline kicked in at the usual volume.

32. BACK TO AFRICA

Robbie decided to hop on the bus, even though the traffic was standing still in the evening rush hour and it would be quicker to walk. His feet were killing him after pounding the pavement in a sulk earlier and he still felt quite tired from the flight. A number 52A was crawling along beside him, and every time it eased forward a few metres and stopped again the brakes emitted a high-pitched scream, so the only way to avoid GBH on the ear holes was to get on. One of the tourist seats upstairs at the front was free and he slouched down adjacent to a middle-aged American couple pointing excitedly at an old wino who was standing in the middle of the road ahead of them waving his can of Special Brew at a lorry. Robbie took his new CDs out of the bag and opened them up to peruse the sleeve notes. At that moment a beautiful girl sat behind him, looked over his shoulder and remarked on his great taste in music, they got chatting and she asked if he would take her to a club. Of course, that did not actually happen, but Robbie held up the CDs for as long as possible on the off-chance, turning them over and nodding to himself. It was force of habit and the reason was by now subconscious, but there was precious little else to be gleaned from the notes, other than spelling mistakes in the titles of the songs, some of which were adapted from unknown original artists, and that Jah was indirectly responsible for the whole recording. Eventually he returned them to the bag and rested it on the seat, still with the distinctive logo facing outwards, just in case the girl was waiting at the next stop. But no one with any pressing engagements that evening was getting on the bus, as a disabled person's mobility buggy was overtaking it on the inside.

Tired of the unchanging view, even the American couple got off and made for the tube, leaving Robbie alone on the top deck. He leaned back and stared blankly out the window. The storm had cleared to reveal a beautiful long summer evening. This was something else he realised that he had missed when he was away, as the days nearer the equator were beautiful but always about the same length. The long hours of daylight made him want to do something to make the most of it, but not knowing how to make hay he decided the best thing to do was just to be out and watch it from the comfort of the top deck of a bus. It was a good place to think, he decided. It could be his imagination, but there seemed to be a slightly different mood in the air in London, apart from the usual pre-Carnival buzz. A sense of unease mingled with defiance on the streets, an almost a blitz-like camaraderie. He could not work out why, but it seemed people were making a statement by coming out on the streets and just carrying on with their normal business. Dismissing this sensation as another symptom of jetlag and getting bored of thinking by himself, he reached over to the seat behind him and picked up a discarded newspaper and read:

Nail bomber targets London's minorities

A police spokesperson confirmed yesterday that the attacks in Brixton, Brick Lane and Soho were related. It appears the bomber has deliberately targeted the heartlands of the African -Caribbean, Asian and gay communities. No group has as yet claimed responsibility for the bombings and police have hinted that they are looking for someone working alone. The public have been warned to be on their guard, especially around Notting Hill, in the lead up to the Carnival, which is likely to be a target as the symbol of multi-racial Britain. Black, Asian and gay groups have been united in their defiance of the bomber and have urged people to carry on their lives as normal, but to be vigilant.

Robbie could not believe what he was reading. It was like something from apartheid South Africa or the Deep South in the sixties. That this could be happening in London at the end of the twentieth century was beyond his imagination. Born and bred as a Londoner, he did not understand how anyone could hate everyone and everything around him so much. He felt the attacks were directed at him, his friends, family, neighbours and everyone and everything he loved and believed in.

Obviously, he knew racists and bigots had always existed, but it was they who were the true minority, frightened to walk the streets. Maybe things had been getting worse since he had been away. Thinking back to his childhood, he used to play football and cricket out in the street every evening with kids from all different backgrounds. At school as he got older, he had his first kiss, his first fight and his first drink with people whose parents had come from all over the world. But they all grew up together as Londoners, he could swear race had not been an issue. With a jolt, he suddenly thought that was because he was white, but then again, with another jolt, which was the bus actually moving all of a sudden, he thought it was because he wasn't white after all. Maybe he had just been lucky, growing up in a relatively middle class, multiracial area. But that was when he was a kid, things were different now, and most of the people he had grown up with had gone their separate ways. Thinking about it, James, Ravi, Angela, and himself were the exception in that they had kept in touch with each other, despite coming from different backgrounds. Robbie had always thought he and they had not let the colour of their skin, or the origin of their parents define them and rule their choice of friends, partners and lifestyle. But then of course it was important, or why would he have travelled halfway across the world in search of his grandfather?

He shook his head at the irony and wasted opportunity, that the only people he had got to know on his travels were from Manchester, Surrey and Hounslow. A second thought formed slowly in his head that maybe that was the point, and that the fact of where they had come from had really not mattered as much to Julian, Trevor and Sarita as where they were going. It had not stopped them from deciding, for different reasons, that their future was in Africa, and making real connections with people there. He had bumped into them by chance and there was a potential for him if he followed his heart to find something similar of his own making. But it was something inside himself that had held him back, a reliance on the familiar life he had known, but had come back to find in tatters. He thought how easy it had been to fall into the role that everyone expected him to play as the white tourist. It took too much effort to shed this skin and get to know everyone he met, especially when he thought they were only interested in the stereotype of him as a rich western traveller, but this was just his own prejudice. Two thousand miles to discover a label hanging out of the back of his jacket that he had grown up not realising was there all the time. Now he felt like his jacket had been nicked and London was the coldest, loneliest place in the world. Viewed from the top of the bus, it struck him that his fellow Londoners never talked to each other, and rarely even looked at each other. Maybe the rosy image of all communities living together in harmony had never existed anywhere, except in his head. Robbie shrugged and closed his eyes, looking at the pinky orange glow of the evening sun on the insides of his eyelids. He wanted to cry at the sudden damage he had experienced in a few hours to his relationship, friendships and now his hometown. Drifting off, he felt that he could be back in Ethiopia if he concentrated really hard on the warmth of the sun on his skin and the steady motion of the bus.

In the distorted circular mirror above him, Robbie noticed a short guy in a scruffy yellow and green tracksuit bounce up the stairs and sit in the adjacent seat. He immediately seemed familiar, and Robbie leaned forward slightly to get a better look at him out of the corner of his eye. The man had dreadlocks tucked into a woolly tam, and a light brown, mixed-race complexion. He lounged back in the seat, resting an arm on the back and slowly nodding as he looked out of the window. He had a wrinkled brow and a flat nose, making him look a little bit like a lion. The dread slowly turned his head and met Robbie's eye, letting his smile break into a gentle laugh as his eyes gleamed with recognition. He reached his fist out towards Robbie, who leaned over and touched it with his fist, noticing the unmistakeable gold ring on the dread's finger, set with the familiar black stone and clearly engraved with the Lion of Judah.

'B-Bob?' stuttered Robbie.

'Yes, me friend, me deh pon street again,' the man said in a musical Jamaican accent.

'But you've been dead since 1981.'

'Is a foolish dog, bark at a flying bird.'

'But what are you doing here, on the number 52A from Ladbroke Grove to Acton?'

'One bright morning when my work is over, I will fly away home,' Bob whispered, his eyes glazing over as he stared off into the sunset over the North

Circular Road.

'Home? What, to Africa? Ethiopia?' asked Robbie excitedly.

'I've got my home, in the Promised Land, but I feel at home, do you overstand?'

'Yeah, man. You know I was there yesterday - it was brilliant! But I did not think I could stay; I did not feel like it was my home.'

'Open your eyes and look within. Are you satisfied with the life you're living?'

'Not really, are you saying I should go back?'

'Soon we'll find out who is the real revolutionary.'

'Yeah, of course – Sarita and her group –should I join them?' asked Robbie, thinking the long-dead superstar may have some insight into his recent experiences.

'Emancipate yourself from mental slavery, none but ourselves can free our minds.'

Bob turned back towards the window and Robbie nodded slowly, thinking that he understood the dead Rasta's message. At this point there was a sudden orange flash from the pavement below, and a bang that seemed to make the bus, the road and everything tilt forty-five degrees sideways. The glass shattered into thousands of tiny ice-like crystals as hundreds of rusty iron nails entered the top deck of the bus so fast there was not even time for Robbie or Bob to blink. Robbie's face felt numb as the fragments of glass and bent nails imbedded themselves deep into his skin. He turned his head and saw Bob, smiling casually as a line of nails wound their way around his forehead. Bob raised his hands and waved at Robbie, who noticed a particularly deep, dark wound on each palm. Robbie sighed and relaxed, relieved to discover that he was not bleeding and he felt fine. Of course, by now he realised he was dreaming, but he did not want to wake up until he had a chance to talk to his hero some more.

'Bob, is Haile Selassie my grandfather?'

'Some people think great God will come from the sky, take away everything and make everybody feel high. But if you knew what life was worth, you would look for yours on earth.'

Robbie screwed his eyes shut and tried to stay in the dream, but he was already wide-awake. He opened his eyes to find the other seat empty and he was alone on the top deck as before, windows intact. The bus picked up speed and trundled through Acton as the rush hours cleared. Robbie sat still, staring out of the window and thinking. He did not even notice when the bus came to a longer than the usual perpetual stop, until the driver flashed the lights on and off. Slowly he got up and made his way downstairs, stepping into the still warm evening. He walked away from his flat, away from his parents' house and towards Acton Town tube station. He checked his inside pocket to see that his passport was still there, taking his debit card out of his wallet and stopping at a hole in the wall. With a twinge of guilt, Robbie withdrew all the housing benefit that had been paid in over the past few months, which the landlord was waiting to collect. He strolled on, breathing in the fresh traffic fumes and admiring a few birds flying over the park in the fading summer light. He trotted down to the platform and waited a couple of minutes for a Heathrow train. As the lights of the tube train got nearer, he thought about what he was doing and whether he should change his mind. Robbie then got on to the tube all the way to Heathrow, where he bought a one-way ticket on the next flight to Addis Ababa.

Epilogue: FORWARD TO ZION

'This is Roger Burke for the BBC in Ethiopia. In the distance behind me, you can see the queue stretching all the way back the four miles to the nearest town of Harar. The weak and the dying have come from all over north and east Africa to witness what some are calling a...Bollocks!'

Roger dropped the mike to his side and motioned for his camerawoman to cut.

'Someone tell those kids to piss off,' he said, shooing away the handful of children who were waving and smiling playfully in the background. The interpreter shouted a rough translation at them and they turned and fled, before regrouping in a larger number and creeping back towards them.

'How about if we take a long shot from on top of that hill, and pan all the way up to the church?' suggested the camerawoman.

'Yes, nice idea, Sophie. I'll do the interviews now and then we can go up there to do the opening shot later, should look quite dramatic. Let's try to grab someone coming out.'

Two unsmiling men in long black robes stood at the gate of the church, looking a little bit like bouncers outside a dodgy nightclub. Roger asked them something, and the one on the right raised his hand and pointed into the distance at the back of the queue, snaking somewhere over the hills and disappearing into the morning mist.

'They say we can't come in. We have to join the back of the queue.'

'Haben, ask them if they know we are from the BBC.' asked Roger.

Haben said something quickly in Amharic, ending with 'BBC', but producing the same response.

'Well, can we interview someone in charge?' asked Roger impatiently.

Haben engaged in a long debate with the two bouncers, involving lots of shaking heads and pointing into the church and up the road.

'Yes,' he replied eventually.

One of the bouncers shouted something towards the doors of the church, and eventually a small, rotund balding man in white robes emerged. Haben spoke with him for a few seconds, resulting in a warm handshake and smiles all round.

'This is Father Ernest Dawed. He can speak a little English.'

'Good day friends, what brings you to my humble church?'

Sophie quickly started the camera rolling and Roger checked the mike and got back into character.

'Good day, Father Ernest. Can you tell us why all these people have come here?'

'Simply to give their thanks and offer up their prayers to the almighty.'

'Of course, but we have heard stories of people arriving sick and leaving well, can you confirm that?'

'I am a mere servant of God, I am not a doctor. All I know is my faith in the holy scriptures.'

'People here have come from all over Africa to see your statue, is that right?'

'Yes, the word of God has travelled far and wide.'

'Could we film the statue?'

'No, I am sorry. In our country, we never allow cameras inside our churches. Like the Holy Ark at Aksum, these treasures are only for the faithful. If you are a believer, you may join the end of the queue.'

'Does the statue do anything at all? Does it cry?' asked Roger as he looked around in frustration, knowing he had to get the story wrapped and back on the road before the hottest part of the day.

'No, no crying. The statue does not do anything. It just stands still, as it has done for hundreds of years. It is a statue,' replied Father Ernest simply.

'Of course, silly me,' muttered Roger. 'Thank you very much for your time,

Father Ernest.'

The priest returned inside his church, patting a little girl on the head as she emerged, carrying a small child.

'Quick, ask this girl what she saw,' whispered Roger, as they moved a few steps away from the church gates. Haben bent down and smiled, the camera still rolling behind him as he spoke a few words. The girl had the skinny frame of a malnourished eleven-year old, but her hard eyes bore the pain of an old woman. She shook her head and tied her bundle closer to her as the child started wriggling and squirming in her arms.

'She does not speak Amharic. She is from Tanzania. My Swahili is a little patchy,' said Haben, who like most Ethiopians had a familiarity with neighbouring languages. He changed language and started chatting with the girl. As he spoke, she relaxed and started smiling, her eyes lighting up with a long-buried happiness. The small boy had wriggled free and took a few tentative steps on the ground, grinning as the older girl pointed at him and laughed, saying something to Haben. The interpreter looked shocked and asked her something again. She nodded and ran after the little boy, picking him up and playing with him. Haben turned back to his colleagues and shook his head. He opened his mouth a couple of times and then laughed incredulously.

'I don't know how to tell you this, guys. She says her mother and father died of the virus. Her baby brother had it as well, and has barely been able to open his eyes for the past few weeks. She says they went into the church and touched the statue on the hand, and now, look at him,'

Roger turned and stared at the little boy, who was now swinging on the arms of an older boy, as they had teamed up with the other children playing outside the church.

'That'll do for us. Quick, get the shot with the queue behind me on one side and these kids on the other,' Roger instructed as he grabbed the mike.

'OK, that's perfect,' said Sophie as she steadied the camera on her shoulder.

'This is Roger Burke for the BBC in Ethiopia. For the first time in my decades of reporting from this seemingly godforsaken continent, comes a good news story. The children playing behind me - carefree, healthy and happy, like children all over the world - only yesterday were dying of AIDS. That at least is the astonishing claim made by the local people here, who are closely guarding the secret of this little church in the hills as the queue of the desperate and the dying from all over Africa swells. From far and wide they have come, spurred on by the rumours of a miraculous statue that heals the sick. Doctors are apparently baffled by reports that people have entered the church suffering from illnesses and have left suddenly fit and healthy. Investigations continue as to whether there is something occurring naturally in the water in this area, which has seen an unprecedented amount of rain in recent months, after years of drought. Other suspicions have centred on a shadowy popular movement, which has taken de facto control of large areas in the north of Ethiopia. The band of rebels, led by a mysterious Indian woman who has apparently cheated death on numerous occasions are, allegedly, unarmed and yet have won support in the villages with a programme of self-reliance, healthcare and education. Meanwhile, from Somalia, Kenya, Tanzania, Sudan, Uganda they come, the superstitious, weak and vulnerable, queuing in the hot sun to touch the hand of a statue in the hope of a future.'

Roger motioned to cut. Sophie gave an uncertain smile.

'Don't you think that's overdoing it a bit?' she asked.

'Trust me, girl, I have been in this business for years, they will lap it up.'

'But you can't just repeat every rumour we have heard without any evidence.'

'Evidence? You want evidence, look in front of you! This is a story whether we believe in it or not. They do, and they are not going away.'

Roger waved his hand into the distance, motioning the thousands-strong queue winding its way up and down the hills, their long shadows stretching behind them in the early morning sun like waking lions.